Ten Days in May

Ten Days in May is a character driven story, one that is dependent on growth and change. It works because Cam and Brooke stand up to the challenge; they change in ways that engage readers' hearts as well as their minds. That's largely because Richardson scripts solid developments for these women. She also constructs reliable backstories, ones that make sense for the characters as well as the story. Readers walk away with a clear understanding of who these women are and where they came from. Their pasts are neatly threaded with their present, providing readers with a full-circle romance that is heartwarming as well as endearing.

-Women Using Words

This exquisitely written book is full of food for thought and a joy to read. I loved the characters (including Wendy the dachshund) and their captivating journeys. Dignity and hope come to mind if I had to sum up this book in a few words. A very worthy tribute to the pandemic and how it changed lives and a very worthy tribute to love and second chances and a very worthy tribute to lives lived well.

-Henrietta B., *NetGalley*

Thursday Afternoons

A fun and sexy book that will tug at your heartstrings. The pace of the book is excellent, and at no point are you left feeling uncertain about Ellis and Amy. The chemistry between them is there in spades. I loved the way Tracey Richardson amped up the tension when everything is revealed and the chapters that follow. This made it really easy for me to connect with the story line and the characters.

-Les Rêveur

There's no manufactured conflict here that can be resolved with a frank discussion over a cup of coffee. Ellis's and Amy's careers have them at odds and they both have so much at stake. The side characters gave me even more reasons to become invested in the book and their plotlines are seamlessly woven together. Good stories always make you want to go back to the beginning and start again, and this is definitely one of those. It has everything from steamy, lust-filled sex, to dramatic tension and a great slow-burn romance between two amazing, beautiful women inside and out. If you're looking for a book that gives you everything you're craving at once, then this is positively the book for you.

-The Lesbian Review

I'm Gonna Make You Love Me

Claire and Ellie might just be my favourite couple that Tracey Richardson's written so far. There are some great side characters between Claire's best friend Jackson, and Ellie's roommate and cousin Marissa, plus her family. They help us get to know the leads better and are integral to both of the women's character arcs. Richardson's writing is easy to sink into and this book was no exception. The romance has a nice burn to it that's slow, but not too slow, and I marveled at how natural Claire and Ellie's journey from former boss/employee to happily ever after was. If you're a fan of contemporary romances, especially those with age gaps or opposites attract pairings, I recommend picking up *I'm Gonna Make You Love Me*. I thoroughly enjoyed it and will be reading this one again (especially if a spinoff happens!).

-*The Lesbian Review*

What a fun story with lots of fantastic music to read along to. One of my favourite tropes is age-gap romance and this did not disappoint; I really enjoyed this unraveling of the romance. The pace was perfect and I hadn't realized I had read so long until I had finished the book in one sitting. It was easy to like both characters and the chemistry for both Ellie and Claire was there from the moment Claire returns Ellie's pup home. This story had happily ever after written all over it from that moment on.

-*Les Rêveur*

Heartsick

This was such a sweet story of heartbreak turned friendship turned love. I knew I'd enjoy the story from the get-go because it's a Tracey Richardson book but I was really drawn to the characters over and above the storyline itself.

-*Les Rêveur*

Delay of Game

There are so many things to love about this book. There are great characters working to be together in a seemingly impossible situation. The scenes on the ice were wonderful and visceral, but without slowing down the story. I've heard it said that in some sport romances, the sport scenes can get in the way of the plot, which is definitely not the case here. The action on the ice is as important as what happens off the ice, both in terms of character and plot development.

-The Lesbian Review

With a story set around the very real rivalry between the Canadian and US women's ice hockey teams, this book has a realistic edge to it to go along with the romance that is the main focus of the tale. Although the romance is given slightly more weight, there's enough of the hockey story to keep sports fans truly interested. Richardson clearly knows hockey, and all the scenes around practice, training, and actual matches come across as very authentic.

-Rainbow Book Reviews

Overtime

Other Bella Books by Tracey Richardson

The Candidate
Side Order of Love
No Rules of Engagement
Blind Bet
The Wedding Party
The Campaign
Last Salute
The Song in My Heart
By Mutual Consent
Delay of Game
Heartsick
I'm Gonna Make You Love Me
Thursday Afternoons
Ten Days in May

About the Author

Tracey Richardson has worn two hats most of her working life—that of a newspaper journalist and that of a fiction writer. For a few years now, she's only had to wear the fiction writer's hat, for which she's eternally grateful. Tracey is the author of fourteen romance novels published by Bella Books. She is a two-time Lambda Literary Awards finalist as well as a first-place Rainbow Romance winner (Romance Writers of America) for contemporary lesbian romance. She is also a Word By Word (short story) second-place winner and a finalist numerous times for awards presented by the Golden Crown Literary Society. In 2024 she was awarded the Alice B. Readers Award, an award based on her body of work. Tracey has taught fiction writing and was a founding member of a local writer's group.

Tracey lives in Ontario, Canada, and enjoys spending time with her wife and their greyhound, as well as activities such as hockey, golf and making cocktails from scratch. And reading, of course!

For more, visit her publisher's website at: https://www.bellabooks.com/category/author-tracey-richardson/

Or visit Tracey on Facebook, Instagram, Threads and Bluesky.

Overtime

Tracey Richardson

BELLA
BOOKS

Bella Books, Inc.
P.O. Box 10543
Tallahassee, FL 32302

First Edition - 2025

Editor: Medora MacDougall
Cover Designer: SJ Hardy

ISBN: 978-1-64247-630-9

PUBLISHER'S NOTE

Acknowledgments

Thank you, dear readers, for all of your encouragement and support over the years. I couldn't do this without you, nor without the support and professionalism of my publisher, Bella Books. I admire their commitment so much. A special thank-you to my editor, Medora MacDougall, whom I've worked with on most of my books now. She <u>always</u> helps me make them better. I am so thankful that I get to do the thing I enjoy doing most. Thank you to my wife, Sandra, for walking through this life with me, and to my friends as well, who make the journey worthwhile.

As we all enter unknown times ahead, hold your loved ones closer, stay strong, and read books!

Dedication

To all women who enjoy the sport of hockey as much as I do. Keep playing, keep encouraging, keep watching, keep cheering.

CHAPTER ONE

Sarah Brennan was good at figuring things out. Good at being on time, too. But good at being a university student again? Not so much. There was a decade and a half of rust on her old textbooks and rust on the ability to get herself to the right building and into the right classroom on time, it seemed. The feeling of ineptitude squeezing her insides was unfamiliar—and unwelcome. Suddenly she was that eighteen-year-old freshman on a hockey scholarship all over again, steeped in her own insecurities, faking it until she got comfortable.

The University of Toronto was not Sarah's alma mater. If it were, she wouldn't be left staring up at the indistinguishable gray buildings, retracing her steps twice, before arriving at yet another marble corridor lined with identical classroom doors. If finding the right classroom was some kind of IQ test, well, she'd failed miserably. She tried to console herself with the thought that professors were rarely on time anyway, but her galloping heart was not so easily convinced. She crossed her fingers.

Fuck. The door was locked. The door that announced classroom 1112. It was the right classroom, Sarah confirmed by frantically checking the email on her phone. So why the hell was it locked? Placing her ear against the frosted glass, she could hear the professor speaking. *Shit.* She put her knuckles up to the window, but paused, taken aback by her own cowardice. It surprised her, this sinking feeling in her stomach, the hesitation to knock, the feeling of being a helpless kid. She was a pro hockey player, for fuck's sake. This was just a class on modern Irish literature. No one was going to bench her or saddle her with a fine or otherwise punish her for being late. There was no need to worry about getting expelled from the course or even a failing grade; she already had a university degree. This was strictly for fun, an interesting distraction from the grind of games, practices, workouts. Something to keep her mind sharp, because if today's tardiness was any indication, her mind needed a little sharpening.

Sarah tapped lightly after considering—and discarding—the idea of going home and forgetting about the whole thing and withdrawing from the class. But that *would* truly make her a coward, and she was no coward. The door opened suddenly, pulled by a woman not quite as tall as Sarah and with a hardened expression on what was otherwise a pleasant face. Glasses covered inquisitive blue eyes. Her hair was so dark it almost looked black, but up close, Sarah could see swirls of subtle shades of brown and auburn, all pulled back in a severe ponytail.

"Yes?" asked a voice as sharp as a skate blade.

"I, ah…"

Sarah hadn't felt this incompetent, this blameworthy, since she was eleven and accidentally let the cat out the back door. Poor Alma ended up being taken in by another family who thought she was a stray that they therefore didn't have to give back. Sarah's mother told her she would just have to live with the fact that Alma had a new family.

"I think I'm supposed to be in there."

"A little late, are we?"

"I'm very sorry. Are you Professor Joyce?"

An obnoxious tilt of the chin, eyes narrowed to slits behind the glasses. "I am. Who's asking?"

"Sarah. Ah, Sarah Brennan."

Professor Joyce looked her up and down, pursed her lips in silent judgment, clearly displeased at the interruption. It seemed like an hour before she stepped aside to let Sarah pass, and it was like walking past a cool breeze. Sarah rushed to the nearest empty seat at the back of the room as three dozen or so pairs of eyes swung in her direction. Whatever. Sarah ignored them, fished around in her knapsack for her iPad so she could take notes. She'd made far more embarrassing mistakes on the ice in front of thousands of people; this was nothing but a momentary irritation. *Move on, people, nothing to see here.*

"Let's get back to what I was talking about before the interruption." The professor's faint Irish accent resembled a blunt instrument intended to pound Sarah a little more before she let her off the hook. Undaunted, Sarah smiled. The professor was actually kind of cute when she was pissed off.

"Some of the…the…ah."

Sarah's smile spread wider. Something about getting under the professor's skin shot a little thrill through her. Oh yeah. She was going to enjoy this class.

"Excuse me, ah, the things I want you all to concentrate on, as we make our way through the reading list, is to be alert to the central role played by cultural nationalism in shaping Irish writing. And vice versa, of course. We will look at how Irish literary culture was both promoted and suppressed, historically. How censorship impeded and inspired Irish writers. We're going to identify major themes in Irish literature over the last hundred and thirty years or so and how those themes were influenced by historical and political challenges. You will see fairly quickly how Irish writers, in a country subjugated, ignored, and oppressed by the British, broke free of those invisible chains and demanded to be heard. And ultimately, we will discuss the importance of the role of writing in Irish society, its transformation over the twentieth century from a revolutionary tool to something celebrated and respected around the world."

Sarah took a steadying breath. She had always been good in school, had proved herself as much more than a Division 1 scholarship jock at Boston College by completing her applied mathematics degree summa cum laude, plus tacking on a minor in literature. She'd always been a sucker for reading novels in her spare time—on buses, in taxis, on planes, whenever she had a few minutes. The minor in literature had been for her own pleasure, same as this course. She could do this course, she knew she could, though at the moment she felt woefully out of practice.

The professor spent the next thirty minutes summarizing the history of Ireland from the mid-1800s to present day, before reminding everyone to start reading the first couple of books from the syllabus—the syllabus Sarah hadn't received because she was late.

"Oh, one more thing." Professor Joyce looked at Sarah. "Sarah Brennan, please stay after class and see me."

Sarah stuffed her iPad in her knapsack. If Professor Joyce wanted to wield her power over her some more, like, if this shit was *fun* for her, well, have at it. Sarah could take it.

"Come with me to my office," the professor said as she gathered her things, slid them neatly into a leather messenger briefcase that looked like it had a few miles on it. The woman didn't look at Sarah, but clearly expected her to be right behind her as she strode down the corridor and up a set of stairs, her comfortable heels hitting the floor in perfect rhythm. More doors. Claire Joyce stopped at one marked 2340, opened it with a key from her pocket, and promptly ignored Sarah for another minute while she removed her papers from her case, made room on her desk, adjusted her glasses, draped her tailored suit jacket on the back of her chair, powered up her laptop, and finally sat down.

"Have a seat, please."

Power tripper. Sarah kept her mouth zipped and sat.

The professor clicked a few buttons on her laptop, peered at the screen. "I haven't seen you around here before, Sarah Brennan. It says here that you're a mature student, that you already have a degree from Boston College. In mathematics. And...literature, it seems. Hmm." A grunt that could be interpreted as approval or dismissal, it was hard to tell. "I'm curious. Why are you here?"

The question sounded innocent enough, but those blue eyes on her were unsettling. Things were going on behind those eyes that Sarah had no chance of deciphering. "I'm just here to take a course. Your course. I thought it would be interesting."

"I see. Why?"

Sarah flashed her most earnest, winsome smile, the same one she'd used in that deodorant commercial she did three years back, when the professional league she belonged to was getting underway. The smile was her default whenever she felt nervous. And she hated feeling nervous. She dropped the smile. "I, ah, want to keep my mind sharp. I feel like, in my line of work, it's... it's a different kind of mental sharpness. Not the book kind. And I want the book kind. I miss the book kind. I mean, I read a lot, but it's not the same as critical evaluation and analysis. I would like a better understanding of the genres, modes, styles, and cultural history of Irish writing. And...all that." Sarah closed her mouth to keep from rambling any further.

"I see," was all the professor said.

You should be a poker player, Sarah thought without admiration. "May I have the course syllabus?"

The professor slid a piece of paper across the desk to Sarah. The reading list: Wilde, Yeats, O'Brien, Joyce (James, not Claire), Williams, Doyle, Keegan, Boyle. Okay, not too bad. She could get through those easily enough in the next four months. Not much else to do on the long bus and plane rides. She folded the piece of paper and stuffed it in her back pocket.

"I don't like to email my students the syllabus, or, funnily enough, they don't bother showing up to the first class. Speaking of which, if you plan to make a habit of being late, please don't bother to come. It's disruptive to the class."

"It was an aberration that won't happen again, I assure you."

The professor nodded. She seemed to soften a little, perhaps realizing she was being a little hard on her newest student or that she'd made her point as a hard-ass and could let up now. There was almost a smile at the corner of her lips. "Tell me, Sarah Brennan. What is it that you do when you're not running around trying to find classrooms in strange buildings?"

"When I'm not lost on university campuses, I'm trying not to look lost on the ice."

A blank stare.

Sarah cleared her throat against her joke that fell so decidedly flat. "I play hockey. For the Toronto team." Another blank stare, and Sarah wanted to roll her eyes. "In the women's professional league."

"Oh."

Exactly the kind of uninformed response that was all too common—even in her own family—and it drove Sarah nuts. Clearly the professor had no idea that women played professional hockey or that the city had a team and that Sarah was a member of that team. It wasn't that her ego needed stroking by having a stranger recognize her name or her face. What bugged her was that Professor Joyce's ignorance was another dismal reminder of how far women's hockey had yet to go. Three years and still the league was invisible to far too many people.

Briefly, Sarah thought about turning the tables, giving the professor a little lesson on the appeal of hockey and the importance of women's sports. She decided not to engage because it was probably a waste of her time. "I'll be seeing you, professor."

"Right. Next Tuesday, I suppose."

"Next Tuesday," Sarah replied without enthusiasm.

She felt the professor's gaze, less condemning and more curious this time, follow her out the door.

CHAPTER TWO

"Mom, Mom!"

Maddie burst through the front door, holding her Wonder Woman overnight bag in one hand and something else in her other hand, a rolled-up poster, by the look of it.

"Hi, sweetheart." Claire hugged her daughter to her chest, ignoring the pinch from the plastic shell of the little suitcase digging into her side. "Matt. Hi."

"Heya, Claire."

Claire's ex-husband towered over them both as he stood in the foyer, his big hands spread out awkwardly like he wasn't quite sure what to do next. It had been more than five years, these acts of shuttling Maddie between their homes. Maddie had long ago learned to take it all in stride. The adults, however, had been a little slower in getting used to the new order of things, but they had a routine down now that worked, with co-parenting drama kept to a minimum.

"How were things at Dad's?" she asked out of habit, her arm still around her daughter's shoulder. She both loved and hated it when Maddie was away. Curling up with a book and a glass of wine without attending to anyone else's needs was heavenly to Claire. For about an hour or two. Then she'd start missing Maddie like crazy, but she kept her loneliness to herself.

"Good, Mom. I got another birthday present!"

"Your birthday was a week ago, *alannah*." Maddie seemed to think turning ten was a particularly noteworthy milestone, like thirteen or sixteen or eighteen, and deserving of weeks of gifts and attention. She was into her second decade, she had smartly reminded her parents. Wasn't that worth something big?

"I know. But Dad and Laurie got me this fantastic new poster. And it's my favorite hockey player!"

Not this again. Ever since Maddie started playing hockey last winter, it was all she talked about. Summer brought no reprieve, because she had insisted on participating in two different hockey camps. She supposed her daughter was right in her insistence that her dedication and all the extra coaching would make her a much better player, but she knew nothing about hockey. Less than nothing. She flashed a look of frustration at Matt, but his response was a guilty smile and a what-can-you-do shrug. He wasn't fooling Claire; he was thrilled that his daughter had taken up playing sports. A chip off the old block.

"Dad, wanna help me hang it up in my bedroom?"

"I'll let your mom help you with that later, sport. I gotta run. I promised Laurie I'd cook tonight."

Matt was out the door and down the front walkway before Maddie's shoes were off and she was tugging her mother's hand. "Come on, Mom, let's go put the poster up. Can we please?"

"Supper's almost ready, honey. How about we put it up later?"

"But it'll be dark soon. I want to make sure it's not crooked. And I want the afternoon light to hit it just right."

Claire laughed. "What are you, an interior designer?"

"Maybe someday. After I'm done being a professional hockey player."

Claire blinked in surprise. "Sorry? What's this about a professional hockey player?" Last month she wanted to be a veterinarian. The month before that it was a chef.

"Dad says I can if I want to. I mean, if I'm good enough. But I have a lot of catching up to do because some of the kids on my team have been playing twice as long as me. He says I have a lot of work to do the next year or two, but that I can do it if I really try." Maddie raced up the stairs.

Claire swore under her breath. Why did he have to encourage this kind of nonsense? A life in pro sports was the last thing she wanted for Maddie—a short career fraught with all kinds of unknowns. She'd need to have a talk with him, tell him to cool it with the hockey stuff.

"Well, look, honey, he's right in that you can do anything you want, as long as you try really hard and put the work into it."

"I know all that, Mom. And I can't wait."

Claire followed Maddie up the stairs, though much less energetically. So she wanted to be a pro hockey player like her new student, Sarah Brennan. Great. Just great. At least Maddie was only ten. There was lots of time between now and adulthood for her to change her mind at least another fifteen times or so.

In her bedroom, Maddie made quick work of unfurling the poster. She took it to the wall over her bed and held it up, pinning one corner, directing her mother to pin the other. They stepped back, Maddie wide-eyed and grinning at the poster with almost religious zeal. Claire's stomach took a major altitude drop. The poster was of none other than Sarah Brennan, dressed in her hockey uniform, her face smiling like she hadn't a care in the world. Which was probably accurate. Cares and Sarah Brennan seemed to be strangers.

"Isn't she awesome?" Maddie gushed. "And she's so pretty, too. Don't you think, Mom?"

Claire couldn't find her voice, so deep was her shock. Or maybe it wasn't shock so much as irritation at this little invasion, at this persistent stone in her shoe known as Sarah Brennan. It was bad enough that Sarah had gotten off on the wrong foot in class, now she was right here, taking up all kinds of space in her daughter's head. Claire stalled, trying all kinds of mental gymnastics to convince herself that nothing would come of a harmless little crush on a hockey player—even if the player was an unworthy idol in her mind. It would pass, she told herself. Her composed smile came late and was forced, and she could see that she hadn't fooled Maddie, who stared at her mother in a silent challenge, her arms folded defiantly across her chest.

To put things right, Claire conceded that Sarah Brennan did, indeed, look like a really great player.

"She *is* a great player. She's the captain of the team. And she's been to the Olympics with Team Canada and everything!"

Claire made herself look at the poster. Really look. For Maddie's sake she could admit Sarah Brennan was likely a very good player, but she would not admit, *never* admit, that Maddie was right about Sarah being pretty. In class, she'd been too annoyed, too exasperated, to register anything but the collar-length blond hair. But now she studied the hazel eyes that changed with the light and perhaps with her mood, too, and yes, they were indeed gorgeous. Her smile was killer, too, and could probably light up an entire city in a blackout. No wonder the team had made her their poster child. *I'd probably have made her the poster child, too.*

Claire reminded Maddie that dinner was going to burn if they didn't get to it. She didn't have time to admire posters any longer or to talk about hockey.

"But we just put it up."

"How about you stare at it after supper. *If* your homework is done. And it will be right there on your wall in the morning when you wake up, all right?"

Maddie thought for a moment. "Mom, do you think someday I might be as good a player as Sarah Brennan?"

"You never know, darling, you just might." Claire was astounded to think that—okay, yes—those gorgeous eyes and that ridiculously bright smile would be staring down at them later as she tucked her daughter into bed.

Over dinner, Maddie said, "Mom, do you think I'll ever get to meet Sarah?"

You're not missing much so far, Claire thought churlishly, but that was chased by a wisp of regret. It was entirely possible that she had been a little hard on Sarah. Not likely, but, well, maybe. "You never know, darling, you never know."

"She lives right here in Toronto. I'm sure we'll see her on the street or at the mall or something, won't we? Like, she must walk around and shop like regular people. People like us."

"I'm sure she does." And maybe even takes a course at the university because she's bored with her life or something. Who knew?

Later in Maddie's bedroom, the two spent time reading their own books until Maddie started nodding off. Claire turned out the light and softly closed the bedroom door behind her. She pressed her ear against the door long enough to hear Maddie whisper, "Good night, Sarah."

Defeat made Claire lean against the closed door. She was outnumbered by Matt and Maddie. Sarah too. All of them athletes, all of them into sports. Matt had played professional football for a decade, his Canadian Football League career straddling the years before and after Maddie came along. By the time cumulative injuries forced him to retire at the age of thirty-five, Claire was long gone from the marriage. They eventually shared custody of Maddie, but not until after he figured out how to adapt to a world that was no longer consumed by practices and games and travel. From afar, she had watched as he descended more and more into a bottle and into his own grief at losing the career he loved. It took the help of a therapist, but he pulled himself together, found Laurie, started a new career building high-end homes. He seemed happy for the first time in many years, and while he and Claire had become sort-of friends, there was occasional friction. Like with this hockey stuff. She knew Matt wouldn't agree with her about it. Sports was the one thing they had never agreed on. But she didn't want to fight, and she didn't want to be that person who discouraged her daughter from something she was so passionate about.

No. Her best course of action was to hope another hobby came along. Or at least another idol.

CHAPTER THREE

The B-minus in bold red pen on her paper shouldn't have upset Sarah. It wasn't a big deal for a course she was simply taking for her own amusement, but it did bother her. It bothered the hell out of her. She didn't do things in half measures, and she didn't like her work—whatever work it was—labeled substandard. At Boston College, she worked her ass off to maintain a 4.0 GPA while playing on the team's first line. It was why she didn't have a social life for years, because she was either on the ice, in the gym, or in the school library. Her teammates called her Serious Sarah, and when it wasn't that, it was Solitary Sarah. Whatever.

Sitting at the back of the classroom, Sarah fired up her iPad and continued to fume. She looked around the room at her fellow students hanging on Professor Joyce's every word—every *sacred* word—Joyce the guru on all things Irish literature, her disciples paying rapt attention. Sarah's analysis of the use of color as symbols of meaning in the classic Oscar Wilde novel *The Picture of Dorian Gray* had been inventive, she thought, a good paper on the topic. They had been tasked with reading the novel and choosing a theme, a motif, a character, or symbols and to expound on their meaning. Sarah argued Dorian Gray's innocence and then his degradation could be charted by Wilde's use of colors. For instance, phrases describing Gray's boyhood as "white purity" and sins described as scarlet in one passage. And a secondary character near the end, when Gray's sins had nearly destroyed him, was described as having a face like a "white handkerchief." Or, in other words, the passage was symbolic of Gray's surrender and death. They were like little trail markers Wilde left for the reader, Sarah explained in her paper. Little breadcrumbs. Had she been wrong? She didn't think so. But she did begin to wonder if the professor was on some kind of vendetta against her. Had being late for the first class really pissed her off that much?

Professor Joyce asked a student named Jackson Dunn to stand up and explain to his classmates why his paper received an A (the only one to do so, Joyce announced pointedly). Sarah watched as the gangly, pimply-faced young man described almost exactly the same summation she'd made in her own paper. After that, she spent the rest of the lecture fantasizing about all the ways she might verbally—or not so verbally—tear a strip off the haughty professor. If she were a hockey player, Sarah imagined, she would squeeze her into a corner using her shoulder and hip, squash her good, right into the boards. Or maybe twist the blade of her stick between the professor's feet until she corkscrewed to the ice. The fantasy wasn't making her feel any better about her mark, unfortunately. There was only one way to find out why she was being treated so unfairly.

At the end of class, she approached the professor. "Can I speak privately with you, Professor Joyce?"

The professor took her sweet time shuffling her papers, slipping them practically one page at a time into her messenger bag. Students filed past solo or in groups, but a couple of them lingered, jettisoning any chance of a private conversation. Just when Sarah was about to give up, the professor said, "Follow me to my office."

Neither spoke on the way up to the next floor. Sarah decided she would not lose her temper. She would not give Joyce any reason to kick her out of the course, would not give her the satisfaction of watching the star hockey player leave campus with her tail between her legs, a failure. *Well, not this hockey player.*

With the door closed and the professor seated, Sarah stood clutching a printout of her essay in her hand.

"All right. What is it that's so urgent?" Calm and cold as an ice-covered lake. Did she want Sarah to genuflect, too? Kiss her ring?

Evenly, Sarah said, "I don't deserve a B-minus on this paper. I would like you to consider a revision."

A skeptical peer over her glasses, her eyes shards of blue. "And you're basing this on…?"

"On the fact that Jackson Dunn said basically the same thing and he got an A."

"I see. And do you know Jackson Dunn? Outside of class?"

"Are you suggesting I *cheated*?"

"I'm simply doing my due diligence in asking the question."

Sarah's blood pounded in her temples. This was absurd. "Ask something else. Because I did *not* cheat."

"All right, then, how about this. So you're a professional athlete wanting to expand your mind. Why *my* course on Irish literature?"

Should she be impressed that the professor remembered she was a pro athlete? "I like to read novels. I find Irish authors particularly appealing, and I want to learn more about the authors and their work."

"Are you sure this isn't some experiment in tracing your family roots? Immersing yourself in the culture of your ancestors? Because with a name like Brennan…I suppose you might be *curious* about your roots."

The woman was infuriating. Did she really think it was any of her business *why* someone wanted to take her course? Sarah was in no mood to indulge the professor's ego.

"With a name like Joyce and with your accent, you're clearly Irish. Is teaching this course a way for you to immerse yourself in the culture of *your* ancestors?"

Sarah regretted her words as soon as they were out of her mouth, and not because Professor Joyce's jaw clamped so tightly that her mouth practically disappeared. What she regretted was dropping into the gutter with her and slugging it out, because it was the high road she usually took, not…this. Opponents on the ice were always trying to get under her skin, throw her off her game, and she had no trouble rebuffing and ignoring that crap there. Did she have to put up with it here, though, in the halls and classrooms of higher education?

"I was born in Ireland and lived there until I was almost eleven. I can assure you I'm not on a path to discover things about ancient ancestors."

"Neither am I." A truce might be a good idea. Sarah tamped down her insolence. "Will you please look at my paper again?"

They stared at one another until the professor blinked. "Is that your essay in your hand?"

"Yes." Sarah handed it over, but not before her gaze landed on a framed photo on the windowsill beyond the professor's chair. How had she not noticed it before? The picture was of a young girl in a hockey uniform, skates and stick planted firmly on the ice, a proud smile eating up her face. The kid's hair was the same dark shade as the professor's, same thick waves, same blue eyes too. Sarah smiled. She had been that kid once too, so eager to be in her skates every minute of the day, playing the game she loved. Seeing the kids, the young girls especially, grow their passion for hockey was what kept her in the game. It fed her commitment, her desire to play clean, to play well, to be a good teammate and a good person. She knew those kids watched her every move, looked up to her as one of their heroes. It might seem silly to some, but not to Sarah.

"Who's the young hockey player?" she asked. The girl was around the same age that the game had begun to consume Sarah, and consume her it did. The night before game days, she would set out all her equipment, pack it and repack it in her bag, and the next morning she'd make her parents drive her to the arena at least two hours early. She could still remember the tingle of nervous excitement in her belly that turned to fire in her veins whenever she stepped onto the ice. She still got those same butterflies before every game, the fire too.

The professor didn't reply. She didn't even look up from reading Sarah's essay until she was done. "All right. I'll bump your mark up to an A." No apology, no further explanation. Not even a facial expression as she handed the essay back to Sarah.

"Thanks." Sarah turned to leave, then changed her mind at the door. "You know, if you give me half a chance, you might come to realize that I'm not such a terrible person."

The professor looked up at her. "Okay. I'll remember that."

With a nod, Sarah indicated the framed photo. "You should bring your…daughter?…to one of my games. She'd enjoy it. As might you."

Professor Joyce's eyes widened and her mouth slackened into an O.

Sarah winked at her before leaving.

In the hall, she threw a triumphant fist into the air.

CHAPTER FOUR

"You know," Claire said to her colleague and friend, Nora Farouk. "I think I'd rather go to the dentist than to this thing tonight."

Nora snaked her arm through Claire's and laughed. "I know you would. A root canal to be exact. Am I right?"

"You're always so much more graphic than I am."

"I like vivid descriptions. Which is why I teach creative writing, remember? And you, literature."

"Yeah, okay, so I'm an aesthete who enjoys *other* people's writing." It wasn't a new joke between them. "Remind me again why I couldn't have just sent Darlene flowers and a nice note?"

Darlene Levy was the head administrative assistant in the English Department, who was calling it a career one day after her sixtieth birthday. Nora and some of the other professors and admin folks had organized a farewell dinner for her at the Northbound Brewery, a popular pub in the city's Distillery District.

"Because Darlene was the best, and we all love her. Including you."

Claire did love Darlene, but get-togethers like this? Not so much. She couldn't remember the last time she'd been in a brewery or pub. The noise assaulted her the instant they stepped inside, and she had to close her eyes and take a deep breath to get her bearings. The noise was mostly talk, the music dialed back to a reasonable level. It was warm and people were laughing loudly. They were happy, and for a moment Claire envied their ability to have fun, to discard their worries so easily and so publicly. She had never been one of those people to dive right into a party, to let loose, the way Matt could or the way her parents did when she was young. The whole concept of a cocktail party sounded like torture to her. As proof, it had been years since she'd been out for a night that involved a little alcohol and lots of conversation. Apparently people still did those kinds of things.

Claire and Nora joined the large table of ten after bumping their way through the throng. The server was efficient—she was on them instantly for drink orders. Nora ordered a negroni. "Would you like one too, Claire? They're all the rage."

"What is a negroni? Actually, forget it. I'm afraid to know." Wine, a gin and tonic, a hot whisky—these were the sum of her drinking adventures.

"How about a gimlet?"

"I don't know what that is either."

"A cosmo? An old-fashioned?"

"You can go through the whole alphabet, and I still won't know what these are. Luckily, I *do* know what wine is."

"At forty-one, it's time you learned your cocktails, Claire." Nora promptly ordered a French 75 for her friend before Claire had a chance to object.

"You're looking to get me drunk on whatever a French 75 is?"

"Yes. You've stumbled upon my plan to successfully convince you to take that daughter of yours to a women's professional hockey game later this fall." Nora's family was hockey mad. "I figure a little alcohol will help me state my case. Or rather, help *you* respond positively to my case."

"Well, bring on the drinks, because it won't work. Matt can take Maddie to see a game sometime, since he seems to think this hockey thing is such a fantastic idea. Maddie's already been bugging us to go. When does the season start anyway?"

"I think it starts soon. A couple more weeks or something."

Months ago, Claire had confided in Nora how much Maddie loved hockey and how badly Claire wished she didn't. How had her life taken this unexpected veer into the world of sports again after all these years? She was supposed to be done with going to sporting events, talking about sports, pretending first that it was football she liked and now hockey. For Maddie, she would at least try. For now. *But please, god, get her off this hockey kick soon.*

"It's just one game, that's all. No biggie."

"Have you met my kid? A game or two this year, and next year she'll want season tickets."

Claire took a sip of her cocktail. Gin, lemon juice, simple syrup, and prosecco, Nora explained. It was actually amazingly good. More precisely, it tasted like a fist in a silk glove.

"Okay, so you can go to a couple of games for now. You'll survive it, I promise, and it might even be fun. Who's Maddie's biggest hockey hero at the moment? McDavid? Crosby? That Bedard kid in Chicago?" The names rolled off Nora's tongue like everyday household words.

Claire rolled her eyes. "None of the above. It's Sarah Brennan. She plays for the Toronto team. Maddie even has a poster of her to prove her undying loyalty." Nora didn't need to know that Sarah Brennan was in one of her classes, because she was just another student. No need to belabor the conversation.

"Ooh, nice! It's a woman player she's styling herself after. I like it. Way to go, Maddie, good choice. And it's perfect that this Sarah Brennan plays for the Toronto team." Nora spoke casually to the others around the table, glancing occasionally at her phone in her lap and furtively tapping away. She turned to Claire and whispered, "Oh, wow, she's a hottie!"

"Who?"

"Sarah Brennan."

"You're *Googling* her?"

"Of course. She's quite the star player. Thirty-six years old, been to three Olympic Games. Maddie could do worse, you know. In fact, I think Maddie should meet her idol one of these days, wouldn't that be cool? She'd love that. It can't be that hard to arrange a meeting. All you have to do is look at the team's social media accounts, they usually say what the players are doing for public appearances. Want me to keep an eye out, Claire?"

Over my dead body, Claire thought. "Look, I'd do anything for Maddie. I just don't—"

"Holy crap!"

"What?"

Nora ignored her and leapt out of her chair so quickly that it wobbled and nearly toppled over. She grabbed Claire by the arm and tugged. "Come *on*."

"If you think I'm going to dance…"

"No, no. There's someone you need to meet."

Claire followed her friend through a labyrinth of tables before coming to a stop in front of a group of rowdy women, more than a dozen of them in all. They were boisterous, but they didn't seem to be drunk, and they weren't obnoxious like the kind of bar people who wanted everyone in the place to hear their precious and spectacular conversation, sprinkled with bouts of appropriately loud laughter. Only a few glasses of beer stood on the table—no shot glasses, no pitchers. Nora tapped on the shoulder of a blonde who was seated before them. The woman turned and settled hazel eyes on Nora.

Oh. My. God. It was Sarah Brennan. It was bad enough that they'd been talking about her, now she was here? In the same pub? Was there no escaping her? *Bloody hell.* Claire tucked herself further behind Nora in the vain hope of becoming invisible, and prayed Sarah wouldn't notice her.

Nora reached for Sarah's hand to shake. "Oh, it—it really is you! I'm so happy to meet you. I thought that was you over here. From your photos."

Sarah rose from her chair, shook Nora's hand. "I'm Sarah. Nice to meet you, too."

"It's not often I get to meet an actual professional hockey player. Matter of fact, my friend's daughter is a huge fan of yours, like the biggest ever, and we just had to come over here and meet Maddie's idol."

Claire took a minute to furtively watch Sarah. Her smile was easy and unhurried, her expression open and friendly. Did she have to be so...so...damned *nice* about being interrupted? So gracious? She was explaining to Nora how she loved meeting fans, loved talking about hockey, especially with girls who had hockey dreams.

"This is almost our whole team. We're sort of celebrating that training camp starts in a couple of days. It's...not something we do a lot...Here, I mean. This." She motioned to a half-empty glass in front of her, as though she didn't want Claire and Nora jumping to the wrong conclusions. It was sort of...cute.

As if reading her mind, Nora turned and whispered to Claire, "Could she be any more adorable?" To Sarah, she said, "My friend's daughter would absolutely love to meet you one day or get you to sign a puck for her or something. It's funny, because we were just talking about that. Weren't we, Claire? Where *are* you?"

Nora stepped aside, exposing Claire, who wanted nothing more than to disappear into the floor. While she tried to think of something to say, since running away wasn't a mature option, she noticed the expression on Sarah's face go from friendly to surprised to guarded, then back to friendly again, all in the blink of an eye. It wasn't something she expected Nora to notice.

"Hello," Sarah said to her. Not exactly warm, but not cold. "Nice to see you again, Professor Joyce."

Oh, crap. She could feel Nora's eyes drilling into her. She'd be upset that Claire hadn't fessed up about knowing Sarah, and she had no defense, no excuse. Sweat trickled down her back. She was burning up. Was she getting hot flashes already? *Christ.*

"You..." Nora pointed in surprise from Claire to Sarah. "Know one another from class? What class?"

"I'll tell you later," Claire supplied, stepping on Nora's toes to get her to shut up about it all.

"Oh, wait," Nora said to Sarah. "She even has one of your hockey posters on her bedroom wall, you know."

"Does she now?" Sarah's slow smile was way too cocky for Claire's liking. She might be enjoying this little exchange, but Claire was mortified. She would never live this down, not with Nora and not with Sarah.

"Oops." Nora giggled. Clearly her negroni had turned her into a starstruck buffoon. "Of course, I mean Claire's daughter, Maddie, has the poster in her room."

"Wow, that's cool," Sarah replied, not taking her eyes off Claire. "I'd love to meet Maddie one day. She plays hockey, right?"

Nora again. "She does. And she's dying to go to one of your games."

"Well, I think I can help with that."

Claire finally found her voice. "Really, it's okay. I'm sure we, I mean my ex, can figure out how to get tickets sometime. But thank you." She turned abruptly and began weaving her way back to their table, Nora hurrying to keep up.

"What was *that* all about?"

Claire played dumb. "What?"

"You know Sarah Brennan and you didn't tell me?"

"Why would I tell you about some random hockey player in one of my classes?"

Nora waved to the server and asked for two more drinks.

"Are you nuts?" Claire protested. "You're going to get me drunk as a skunk!"

"Good! Then you can tell me all about Sarah Brennan being one of your students." Nora's smile arranged itself into something far too animated for Claire's liking. "Is she single?"

"How the hell would I know a thing like that?"

"Because…"

She dared Nora to spit it out. "Yes?"

"Nothing. It's just, she's so attractive, that's all."

"So are any number of people in this city. Look. She's not *your* student, so you go ahead and date her if you want." It wasn't a secret at work that Claire was bi. A couple of years ago she had offered to teach a graduate course on how bisexuality was handled in Victorian and early twentieth-century literature. Outing herself had gone surprisingly well; nobody had batted an eye.

Nora cackled. "If I wasn't straight, I might actually consider that." She tipped her glass in a toast to Claire. "She won't be your student forever, you know. I'm saying she's a catch, that's all. And, you know, you're single."

"Oh, stop. Sarah Brennan—or any athlete, for that matter— would be the last person I'd ever date. If dating was even something I cared about. Which I don't." And Nora damned well knew it; it was the booze talking.

Nora waved a finger at Claire. "You should never make such declarations."

Claire hadn't dated anyone seriously since she and Matt ended their marriage six years ago. Her job and being a co-parent to a busy girl didn't allow for much intimate socializing. But she did puzzle over why she'd told Sarah that her ex could look into getting tickets to a game. Her *ex*. Why hadn't she called him Maddie's father or even just Matt? Her intentional evasiveness troubled her. To Nora, she said, "I think I know my own mind, thank you very much."

"Just remember, my friend. Declarations like that have a way of coming back and biting you in the ass."

"Ha! Not this ass."

CHAPTER FIVE

Sarah squeezed analgesic topical onto both her knees and rubbed vigorously. Her thirty-six-year-old knees weren't exactly screaming at her, but they were grumbling. And when they grumbled, she paid attention.

Brett Quincy, Sarah's teammate and best friend, plopped down on the bench beside her. The two had first become teammates more than a decade ago at tryouts for Team Canada in Calgary. Brett's car had broken down on the way to practice, and Sarah had happened upon her. Missing practice, unless you had the excuse of being on your deathbed, was not something to be trifled with. Brett, profusely thankful, promised Sarah her firstborn, and Sarah said she'd settle for being friends. It was pure luck they were drafted to the same team three years ago for the inaugural women's pro league.

"Oh, man. I'm too old for those damned suicide sprints," Brett whined. She'd never been one to keep her complaints to herself, and yet nothing could tear her away from the game. Every training camp was a marathon of pain and exhaustion, something to be endured. But there was nowhere else either of them wanted to be.

The locker room remained faintly redolent of sweat, and Sarah and Brett were the only ones left behind. As the two oldest players on the team, it took them longer than it did the younger players to manage their bodies after a practice or a game. Long stationary bike rides to cool down their legs, ice baths, sometimes a massage or a chiropractic treatment were all par for the course. Occasionally they were the butt of practical jokes. Like the time a cane was left leaning against Sarah's locker. Another time it was a box of adult diapers for Brett. Crude, but all in good fun, and Sarah and Brett exacted their revenge in time. Once, they took over the music in the locker room and blasted out old tunes from the 1950s and 1960s. Another time, they wove little jingle bells through the laces of the two youngest players. "So we can hear you coming on the ice," Sarah explained. "You know, the old hearing starts to go when you're over thirty."

Sarah was in no mood to laugh about her age now, as she waited for the topical on her knees to take effect. "Do you think in my next contract I can have a clause for optional practices?"

"Sure, if you want to be paid half as much."

Sarah laughed. "Half of almost nothing is, well…Not much." They might be professionals, but that did not mean they made the salaries of professional male hockey players. Not even close. It was a living, and it paid her more than twice what she'd made during her years as a carded Canadian athlete under the national athlete assistance program. In any case, to stretch her money further, she rented a tiny fifteenth-floor downtown condo that was barely big enough to turn around in. Brett, on the other hand, didn't have such worries; her wife, Kelly, was a physician. They lived in a nice two-story, brick and stucco Art Deco style home in Cabbagetown, only a few kilometers from Sarah's building.

"Hey," Brett said, zipping up her duffel. "Before I forget, join us for dinner tonight? I was supposed to text you about it last night, so please don't get me in shit with my wife by telling me you already have plans."

"Ha, me have other plans? For dinner?"

"Well, we do keep wishing you'd let us set you up with one of Kelly's single colleagues, but you keep pretending to enjoy the single life."

"I do enjoy the single life."

"You simply enjoy not having anyone to answer to. In other words, you enjoy being alone."

"Hey, my place is too small to feel alone. Sometimes I even get on my own nerves."

Brett laughed. "Figures. But look, even *you* need to get laid once in a while."

"True that. But I'm picky, so…"

"If you were any pickier, you'd be a nun."

Sarah lightly smacked Brett's shoulder. "You want me to say a Hail Mary for you?" She'd never forget her punishment for stealing the teacher's apple off her desk one day. At home, her mother had made her sit in a corner and say the entire rosary three times over.

"I think I can do without the Hail Mary, thanks. Though, on second thought, maybe you can pray for me to score a goal our first game? Coach has been getting on my ass to increase my point production this year."

Brett was a solid, defensive-minded forward who usually played on the third line and killed penalties. Her play was an important factor game in and game out, but it wasn't the kind of skill set that drew a lot of attention.

"Huh. Maybe we can become one player? Coach has been on *me* about improving my defensive play."

"Cool. Maybe my wife knows how to surgically make us into one person. Hmm, probably not though since she's a pediatrician. Come with me to the house now? We'll have a glass of wine and watch Kelly cook."

"You mean we'll have a glass of wine and *help* Kelly cook." Sarah rolled her eyes. "How is it that you manage to stay married?"

"Oh, I have my ways of keeping my wife happy. In fact, last night, I—"

"Okay, okay, I don't need to hear all about your very active married sex life when mine is nonexistent."

Brett sighed. "I'm taking back the erotica book I got you last Christmas, since clearly it's not helping you with the ladies."

"No, please! Book sex is the only sex I get these days. Oh, wait. I need to hit the box office first. Gotta pick up some tickets for our first home game." The team had a couple of exhibition games to play before the season started for real the week after next. "Meet you at your place in a bit?"

"Ooh, do tell who the tickets are for. It's not your family in town, is it?"

Sarah pulled a face. "Yeah, right. They only come to town for conferences." Sarah's family lived in British Columbia—her pharmacist parents, her physiotherapist brother. They were all patiently waiting for her to move onto a *real* career—one that involved more brains and less brawn. Use your mathematics degree to go into engineering, they urged her. Or health care, like them. Or…anything that would result in a long and rewarding career. Yeah, yeah, she kept telling them. Someday.

"Oh, right, sorry." Brett looked away, patted Sarah's knee. "I'll see you when you get there."

* * *

Kelly was a fabulous cook, and she regularly hassled Sarah about eating properly. Or at least eating regularly. "I'm from a big Italian family on my mom's side," Kelly once explained to her. "Food is how we take care of each other."

Sarah peeked in the oven and nearly drooled. It was Kelly's famous lasagna. "Oh, I'm in luck tonight. Thank you, God."

"How was training camp today?"

"A grind but good. We're ready for Boston this weekend, though our power play still kinda sucks. It's coming, though."

Brett pretended to clutch her heart. "For a minute I thought you said the penalty kill sucks. Which would mean that I suck. But since it's the power play, it means *you* suck, my friend."

Sarah took a sip of red wine and smiled around the rim of her glass. "Good one, Quince. You surprise me once in a while."

Kelly pointed her salad tongs accusingly at them. "You two never stop. Are you sure you're not siblings separated at birth?"

"Nope." Brett snapped off a three-finger salute. "Scout's honor. If we were, though, it's obvious I'd be the smarter one."

Sarah grinned. "Oh yeah? Well, I'd be the better-looking one." That earned her a middle-finger salute from Brett.

"Hey, speaking of being smart," Kelly said, "Brett tells me you're taking a university course in your spare time. Irish literature or something. What, hockey doesn't take up enough of your soul?"

"I do have a cultured side, you know."

Brett popped a small tomato into her mouth. "Debatable."

"Man, you guys are so *mean* to each other."

It wasn't something easily understood by outsiders, but Kelly was right. They weren't trying to be cruel or hurtful; it had to do with team bonding. Sarah, Brett, and their fellow players could rag on each other, but if an opponent or any outsider did the same to any one of them, there would be hell to pay. It was also part of learning to maintain a thick skin, which every athlete needed.

"Nah, we're not mean," said Brett. "You know we love each other."

"I do know that." Kelly handed the bowl of Caesar salad for her wife to finish mixing, then planted a kiss on her cheek. "Luckily I'm not insecure."

"Luckily," said Brett, turning the cheek kiss into a full mouth kiss, "I love you best. Cuz you *are* the best, babe."

Sarah sighed loudly for effect. "I'd be happy to do takeout with this if you two would like to be alone." She had heard enough hints from Brett that the couple enjoyed sex. Like, a *lot* of sex. Which was super impressive considering they'd been together six years and married for four. They still acted like newlyweds, pawing each other, kissing.

Kelly broke away and playfully swatted Brett's ass. "Not a chance. First exhibition game this weekend, we need you to eat well, Sar."

"Maybe I should just move in. Oh, wait, no." Sarah remembered about all the sex. No way did she want to be in the next room listening to her friends having sex. That would be… eww. "I'll stay where I am, unless this place has a massive guest wing that I don't know about."

Kelly arched her eyebrow. "What are you talking about?"

Brett stifled a giggle while Sarah bit her tongue until it stung. "I love your house just the way it is. And I'm fine where I am. I like it on my own."

"Speaking of which…" Brett topped up the wineglasses and shot a questioning look at Sarah.

"Oh, leave her alone," Kelly said. Sarah liked Kelly. She was honest, kind, and always took up for the underdog. Which, at the moment, Sarah happened to be. "Not everyone wants or needs to be partnered with someone. In fact, you seem to be doing just fine on your own, Sarah."

"Thank you. I try."

Sarah carried the bowl of salad to the table, while Kelly removed the lasagna from the oven. Brett sliced the garlic bread on the counter. The three had shared dinner so many times that they slid into their tasks as routinely as putting on the day's socks.

"So this literature course you're taking," Kelly said over dinner. "Enjoying it?"

"I am. It forces me to read good books, and in a critical way. I have a minor in literature from Boston College, so it's not super tough or anything, but it does challenge me."

"And the professor? How is he?"

"It's a she." Sarah kept her tone casual. "She's good, but a bit tough."

"I can tell she's tough," Brett said. "The way you're always reading and making notes whenever we're not on the ice. She must get the whip out in class, huh?"

"Sorry to disappoint you about your little whip fantasy. Any whips in class are purely figurative."

"Damn!"

As they cleaned up from dinner, Brett turned to Sarah. "Did you get your tickets for our home opener?"

"I did. Hey, what are you wearing for the catwalk this weekend?"

The players called the game day stroll from the bus to the arena or the walk from the arena parking lot to the back doors the catwalk. They were expected to dress up coming and going to work because there were often fans and media watching or snapping photos. Some of the players welcomed it as an opportunity to make a fashion statement or to ham it up a little. Sarah and Brett were usually on the same page with their style: custom suits, a colorful blouse, sometimes a tie, sometimes a scarf and maybe a fun hat like a beret or fedora. But no dresses or skirts, and no heels. It was their unbreakable rule.

"Nice try on the subject change." Brett pointed the spoons she was washing at Sarah like it was a holdup.

Oh, why did I say anything to her about needing tickets? Brett was a dog with a bone about things. It made her a good hockey player but a pain in the ass as a friend sometimes.

"So," Kelly interjected. "Someone special coming to the game? Someone you're interested in dating, by any chance?"

It was common knowledge that there weren't often special invitees who came to watch Sarah play, since she hadn't been dating anyone lately and her family was on the other side of the country. Sarah would never admit it to anyone but herself, but it would be nice to have people at the games for her once in a while. It sometimes made you play better, made you more accountable, knowing they were in the stands.

"Nope. It's just for, ah, somebody I know who has a young daughter who plays hockey. And the home opener is always tough to get tickets to, so…"

Brett and Kelly looked at each other like they didn't quite believe her. Or maybe they simply hoped that she was trying to romance someone on the down-low.

"What?" Sarah played dumb. She wasn't about to explain that there was this professor, *her* professor, who was driving her nuts, but who was also kind of intriguing in a way Sarah didn't understand. Something quickened her pulse whenever she was around Claire Joyce lately. And yes, for some weird reason, she wanted her to come watch her play and to bring her daughter. That was the crux of it, really. She got to see the professor each week in her element, in the place where she excelled. Now she wanted Claire to come see her in *her* element, in *her* place of excellence. Maybe Professor Joyce would miraculously muster some respect or even admiration for her. Or… Well, that probably wasn't going to happen, but at the very least, Sarah could offer some encouragement to a young girl who loved hockey.

Plus, there had been that chance meeting at the bar the other night, when that brash woman had dragged Claire over to her, with Claire trying to hide, then blushing furiously when she could no longer take cover behind her friend. What was that all about? Why had Claire been trying to hide from her? Why had she been so embarrassed? So uncomfortable? Well, at least she'd shown some emotion. At least she was actually human, had actually had to humble herself in front of Sarah. Sarah caught herself grinning.

"You're smiling," Brett said. "You sure it's not anyone we should know about?"

Sarah carried her plate to the sink. "Nope. Nobody at all."

CHAPTER SIX

Predictably, Maddie was on a massive hockey high, which looked an awful lot like a sugar high. From the minute she, Claire, Matt, and Matt's wife, Laurie, entered the downtown arena, Maddie was a whirling dervish of excitement. First, there was much leaping and skipping and twirling up the crowded stairs and along the concourse. Once in her seat, she bounced and cheered wildly at every little thing—even at mundane PA announcements. She kept flashing her homemade cardboard sign that said "Brennan Is The Best," shaking it emphatically like somehow it might cast a spell—the good kind—on her hero. The kid was going to be exhausted for days, and the game hadn't even started yet.

"When can I meet her? When can I meet her?" Maddie was a needle skipping on a record as Sarah and her teammates skated onto the ice, bathed in colorful spotlights.

Claire didn't mind the exuberance, mostly out of guilt. The look on Maddie's face yesterday when she'd told her Sarah was responsible for getting them the tickets to tonight's home opener. And then when she admitted, reluctantly, that Sarah was her student. Maddie was hurt and angry at having been kept in the dark and dissolved into tears. The betrayal was something she didn't want to do to her daughter again any time soon.

All the trouble the tickets had caused, and she hadn't even sought them out. And she never would, either, because the less she had to do with Sarah Brennan outside of official school business, the better. But Sarah had slipped an envelope with four game tickets beneath Claire's office door ("For your hockey-playing daughter," the scrawl on the envelope said). Claire wanted to decline the tickets—the thought of accepting a favor from Sarah was a place she didn't want to go—and not just because it could be construed as a bribe. As a rule, Claire didn't fraternize with her students. But Matt told her that the game was sold out and that he really wanted Maddie to see her idol in action. For Maddie's sake, Claire gave in. Not like she had much of a choice. After her confession about knowing Sarah, Maddie had demanded to know exactly how her mother was going to make up this duplicity to her. As in, draw up a list. Now.

"I don't know yet. But I promise you I will make it up to you, okay? You'll have to trust me on this, kiddo."

After Maddie went to bed, Claire wasted no time in emailing Sarah—and falling on her sword. She thanked her for the tickets and asked if it might be possible sometime to get an autographed puck or poster for Maddie. There. Just a couple of quick sentences with a very simple request. Within minutes Sarah emailed back a cryptic, "Sure, no problem. I'll think of something for Maddie."

Claire fiddled with the silver Celtic knot ring on her right hand. She would be indebted to Sarah Brennan now.

The starting lineup was announced over the loudspeaker, the lights dimmed, and blue and yellow spotlights lit up the ice surface. When Sarah came gliding out, waving to the crowd in her bright cobalt-blue jersey, Maddie screamed her name and leapt to her feet.

Matt gently pulled his daughter back down. "She hasn't even scored yet, champ. Better save some of those cheers."

"Don't worry, Dad, she will. And I've got plenty of cheers left."

The puck was dropped at center ice and the players were off, battling for the little rubber disc. Sarah was on the first line. She was a forward, it seemed. Claire was going to have to brush up on hockey and all the jargon. No more excuses, with Maddie in her second year of playing, and, well, if they were going to attend a real game occasionally or more than occasionally, she didn't want to sit mute in her seat, trying to decipher what was happening in front of her. She could no longer ignore the evidence that Maddie's obsession with hockey was anything but transitory in nature. Maddie had it bad for hockey.

The crowd oohed as the Toronto team nearly scored. Sarah wore number seventeen, and she seemed always to be in the middle of the scramble in front of the net. Beside Claire, Maddie was quiet and scooted to the edge of her seat in anticipation, her eyes glued to the ice. The concentration and fierce determination on her face didn't escape Claire, and she wondered: Did she get that from me? Or from Matt?

The puck popped loose and sat in the goal crease for what seemed like forever. Nobody was able to find it until Sarah, diving for it with her stick, batted it into the net one-handed. It was highlight reel stuff, and the crowd knew it. They were on their feet for a standing O before Sarah could get up and collect the high-fives from her teammates.

Maddie let loose with a giant "Woohoo" and stomped her feet. Matt gave her a hearty high-five.

"Isn't she great, Mom?" Maddie turned to high-five her as well.

"She is, honey. She's very good."

"She's not just good, she's the best, you know."

Claire smiled in concession, her eyes following Sarah as she headed to the bench. "I think you may be right. She seems quite brilliant out there, doesn't she?"

Even though Claire barely knew a thing about hockey, it couldn't be more obvious that Sarah Brennan was one of the best players on the ice—on either team. Grace, strength, athleticism were on display every time she moved on the ice. It didn't quite fit with the image of the woman at the back of the classroom each week, her nose buried in her iPad as she typed notes. Her essays were, Claire had to admit, always on time, always articulate, and always better than ninety percent of what her classmates handed in.

Her eyes drifted back to the ice and to Sarah. Who seemed to be looking in the direction of the four of them. There was a moment of the tiniest hesitation, Claire swore there was, as Sarah scanned the crowd. There were six thousand people here. How could she possibly be looking for them? Oh, right. She had bought them the tickets and knew where the seats were. When Sarah's eyes landed right on the four of them, Claire's heartbeat accelerated. Suddenly she wanted Sarah's team to win and she wanted Sarah to score a bunch of goals. Did that make her a fan now? *Jesus.* Probably.

The first period was close, each team scoring a goal. A bone-rattling body check against the boards in its final seconds had everybody gasping, including Claire, who relaxed as soon as she saw that Sarah wasn't involved. There would be heartrending tears in her household if Maddie's hero got hurt.

The second period was another close one, with an additional goal from each team. Heading into the third period, the score was 2-2.

"Do you think Sarah will score again, Mom?"

"Gee, I don't know, honey. It seems like a pretty tight game."

"Don't worry. She will. Right, Dad? She'll get the game winner, I know she will."

"Right-o, Mads. The really good players always find a way to score when their team needs it the most."

"But how? How do they score like that when they really, really need to?"

Yeah, Claire wondered, how do they do that? Batting around a tennis ball was about as much as she could handle. Which was marginally sportier than the couple of games of golf she played each year. Matt was the athlete in the family, and yet Claire had never asked him a question like Maddie's. She'd never truly warmed up to sports, not even while she was married to him. Athletics were simply not as deserving of her time, her energy, her passion, as her precious books. Producing Maddie was the summit of their time together as a couple, the best thing Claire cared to remember about that time in her life.

"Well, honey," Matt said. "You do it by being super focused. Like, you have to tune out everything else…the crowd, your opponent, even your teammates. It's almost like you're moving through this tunnel real fast, just you, and there's only the tunnel and the light at the end of it. And you know that's exactly where you're going and when you get there, you know you're going to score. You believe it with every molecule of your body. Concentration and believing in yourself are your superpowers."

Claire listened intently, trying to understand his explanation, but Maddie got it. Sports was a language father and daughter shared. But Mom was going to learn it too, dammit, even if it meant more sitting on hard seats in cold arenas and feeling stupid.

Midway through the third period, an arena usher stopped at their seats and asked if they could wait a few minutes after the game, that he would come back and retrieve them.

"What's that all about?" Laurie asked.

"Beats me," Matt said.

Claire didn't have a clue, either, but at least the suspense wasn't getting to her daughter, because her eyes remained glued to the ice. As the minutes of the final period ticked by, the tension in the arena ramped up. Chants grew louder, conversations were silenced, all eyes followed the puck. Back and forth the play went, both goalies making a couple of spectacular saves at either end. Maddie clutched her mother's hand. "I almost can't look."

"You must look, sweetie, in case Sarah scores. You won't want to miss that."

"Oh, right. Thanks, Mom."

Two minutes left. Toronto had possession of the puck and Sarah's line was on the ice. They passed to one another with perfection and ease, waiting for the perfect opportunity for

Sarah to head to the net. An opponent unexpectedly caught an edge and went down, opening a lane for her to dart through. Just as she arrived at the net, her teammate hit her stick with a perfect pass. Before the goalie had time to react, she one-timed the puck into the back of the net.

The crowd went nuts. Maddie jumped to her feet and did a little dance. She cupped her hands around her mouth and tried to start a chant. "Sar-ah! Sar-ah! Sar-ah!"

Claire grinned, because what else could she do?

It was her daughter's first crush.

CHAPTER SEVEN

Sarah stepped out of the hot shower and hurried to change into a dove-gray tailored suit and lavender blouse, purposely avoiding Brett's gaze. She could feel her friend's curious eyes tracking her movements, but she didn't want to have to explain why she was in a hurry, why she didn't want to hang out in the locker room and dissect the game.

Near the door, Sarah stopped Maxine, the assistant equipment manager. "Okay if I give my game stick away to a special fan today?" The team owned most of the players' equipment, including sticks, which could cost two or three hundred dollars apiece. Each player had at least five, most of them locked away in an equipment closet. Maxine guarded the equipment like a pit bull, because in this league, every penny counted. As did every stick, every puck.

Max hesitated. Of course she was going to say no. Sarah sighed in defeat and went to turn away when she felt the press of Max's hand on her forearm. "It's that stick you cracked in the game, right? The one destined for the trash?"

"Right. That one." *Whew.* "Thanks, Max."

"As long as it's a special fan, we're all good."

"Good. It is."

Sarah grabbed a puck and a couple of Sharpies for her pocket. Outside the locker room and down the hall was a small conference room, and it was there she'd arranged to meet Claire and her daughter. She took a deep breath to banish any nerves, straightened her shoulders the way she did before she entered a room full of reporters or sponsors, and marched in. It was only to meet a young fan, after all.

"Hello, everyone." She gave them her best television smile. That's what she and the players called it, when you smiled so hard your face hurt. "Thanks so much for coming tonight."

"Thank you again for the tickets." The frost on Claire had definitely melted, and it came as a surprise to Sarah that, away from campus, she was almost human. "And…congratulations on the game."

"Thank you." She held Claire's eyes until Claire looked away. "And you're Maddie, right?" Big blue eyes locked onto Sarah's. The girl was completely dumbstruck; it was cute. She looked so much like her mother. "I hear you just might be my biggest fan."

No reply, just an ear-to-ear grin.

"And I also hear that you play hockey, too. What position do you play?"

Maddie shrugged sweetly. In Sarah's experience, kids were often shy when meeting the players. A little ice-breaking usually did the trick.

Claire cleared her throat. "She's a defenseman."

"But probably not for long, now that she's seen you play." The man Sarah assumed was Maddie's father was a big guy, probably six-four, and built like a truck. He stuck out his hand to shake Sarah's. "Matt Hendry. Maddie's dad. Nice to meet you. And that was a helluva game."

"Thank you."

Claire winced. "Sorry, I—This is Laurie, Matt's wife."

Sarah shook hands all around. "Hendry. Why does that name sound familiar?"

Maddie spoke up. "My dad used to play football." She gushed with unabashed pride.

"Ah, yes, okay, Toronto Argonauts. I think I saw you play a couple of times back in the day."

Already she could see she'd won him over. "I don't get many people these days remembering that. Been a few years."

Interesting. So Claire Joyce was once married to a pro athlete. Maybe that explained a few things, like her early rudeness toward Sarah in class or her general awkwardness around her. It might be too early for consideration, but maybe Claire's attitude toward her wasn't entirely personal. Which was…something, at least.

Sarah dropped her eyes to Maddie. "I know this stick is a bit long for you right now, but what do you say? It's my game stick today and I'd like you to have it. If you want it, that is, and I'll sign it for you, too."

Maddie squealed. "Mom! Dad! Laurie! This is the best day of my whole entire life!"

It couldn't possibly be, but okay. It never got old, making kids like Maddie happy. With her Sharpie, Sarah signed the blade of the stick. Then she signed the game puck she'd brought with her and handed them both to Maddie. The girl was about ready to faint.

Sarah placed a calming hand on her shoulder, bent down, and looked her in the eyes. "Whatever happens in your life, whatever direction you take, just remember that you're a hockey player. And that means you're fierce. Because you know what? There's nobody fiercer than a hockey player. Always remember that you are fierce." She looked at Matt and gave him a triumphant little smirk to drive home her point. *Pfft. Football players got nothing on hockey players, buddy.*

Maddie hung on her every word, nodding sagely, hugging the stick and puck to her chest like they were part of her ensemble. "Did you know I have your poster on my bedroom wall?"

"I've heard." Sarah wanted to laugh out loud at the thought of Claire being reminded of her every time she tucked her daughter into bed. Something along the lines of karma being a bitch popped into her head. "Does it at least show my good side?"

"I think it shows all of your good sides," Maddie answered. "Right, Mom?"

Claire glanced quickly away, and Sarah bit the inside of her cheek to keep from smiling.

"Hey, sport," Matt said, putting a beefy arm around his daughter's shoulders. "Did you know your mom once told me that she had a poster of Martina Navratilova on her bedroom wall when she was your age?"

"She did? Mom, how come you never told me that?"

Claire looked mortified. Her cheeks darkened, and those arctic-blue eyes flashed with something a little murderous. There was no resemblance to the professor who was so in command of her class, the master of her subject, with her nerdy glasses and her laser pointer and her granite composure. This, a hockey arena, was clearly not her preferred environment, and it was sort of adorable, actually, maybe even sexy—all that awkward vulnerability on display. It was a side to her professor she never knew existed and certainly never expected to see. It was fun.

"That was so long before your time, honey, that I didn't even think you would know who Martina is."

"Of course I know. She was only, like, one of the best ever tennis players in the world. Sheesh, Mom."

Matt winked at Maddie. "Hmmm. I wonder if your mom still has a crush on Martina."

Sarah liked Matt. He seemed the brutally honest type. And playful.

Maddie smiled up at her mom. "Do you, Mom?"

Okay, so the acorn hadn't fallen far from the tree, seeing father and daughter together. They had a palpable connection between them, and yet it was clear Maddie and her mother were undeniably close, too. She was a lucky kid to have two doting parents.

"Honey, I'm not much into sports, you know that. Or at least, not since I was a kid."

Not into sports, but apparently into athletes. And perhaps not only male athletes. Well, well. A spark of something hot flared in Sarah's chest—not enough to pay it much heed, but she wouldn't forget the feeling any time soon. Claire Joyce was a puzzle. Perhaps even one that was unsolvable, but the attraction was in trying to solve it.

"Did you ever get to meet her, Mom?"

"Who?"

"Duh. Martina!"

"No, sweetie, I never did."

"Then I'm super lucky I got to meet Sarah today."

"No," Sarah corrected. "I'm the lucky one cuz I got to meet my biggest fan today. And since you did me the favor of coming to my game, I would like to return the favor and come to one of your games sometime. How about that? Would that be okay?"

She was pushing it, and if she kept it up, she'd be on a collision course for earning a D in Claire's class or maybe even an F. Oh well. Some things were just plain worth it.

"Oh, man, that would be so amazing!" Maddie jumped up and down again, nearly dropping her stick and puck. "Mom or Dad, can you text Sarah my game schedule?"

"Yeah," Sarah said, looking directly into Claire's slightly panicked face—panic that her glasses couldn't hide. "Can you? That'd be great. *Claire.*" Sarah couldn't resist having a little fun at Claire's expense. Call it sweet revenge for the professor's behavior toward her on campus. She took the cell phone Claire reluctantly produced and, very slowly, typed her number into it. "There. All ready for you to text me anytime you want." She winked at Claire, because, honestly, she could not resist.

Claire cast her eyes away and took a step back, depositing her phone in her coat pocket. Something told Sarah that they were even now.

CHAPTER EIGHT

Claire's gaze traveled to the empty seat in her classroom, the one where Sarah usually sat. She was on a road trip to New York with her team, Claire knew, yet her eyes kept finding the empty seat like a tongue gravitating to the gap where there was once a tooth.

She blamed Maddie for this slight fixation, or distraction, or whatever it was, as though it were a contagious thing. Maddie couldn't, for more than ten minutes at a time, stop talking about Sarah. The hockey player was her daughter's sun, her moon, her whole galaxy. The signed stick was mounted on her bedroom wall, right over her bed and above the poster, and as for the puck, well, this morning Claire found it under Maddie's pillow. For self-preservation and family harmony, she went along with the little love-in, although kissing Sarah's poster good night, as Maddie had asked her to do last night, was over the line. Way over the line. She would not be kissing a poster of Sarah Brennan. Not a chance.

Claire pulled her attention back to the class. "That Yeats poem I had you all read is a little on the depressing side. But perhaps appropriate in these times. For instance, this line: 'The best lack all conviction, while the worst are full of passionate intensity.' Who wants to give it a go?"

A young man with thick facial hair that made him appear much older volunteered. "I think it means good people, the best people, are kind of sitting idly by, while the worst kind of people are impassioned, driven to act."

"Correct," Claire replied. "Kind of like what we're witnessing all around us these days. What is Yeats saying in the next stanza?"

Another student, another reply, and then a third student weighed in. Claire's thoughts drifted to Sarah's two-page essay on the poem, which she'd emailed late last night. She had added in a personal note about how boring it was killing time at the airport, because the team was embarking on a road trip, and the personal connection had melted something in Claire. Only a little, but still. A certain resistance, like the tautness of a string, had begun to slacken. Maybe they both weren't pulling so hard on it anymore. Sarah clearly wasn't withdrawing from the class, and Maddie was nowhere close to removing the halo from Sarah's head. They were sort of stuck in this triad together.

Sarah's essay on the Yeats poem was spot on. She was spot on about pretty much everything the class had so far studied. "He's talking about the end of the world, or at least, the world rapidly heading in that direction," Sarah had written. "The world on the brink of evil, of destruction." This morning, Claire had marked an A on her paper.

There was no denying Sarah Brennan was one of the best students in her Introduction to Irish Literature class. She was anything but a dumb athlete, Claire knew that, and yet her initial assumption that she was wasn't so easy to banish. The truly smart people chose academics, chose a more intellectually based career, didn't they? It was a belief she'd always held, it was gospel to her. Matt, though he wasn't stupid, was never going to be on a debating team. When they met in university, Matt scraped by, earning marks just good enough to keep his football scholarship. He'd never been able to match Claire's intellect, and he wouldn't be able to match Sarah's, either. So why had Sarah chosen sports when she was equally adept at academics?

In a couple more days she would see Sarah at Maddie's hockey game. Her feelings about that were muddled. Originally, the plan was for Matt to take Maddie, but he was going to be tied up with a plumbing crew on a very large and very expensive home he was building for a client in The Beaches. And so it fell to Claire. The last day or so, her sense of dread about the game had given way to some sort of weird, hopeful anticipation. Weird because she realized part of her *wanted* to see Sarah outside of the classroom again. She just didn't know why...unless it was simply Maddie's contagious adoration of her idol. Yes, that must be it. She was absorbing Maddie's excitement. *Whew. Case closed.*

Claire steered her attention back to her students. "Okay, class, what can we say about the religious references in 'The Second Coming'?"

Claire's eyes landed on that damned empty seat again. *Oh, Sarah Brennan, why did you have to sign up for this class? My class?*

* * *

Claire zipped up her sweater. The arena was chilly. Winter was on the march, ready to shove autumn aside. Maddie's team skated onto the ice as she found a seat in the third row. She had her pick, because the only people who typically showed up for the kids' games were the parents, and Claire didn't know any of them. She didn't really want to, because she didn't want to stand around talking about a subject that resembled a foreign language to her.

"Hey." Sarah slid into the seat beside her, gave a wave to Maddie.

Claire's heart thumped—the thing had a mind of its own lately. "I didn't think you'd show."

Sarah looked at her, puzzled. "Why not?"

Claire's breath caught. That poster in Maddie's room did not do justice to Sarah's eyes. Not even close. They were mostly river green with a thin ring of gold around the iris. They were hazel, she supposed, but whatever color they were called, they were pretty fabulous. No, they were fucking fabulous. If she wanted to compose herself, and she did very much want to, then she needed to look away from those eyes. Now.

"Why," Sarah repeated, "did you think I wouldn't show?"

"I…" *Thought you were a spoiled, irresponsible, inconsiderate brat.* "I thought because you're so busy with your own hockey that you wouldn't have time."

"It's no problem. And for the record, I don't make a habit of breaking promises."

"All right."

They watched the game in silence.

"I see Maddie's playing forward," Sarah said with surprise.

"She is?"

"She's switched from playing defense."

"Oh." God, she felt dumb. She should have noticed. Matt was right when he predicted Maddie would switch to forward because of Sarah.

Maddie and a teammate skated down the ice on a two-on-nothing. Sarah began to cheer them on and Claire, following Sarah's lead, did the same. As Maddie and her teammate drew closer to the opposing goalie, Sarah jumped to her feet, yelling encouragement. The teammate passed to Maddie at the last minute, and Maddie swatted the puck into the net.

"Yes!" Sarah yelled, adding a loud whistle that reverberated around the arena. Maddie grinned like it was the Olympic Games. She waved her stick at them in celebration.

"Now *that*," Sarah said, "was a perfectly executed two-on-none."

"I'm…" Claire shook her head faintly. It wasn't easy admitting she knew almost nothing about something her daughter was so passionate about. And as much as she wished Maddie would find another hobby to obsess over, the writing was on the wall. Maddie was not going to move on from hockey any time soon.

The least Claire could do, for now, was learn something about the sport.

"What?" Sarah prodded.

"I'm not very good at…understanding this hockey stuff." There. She admitted it, and Sarah could laugh at her if she wanted or weaponize her ignorance against her. Whatever. She couldn't learn if she didn't admit to her lack of knowledge.

"That's okay. The main thing is that you're here, because being here shows your support." Sarah laughed. "My parents and my older brother know nothing about hockey, either. In fact, they think it's kind of nuts. But they still love me. They came to all my games when I was a kid, even though an arena was about the last place they wanted to be."

Claire was ridiculously grateful for Sarah letting her off the hook, for instantly making her feel like she was being a good mom. She loved Maddie more than anything or anyone else in the world. It was a love that often swelled and overflowed its banks, even in a cold arena. Softly, she uttered, "Thank you."

Her eyes back on the game, Sarah replied, "You're welcome. Just keep being present. That's all you need to do."

Yes. She could do that.

When the game was over, they waited for Maddie in the hallway outside the locker room. Sarah made sure to high-five all the players as they exited.

"Great game, ladies," Sarah called out. "And you!" She gave Maddie a hug. "Way to go, kiddo! A goal and everything! Wow!"

"Did you see I'm playing forward now? Just like you!"

"I noticed that. Well done, Maddie. You looked great out there. Really great."

"Do you really think so, Sarah?"

"I do. You looked completely comfortable in your new position. And you executed perfectly on that two-on-none."

Claire stood back and watched the two of them, and it reminded her so much of Maddie's relationship with Matt, the shared love of hockey, that immediate bond, the secret language, from which she was excluded. Oddly though, she didn't resent Sarah for it. How could she, when Maddie lit up around her, as she did now.

"Hey," Sarah said to Maddie. "What if I stayed to talk to your coach about giving you and your team a little skills clinic sometime? Maybe at your next practice? What do you think, would that be a good idea?"

"Yes! That would be so awesome! I can't wait to tell the others."

"Oh, Sarah, you don't have to do that." With her own hockey obligations, not to mention the lit class, Claire considered it too generous an offer. "You're too busy, I'm sure. It's fine, really." She didn't look at Maddie, but felt Maddie's foot defiantly, angrily, step on hers.

"I'm never too busy for the kids, Claire. Maddie, I'll go talk to your coach."

Sarah was exceptionally, unexpectedly, good with kids. Nothing suggested it was an act. "Come on, sweetie, we better get you home." It was going to be hours before Maddie came down from her hockey high. To Sarah, Claire said, "It was great of you to come to Maddie's game today." She wanted to say more, to say how much she appreciated everything Sarah was doing for Maddie, but she had no clue where to start. Or even how.

"Yeah, Sarah, thank you so much for coming to my game."

"You're very welcome. And I'll see you again soon, okay, Maddie?"

"Okay."

On the way out, Claire stole a last glance at Sarah, whose mouth wasn't smiling but her eyes were. And there was something else in that solid, green-gold gaze of hers—warmth, respect, a new friendliness that hadn't been there before. She wondered if Sarah was concluding the same thing about her right now.

All right, Sarah Brennan. You win. I was a jerk before.

CHAPTER NINE

Coach Saunders blew her whistle to start the next drill. "Harder, harder!"

The players were practicing one-on-one puck battle drills along the boards. Each pair went at it for close to a minute, shoving, pinning, trying as hard as they could to gain possession of the puck. Sarah and Brett were next.

"Oh, thank God. I got the other senior on the team," Brett quipped.

"Senior, huh?" Using her hip, Sarah firmly bumped Brett into the boards, then kept her pinned there using her shoulder and hip. She grunted from the effort, Brett being one of the stronger players on the team. "I'll show you who's the senior."

They were both the same age, both the oldest players on the team, but they weren't about to give each other any free passes. Mostly because they didn't want to give their teammates, or the coaches, any reason to think they were past their prime. The young ones, those in their early twenties, were not-so-patiently waiting to steal some of Sarah's and Brett's precious ice time.

There were nineteen skaters on the team. Those who got the bulk of the minutes in a game wanted to keep them, and those on the fringes wanted more. Sarah had been one of those players a long time ago, jockeying to show off her abilities, trying with every game and every practice to move up the ladder. There was some latitude with the older players because they brought leadership, maturity, experience—all the intangibles that any good team needed on its roster and in the locker room. But Sarah, Brett too, took no chances with her revered status. Hockey was a business. Players were expendable. Sarah was the face of the team, its bona fide star, but this season, everything was a sliver more difficult. She had to put more time in at the gym, go to bed a little earlier, do a little more PT time after each game. And that was just to keep at the level she expected of herself.

With the blade of her stick, Sarah finally gained hold of the puck, but only for a second, as Brett turned the tables and pinned Sarah this time.

"So who's the cute professor-type with the kid that I saw you with after our game last week?" Brett said in her ear. "Glasses, dark hair, cute ass."

Gasping as they continued to battle for the puck, Sarah huffed, "She actually *is* a professor." *Fuck.* She hadn't wanted Brett to see her with Claire and Maddie and Matt and…Laurie, that was Matt's wife's name. She dreaded what would surely happen next: questions and assumptions, especially teasing. Being on a team was like living in a goldfish bowl, which meant living a companionable and insular, albeit transparent, life. It was the transparency part, not having any privacy, that was the worst. She couldn't date, or even think of dating, without everyone on the team knowing.

"Wait. She's not *your* professor, is she? From the Irish lit class?"

"She is."

Brett's hesitation, not more than a second long, was enough for Sarah to get hold of the puck and skate off with it. Coach Saunders blew her whistle and the next pair took off.

Brett followed Sarah to the far boards, where they watched their teammates take turns with the drill. "Okay, hold on. You gotta tell me more. You got tickets for your professor to come to our game? How come?"

How could she explain something that was so embryonic and confusing that she didn't understand it herself? Yes, Claire Joyce was an alluring mix of fire and ice, of vulnerability masquerading as bossiness. And her kid was the cutest thing going. But there was nothing more to it than that. She and Claire continued to see each other in class, and she'd gone to one of Maddie's games because she said she would. And yeah, she'd go do some drills sometime at one of Maddie's practices. Big deal. That was it.

And yet, it did sort of feel like it was a bigger deal. Something she couldn't put her finger on, but it felt kind of good, kind of exciting. Each week, when it was time to go to class, Sarah looked forward to it. She'd arrive early and sit in the back of the class and busy herself with her iPad, except what she was really doing was secretly watching Claire, studying her as she prepared to teach. She didn't want to overthink things, though. Probably just a little teacher-student crush that would peter out before the semester was over.

When Sarah didn't answer, Brett pressed on. "Wait a second. She's the same woman from that night at the bar a few weeks ago, isn't she?"

Sarah shrugged, fussed with the lace in her skate. She didn't want to see on Brett's face the evidence of her connecting the dots.

"I remember her now. She was with another woman, and she was all shy about coming over to our table to say hi." Brett's eyes widened. "Does she have a thing for you, Sar?"

"Of course she doesn't. She's my professor. I'm her student. That shit's forbidden, or did you ignore that part when you were in college?"

"Very funny. And no, I never screwed any of my professors. But you, I mean, you might not be screwing her, but are you crushing on her? Is that what's going on?"

"Give me a break. Why on earth would you think that?" She could tell from Brett's face that she didn't believe her, not really. She also knew Brett respected her boundaries and knew when to back off. She wouldn't push her much further, thank God, because she was not ready to talk about any of it.

"Well, her loss." Brett grinned. "Or maybe yours. She's pretty hot. But then, I'm partial to intelligent women who wear glasses." Brett's wife wore glasses and was one of the smartest people Sarah knew. "Oh, and the good news? Semester is over in less than two months." Brett waggled her eyebrows. "She won't be your professor then."

Brett was jumping way too far ahead, if she was implying, which she obviously was, that Sarah and Claire would then be free to date. It would never happen. Claire didn't like athletes, and Sarah had never dated an older woman with a kid. She would, however, miss Claire and Maddie once her course was over, because she'd have no reason, no excuse, to keep seeing them. The thought sent her mood tumbling.

Coach Saunders blew her whistle again.

CHAPTER TEN

At the sink, Claire rinsed another bowl and set it on the drying board. Maddie was in the other room watching a hockey game on television, the volume at a ridiculous level. It was Sarah's team, playing against the Montreal team. Maddie wanted her mom to watch the game with her, but Claire kept finding excuses, doing the dishes being the most pressing one.

Out the window, in the advancing dark, she watched the November wind blow the last of the leaves off the sycamore tree in the backyard. Matt had wanted this house because of that tree, with its perpetual peeling bark and its massive canopy of leaves. Matt, of course, had been gone for years now, but the tree remained, a constant to remind Claire that while some things change, many things don't. She loved that tree now. It grounded her, its peeling bark reminding her that things, people, were often more resilient than they appeared.

"Mom, are you coming in to watch?"

"In a minute, honey." It was the third "in-a-minute-honey." She couldn't procrastinate forever. Maddie's feelings were on the verge of being hurt, and yet she couldn't quite bring herself to get in there and watch the game with her. Because it was Sarah's team, Sarah on TV, Sarah was everywhere, and there were times, like now, when it was too much. Sometimes she needed a Sarah break.

Claire closed her eyes, plunged her hands into the soapy water. The crux of it was that even though Sarah had not turned out to be the person Claire thought she was, she didn't want another pro athlete as a regular presence in their lives, didn't want this advancing proximity to Sarah. It wasn't Sarah's fault, that much she could admit. If Sarah were a ledger, the positive column would be full, with a big fat zero in the negative column. She was nice, she was smart, she was talented, and, yeah, she was kind of gorgeous. And she probably knew exactly how gorgeous she was and exactly how smart and how talented she was. Sarah Brennan was bloody well perfect. Except for the pro-athlete part. And that was the part Claire could not accept.

She washed and rinsed another bowl, taking her time. Oh Jesus, how she wished she were attracted to accountants or teachers or chiropractors—to people who didn't move through the world with such cocky intention and with such God-given poise and grace and determination, along with that powerful sense of self that made them stand so obviously apart from others. Claire could admire athletes from an objective place in her mind. And yet the pull was more than academic. It was molecular, almost corporeal. Though she'd been defenseless against her attraction to Matt back in university, she did not, would not, again fall for another athlete. Her life, finally, was exactly the way she wanted it: predictable, manageable, drama-free.

"Mom!"

"All right, I'm coming."

Claire pulled herself together and joined Maddie on the couch.

"Why don't you like Sarah?"

"Excuse me?"

Maddie's eyes, so much like her own, lasered into her. "You pretend you like her, but you don't. I can tell."

"I like Sarah just fine. She's my student, remember? I have to be careful not to appear as though I'm granting her any special favors. It wouldn't be fair to the others."

"But I want you to be Sarah's friend, too."

"Honey, look. It's okay that you idolize Sarah and I don't. Everyone is allowed to have their own friends. There's nothing wrong with Sarah being your friend and not mine."

Maddie crossed her arms over her chest and swung her gaze back to the game, but she wasn't done yet. Not by a long shot, Claire could tell. She had Matt's temper and his habit of wanting to hash everything out the minute he felt like it, while Claire liked to go away and think about things, to process them at her own pace. Processing, on the fly, anything more than what she wanted for lunch was not in her comfort zone.

The pout intensified. "Fine. But you don't like hockey, either."

"It's...I don't understand it, that's all."

"Because you don't *want* to understand it, Mom."

Claire was about to answer back sharply but caught herself. Her daughter didn't understand how she had spent her entire childhood trying to be and do the things her parents wanted, adopting their interests as her own, playing the role of their perfect offspring to be trotted out to impress others. She could mix a perfect gin and tonic by the age of twelve, could recite Shakespeare from memory at seven, because those were the things that pleased her parents. From the hard way, Claire knew what it meant to give all of yourself, even the parts you didn't want to, to somebody else, only to end up feeling hollowed out, like you'd lost yourself along the way. She'd done it with Matt, too, moving to three cities over his football career, taking care of a baby while he was traveling with his team or was at the stadium practicing or working out. She'd earned her PhD by the time Maddie finished kindergarten. No. If Claire wanted to hold back parts of herself, if she wanted to *not* fall for another athlete, it was her right to do so. She'd earned it.

But she's your child, Claire. For the love of God, don't be remote with your own child.

Contrite, she said, "I do want to understand the game. And I will. I promise. I will study up on it and become as much of an expert as you, all right? Just be patient with me. Give me some time. That's all I ask."

Maddie's anger disappeared as fast as it had come on. "Okay, it's a deal. Hey, why don't you learn to play, too?"

"Are you kidding? I can barely even skate."

"Sarah could help you."

"I'm sure she could, but I'm also sure Sarah has about a thousand other things to do besides teach someone like me how to skate."

"I'll ask her. She'll do it."

Panic shot through Claire. "It's okay, honey, really. I've lived forty-one years with being a crappy skater. I promise I can live another forty-one the same way."

"That's just because you grew up in Ireland, Mom. They don't skate there."

Well, that was pretty much true. Indoor ice arenas were almost nonexistent in Ireland, while lakes and rivers and ponds didn't typically freeze in the winter. It wasn't until she moved to Canada at the age of ten that she realized what skating meant to the country's culture. Eventually she had begun joining neighborhood kids on backyard rinks, or on shallow ponds, with her thrift store figure skates. It was either that or sit on the sidelines and watch her friends have fun. So she took the plunge, but it didn't mean she was any good at skating. And she most certainly had no desire to play hockey. That was for the insane.

"That's right. We have football—sorry, soccer to you—and hurling and golf and tennis and rugby. That's about it. Aside from horse and dog racing."

"Hockey is way better than any of that stuff. Hey, look, there's Sarah on the ice now!"

"She has the puck a lot, doesn't she?" She was masterful with it; it was like she had a string attached to it. And the way she skated—fast but incredibly smooth and nimble, all elegance and power, like a Thoroughbred. It was preternatural, and it was goddamned beautiful to watch.

"Yup. That's because she's the best forward on the team. She's got the most points, and she's been to the Olympics three times! Isn't that amazing? Mom, do you think I'll get to go to the Olympics one day like Sarah?"

Claire looked into the shining face of her daughter. If she was filled up by hockey and by this hockey player named Sarah Brennan, well, there were worse things to worry about. The fact that her daughter had a dream and was willing to work toward her dream, well, how could she argue with that?

"You never know, sweetie. You just might." She knew firsthand the hardship of carrying the weight of a dream all by herself. She would not do that to her daughter. She'd let Maddie have her fantasies.

CHAPTER ELEVEN

Sarah slapped her stick on the ice for encouragement as she tracked the girls skating a lap around the ice. It had taken several minutes to get the practice started, because the kids wanted their skates and sticks and helmets autographed. For as long as it took, Sarah obliged. She had been that kid once, seeking autographs from her sports heroes. Haley Wickenheiser had once handed her a signed puck during an appearance at the mall, and for three months, Sarah carried that puck in her knapsack to school every day.

On the ice, she showed the girls stick-handling skills, how to make a saucer pass, then gave them tips on winning face-offs. It harkened back to all the summers she'd spent making extra money as an instructor at hockey camps. There was something about teaching the basics that brought her back to her own early days of learning the game, of all the great mentors she'd had along the way, the friends she'd made. Maddie, she noted, especially loved the face-off drill, same as Sarah. For someone who had only switched to forward a couple of weeks ago, the kid was already showing plenty of proficiency at it.

She grinned up at Sarah from behind the wire mask over her face. "Sarah, can you show us how to do a wrist shot?" To her mother watching in the first row watching, Maddie mouthed "Watch me."

Success was slow to come, as it often was with a wrist shot, which took a timely flick of the wrist intersecting with the puck rolling toward the toe of the stick blade, then following the shot all the way through. After a handful of attempts, Maddie grew impatient and turned up the whining. "I can't get the puck up off the ice, Sarah. I just can't do it the way you do it. Why can't I?"

"You can, it will come. Don't forget, you've been a defenseman. Defensemen don't typically have good wrist shots, so give it time." She watched as Maddie gradually began to raise the puck off the ice a couple of inches. "Good. Try again. Now don't forget that with the blade of your stick, you're rolling the puck slightly forward before you release it, and then it's kind of a quick snap of the wrist. Let's try rolling the puck back and forth on our stick blade without releasing it, just to get the feel of it, okay?"

Sarah spent another ten minutes going over the shot with Maddie and a couple of the other girls who were eager to learn. By the end, Maddie was making steady progress. Her impatience yielded to jubilation at a new skill on its way to being mastered.

"I'll see you again soon at one of your games, okay, Maddie? Now, do what your coach tells you in the meantime." Sarah glanced over to where Claire was sitting, her nose nearly pressed against the glass as she took everything in. It was amusing—and a little surprising—to witness the about-face with hockey. "And listen to your mom, too, okay?"

"Okay, I will. Thank you, Sarah. Bye."

"Bye, Maddie. Bye, girls."

On the other side of the boards, Sarah peeled her skates off and slammed her feet into her Blundstone boots. Maddie had a few more minutes of practice left. She sought out Claire.

"Hey."

"Hi." Claire's smile, though brief, was genuine, almost warm. Definitely room temp, anyway, which was a big improvement.

Sarah raised her chin toward Maddie on the ice. "She's a fast learner. Did you see how quickly she learned to get her wrist shot up?"

"I did. She'll be talking about this nonstop for the next three days." There was an edge to Claire's tone, but she looked at Sarah and smiled. "Don't worry, I'm getting used to all the hockey talk."

"Mind if I join you?"

"Of course not. You…Well, as long as I'm not holding you up."

Sarah glanced at her watch as she took the seat beside Claire. "We've a bus to catch to Detroit later this afternoon for our game tomorrow, but I've got a bit of time yet."

"It's very kind of you to help Maddie like this."

Sarah hadn't noticed before the faint spray of freckles across Claire's nose, barely noticeable on her cheeks. She wanted to tell her they made her look younger, softer, playful. She liked to imagine that the freckles were a brief porthole into Claire as a child—a raven-haired, blue-eyed, freckled girl romping through the green, rolling hills of Ireland. A nice picture that probably was nowhere near accurate. But she liked to think that Claire had a fun, adventurous side to her, even if it was from a long time ago.

"She's a good kid," Sarah replied. "And it's good of you to come to her games and practices when hockey isn't really…your thing." The last part might get her head bitten off, but Sarah would chance it. She would love to know why Claire seemed so rattled by hockey, or perhaps it was all sports that got her ire up.

Claire turned her attention to the practice, a tiny frown line between her eyes. What was she thinking? Sarah wondered. Who exactly was this woman with the faint Irish accent who had a hockey-mad daughter and an ex-husband and who knew everything there was to know about Irish literature but nothing about sports? What did she like to do in her spare time? What was her biggest joy? Her biggest disappointment? Her dreams? Her desires? There were many streams feeding into the river that fed Claire's soul, and Sarah didn't have a clue what those were. She might never, but there was a challenge in trying to unravel the mystery. And Sarah was a sucker for challenges.

"The thing is," Claire said after a time, her voice cracking a little. "I know so little about hockey. Which was absolutely fine with me until Maddie took such a liking to it. And now, well, I need to no longer pretend the sport doesn't exist."

"You want to learn more about it."

"Yes. For Maddie's sake."

"Right. For Maddie's sake."

A sidelong glance. "I would like to support her as much as I can."

"Good. Of course." Sarah could see that Claire struggled mightily with the game—not only with understanding its myriad rules and strategies—but grasping what made it so special, so addictive, so exciting. To her credit, she'd dutifully plucked herself from the world of books and academia to sit in hockey arenas for Maddie's sake. Which pretty much made her a hero in Sarah's mind.

"You know, you're already a big support to Maddie. If you hate hockey, though, you don't have to—"

"I don't hate it."

"Okay." It sure seemed like she hated it. Or used to. "But giving support to someone can be as little as showing up. Being present. You're already doing a great job of that, you know."

"But I want to do more. I can't support her the way you can, out there on the ice, telling her stuff, showing her stuff. I feel…" Claire tucked her chin into her coat.

"What?"

"Inadequate."

"Oh, Claire." *Oops*. It was supposed to be Dr. Joyce, but screw it. Sarah's heart was breaking a little for the woman sitting beside her, this woman who would do anything for her daughter. What she really wanted to do was to put her arm around her shoulders and tell her to stop worrying so much. "Being on the ice with her, teaching her things…Okay, I get that you're a teacher, but you can't teach your daughter everything she's ever going to be interested in or needs to learn in life. That's where others come in. People like me, like her coach out there. She needs you to be her, I don't know, her fearless cheerleader. Can you do that?"

Claire nodded once, hard. "Of course I can do that. But, Sarah?" Blue eyes fixed on her. "I have to confess: I hate being so stupid about hockey. Could you...Do you think you could help me with that a little? Teach me the rules, for instance? Or recommend a book? I want to be able to make sense of what I'm seeing."

Sarah smiled, gently bumped her shoulder against Claire's, because it must have taken a lot for Claire to admit that she wanted help, Sarah's help, to be precise. "Yes. I can help you with that."

"Really?"

"Really. When would you like to start?"

"I can't exactly repay you. I mean, you're my student. So no quid pro quo."

"I wouldn't expect any. Breaking news: You're *my* student now." The tiny flare of panic in Claire's face that preceded her grin shook something loose in Sarah. She liked Claire, she realized. Hadn't seen it coming, but there it was. She *liked* this woman. A lot.

"Hmm. I guess that makes us even."

CHAPTER TWELVE

Claire brought the two cups of coffee over to her desk and handed one to Sarah.

"Thanks."

"It's the least I can do." They were in Claire's office, but Sarah, with her little whiteboard that resembled a two-dimensional hockey rink, was the professor today. As odd as it felt being on the other side of a lesson, Claire looked forward to their sessions, which had begun two weeks ago. Today was their third one. Claire was well past the point of feeling hockey stupid, but only because she'd safely tucked her ego away.

"All right, so we have icings and off-sides down," Sarah said, pointing at the board. "Now I'm going to show you how the team breaks out of their end when the play is happening there. As I said before, there are three zones in the game of hockey. The defensive zone, the neutral zone, and the offensive zone."

With a blue dry-erase marker, Sarah drew 0's and X's to delineate which team she was talking about.

"Okay. So the X's are hemmed into the defensive end by the O's. Now. We have a couple of options here. See what happens if this forward moves to an open spot right here?" Sarah drew an arrow. "Now our defenseman has a place to send the puck so that we can get out of the zone."

"All right. So if that defenseman passes the puck to this person, like you said…" Claire pointed to an X on the board. "What if this other player, an O, suddenly gets in the way of the pass?"

"Ah, good question." Sarah bent closer to the whiteboard in her lap. "That's why ideally we don't want just one open player for the passer. So in this case, the defenseman can either skate with it herself and then pass it, or…" Sarah erased an X and redrew it. "She can pass it to this forward, who needs to immediately get open. It's really important to know where every player is at any given moment."

"I see. So as soon as we have possession of the puck in our end, it's up to our other teammates to get open so they can receive a pass."

"Exactly. And, ideally, your teammates are never stationary, but always moving."

Claire reflexively raised a hand to her forehead. "Wait. I think I could understand the game better if everyone would just stand still."

Sarah laughed. "I think I could understand the game better that way, too. And my legs, and lungs, would definitely like it better. Hey, you could always take up cornhole, you know. I hear that's pretty stationary."

There was no denying Sarah was cute when she laughed. Extremely cute. Her smile went right to her eyes. Her dimples joined in, too. And the gentle teasing was a new and welcome addition. If things were different…*way* different, Claire might actually consider…

Well, no, she'd never date a student. And she needed to remember, like, *really* needed to remember, that athletes weren't her thing. She could, however, admit that Maddie had good taste in choosing her idols. She'd been wrong about Sarah, dead wrong, even if it had taken her weeks to figure it out.

Claire frowned at all the slashes and markings on the board; there was so much to learn about the game. "Do you think I'll ever actually be able to understand hockey?"

"Of course. You must have learned a few things about football, from Matt's playing days."

Matt. Those football-playing years, running parallel to their six-year marriage. Claire had never known such a mix of intense and contrary feelings, the most predominant of which was sadness. Another was loneliness. She'd wanted to be in love, wanted it all: a mate, a career in academics, a child or maybe two. Yet within months of matrimony, she knew she'd made a mistake. She wasn't cut out to be a jock's wife. It was an insufferable role. Posing for pictures at charity fundraisers, attending the right functions in town to keep the team's owners and the fans happy, red carpets (too many), buying cars worth more than a year's salary, expectations of hanging out with the other players' gossipy wives. After Matt's team won the championship one year, he had disappeared with his teammates for four days of drinking and partying and who-knows-what while Claire stayed home with their new baby. It was a reprehensible event and one that eventually became part of the avalanche of grievances that contributed to the breakup of their marriage. How easy it would have been to keep drifting through a life that had so rapidly faded to sepia tones, to float through a succession of reactions to events. Claire lived that way first as a kid, then as a wife. She was done with anything ever again that meant she wasn't her own person. Her needs would not take a back seat to anyone again.

"Honestly, I didn't pay a whole lot of attention to Matt's football career." Her cheeks burned furiously. Instead of learning about football, of truly sharing it with Matt the way she had decided to share hockey with Maddie, she'd run back to the safety of academia. "I went back to school to do my postgrad stuff. I became kind of consumed with my education." It was her salvation, really. Her way out.

"Is that when the marriage ended? When you went back to school?"

"No. Not quite." Claire couldn't remember the last time someone had asked her about her marriage. She'd been divorced for years now, apart from Matt almost as long as they were together. There were so very few people, true friends, with whom she spoke intimately about those days. By nature she was shy, uncomfortable with intimacy. She liked to listen to others talk about fears, problems, secrets…sympathizing but not offering up her own. Strangely enough, Matt was one of the few people in her life she could talk to—she just didn't particularly want to anymore. Sharing with Sarah like this, engaging with her on her own territory, opening up about personal things, it wasn't terrible. And, yeah, okay, she didn't normally have friendly relations with her students, and certainly not personal conversations like this, but technically, Sarah was mostly Maddie's friend. They were doing nothing wrong. Claire relaxed a little more.

"I left him when he came home one day and announced he was being traded. To a team three provinces away. It was his third trade, and I didn't want to live that life anymore."

Sarah paused, her expression unreadable. "That must have been a really tough time. For all of you."

"It was." No doubt Sarah would take Matt's side of things, being a pro athlete herself. But when she chanced a look at her face for confirmation, there was no judgment, only a sympathetic knitting of her brow.

Claire took a swallow of coffee. "It was especially hard on Maddie. She was not quite four when we separated. She couldn't understand why her dad was suddenly never around anymore, why she could only talk to him on the phone for weeks at a time. And I was busy too, finishing my PhD and then teaching at the university as soon as Maddie finished kindergarten."

She would not, ever, go through it all again, that nearly insurmountable mountain of crap from the divorce and solo parenting—the years of tears, guilt, exhaustion. It didn't take much, even now, to remember the sleepless nights followed by the mornings of pasting on a smile and putting one foot in front of the other, making a Herculean effort to grind through the days. For at least two years, she felt like a fraud in carving out her new life, acting like she had it all together. She didn't, but she had made it through to the other side.

"I'm really glad you all survived it all." Sarah's smile was solicitous.

"Me, too." Claire sank into her thoughts. As much as things were better in her life now, even good, there was still a fog of melancholy that periodically ambushed her. She had not fully vanquished the feelings of failure that had accompanied the divorce. Oh, what an unexpected, crappy little surprise that had been, feeling that it was all her fault, that maybe she hadn't tried hard enough. And then there were her parents reminding her, with their constant "trying to figure out what happened," what a glorious marriage they themselves had been blessed with, what a happy example they'd been to their daughter, what a good guy Matt was. In their minds, Claire was a failure and a disappointment, all in one, because she hadn't heeded their lessons.

"So, I thought we could go over how a power play works, what do you think?"

Claire blinked herself back to the present. "Sorry, what?"

"The power play. Special teams are really important, especially in playoffs."

Relieved at being plucked from her brooding, Claire smiled and said, "Special teams? Aren't they all special? The teams?"

It took a second before Sarah got the joke. "Good one, Dr. Joyce. Er, Claire. I'm not sure sometimes what I'm supposed to call you."

The lightness of the moment, watching new slash marks and X's and O's being sketched on the whiteboard, felt good. And it was fun the way Sarah turned her hockey lessons into mathematical equations. Or maybe it was more geometry.

"Claire is fine, except when we're in class, of course. Um. Sarah?" Christmas was nine days away, and she had been wondering for days now if Sarah would have to spend the holidays alone. More to the point was the niggling desire to repay Sarah for the time and effort she'd put into helping first Maddie, and now her, with hockey. She hadn't been sure she'd have the courage to go through with her invitation, or whether she even wanted to try, until now. "What are you doing Christmas Day?"

A noncommittal shrug while the sketching continued. "Hadn't really thought of it. The team only takes a few days off. I'll probably just stay in town and hang out with my friend Brett and her wife, Kelly. I'm, like, practically their kid the way they're always feeding me and—"

"Would you like to join us for Christmas dinner? At my place?" With everything inside her, she really wanted Sarah to say yes. And not only because of how it would make Maddie's entire month. Claire wanted Sarah's company, too.

Sarah looked up, the late afternoon light from the office window catching her eyes and instantly brightening the gold ring around her irises and the little gold flecks nestled in the green. The vision was captivating enough to steal Claire's breath for a moment. "Are you sure?"

Oh, please don't make me second-guess this. "Yes. I—we—would really like you to come." She hadn't said anything to Maddie, in case she'd decided not to extend the invitation or if Sarah declined. Plus, if Maddie knew too many days in advance, she'd drive Claire nuts.

"Okay. Yes."

"Yes?"

"Yes."

Claire didn't realize she'd been holding her breath. She let it out. "All right. Good." She wrote her address on Sarah's whiteboard. "Now…you were saying something about teams being special?"

CHAPTER THIRTEEN

The snowfall rushed down in tiny flakes, as persistent as a rainstorm. Sarah could see it piling up outside the long vertical windows from inside the hotel bar, where she and the rest of the team were killing time. They had played the Boston team that afternoon, but their early-evening flight back to Toronto was postponed until morning. They'd have to stay an extra night, prolonging the start of their five-day Christmas break.

Sarah and Brett each nursed a soda and lime at the bar. The others were scattered—some played pool, others hunched around tables and played cards. Nobody was drinking much.

"Okay, what's going on with you?"

"What?" Sarah said.

"What's bugging you? Is it the flight delay?" Brett gave her a long look. "Big date you forgot to tell me about get postponed?"

"You wish. Nothing that exciting."

Brett's pursed lips signaled that a lecture was coming. And… yup. Here it came.

"You know, Sar, you're a good-looking woman. No, you're a great-looking woman, hot even, and you're—"

"Now, now, don't let Kelly hear you talk about another woman like that."

"Please. She knows you're like a sister to me. As I was about to say before I was so rudely interrupted, you're single, you're smart, you're a catch, Brennan. And if this goes to your head I'm going to kick your ass."

"It won't and you wouldn't be able to." She poked her tongue out and made a face.

"Ooh, very mature. But listen, my point is this: why the hell aren't you playing the field right now? Time to get out there and meet women. Long past time, to be honest. Your last relationship was, what, sixteen years ago?"

"Ha ha, very funny. It was almost two years ago." The ending hadn't come as a surprise, but the rejection had nevertheless hurt when she returned home from the world championships in Sweden and found Ruth gone. If there were torches to be carried, though, there were none for Ruth. They parted because they were never going to be on the same page about life. Ruth was simply the one who had had the guts to pull the plug on their relationship.

"That's an awfully long dry spell for your vajayjay. It must be full of dust webs by now."

"Eww. Thanks a lot for the visual, you jerk. I mean, my friend."

"The single ladies are lined up outside our locker rooms after games. I see the way their eyes follow you. You could have your bloody pick."

"Except you know I'd never choose a girlfriend like I'm at the pet store choosing a puppy. I'll leave that for the twenty-year-olds on the team." Sarah had always eschewed the promiscuous jock stereotype. Not because the opportunity wasn't there, but because it felt more like role-playing, like she was putting on clothes that didn't fit and looked stupid on her. It just wasn't for her. Once she had the time for a real relationship, the true sharing kind, she'd give it her full attention.

"Anyway, enough about dates and vajayjays. Life is good the way it is, thank you very much." She cast a glance at the knot of their young teammates around the pool table. The ones who were constantly on their phones, relentlessly trolling for dates, checking social media to see what people were saying about them. Well, they could have it. Quiet evenings at home with a book, coffee dates with friends, maybe a drink someplace nice was far more preferable than chasing booty.

"We've been losing lately," she said quietly. "That's what I'm pissed off about."

"I hear ya. Three out of the last five. Not exactly a trend yet, but I agree, it's concerning."

They had a good team that, while not pegged to win the championship this year, had lots of talent. They should be winning more than they were. If the losing trend became entrenched, there would be changes, and changes to sports teams went two ways: Either the coaches were replaced or some of the players were. It was ugly. Sarah had lived through that kind of upheaval a few times, including one year when Team Canada's coach was turfed midway through the world championships. As captain of her team, she knew firsthand the shit storm that sudden firings or trades caused. She didn't want to have to go through it again.

"Are you truly worried?" Brett asked. "Or is this more of a grumpy thing that you'll forget about in a few days?"

"I don't know. Yet."

"The season still has almost eleven weeks to go, plus playoffs. Isn't it a bit soon to be worried? Cuz, like, I'd rather not spoil the Christmas break being worried about this. We've both done enough agonizing over hockey seasons to last us a lifetime." Brett rolled her eyes. "Please don't let this be another one of those."

"Your lips to God's ears." Sarah didn't want to spend the Christmas break worrying, either. Her job was to play, she reminded herself, not sort out the team's inadequacies. And in a couple more days, she'd see Claire and Maddie.

"Oh, I almost forgot to tell you. Can I take a rain check on Christmas dinner with you and Kelly and the gang this year?"

"What? You have *plans* on Christmas Day? By what sorcery did that happen?"

"I got invited someplace else. Must be my boundless charm and good looks."

"More like your sad, puppy dog eyes."

"Whatever works. Anyway, you guys will have a full enough house without me." Two years in a row now, she'd spent Christmas Day with Brett, Kelly, Kelly's brother and his wife and kids, and usually a couple of other teammates who were on their own for the holidays. "You won't even miss me, but thank you. And please thank Kelly for me."

Brett pushed her empty beer glass aside. "I won't feel insulted unless your invitation is a better one. So? Is it? Do tell!"

Jokes and hockey talk aside, Brett was Sarah's closest friend. Right before Brett married Kelly, it was Sarah who talked her friend out of her untimely cold feet, reminding her how special Kelly was, how in love they were, and that their fabulous life together could start as soon as Brett smartened up and realized how lucky she was. So…yeah. They could talk about anything. Which was all the more puzzling as to why was it so damned hard to confess her conflicted feelings for Claire. Maybe she wanted more clarity before she talked about it, because things were confusing between the two of them, a back-and-forth that seemed like they were on the path to friendship, but she couldn't be sure. She'd never met anyone like Claire before, had never had this kind of *friendship* with anyone before. It felt like they were dancing around something, something that both awed and scared them, but it was beyond Sarah's understanding.

Brett dropped her voice. "Wait. It's not an invitation from your professor, is it?"

"Actually, yes." *Okay, here it comes.*

"Whoa! Seriously? How did that happen?"

"We've sorta become friends, I think. Because of her daughter."

A curl of a smile that brimmed with incredulity. Brett's dirty mind would never believe there wasn't something more going on between the two of them. "Okay. Cool."

Neither spoke for a few minutes as they each checked their phone for missed texts or emails. It was getting late. Sarah began to push herself off the barstool when Brett touched her wrist. "Wait a second. Do you want to talk more about this?"

"Not really." It was too hard to explain. Plus, what was the point? She didn't understand any of it herself, which meant no one else would, either. All she knew for sure was that she was starting to care about Claire and Maddie. "I'll see you in the morning."

"All right. But you're okay, right?"

Sarah produced a tired smile. "I am. And thanks."

Before heading up to her room, Sarah took one last look out the window at the mounds of snow piling up. Yup. It was Boston, all right.

CHAPTER FOURTEEN

Maddie tore open the wrapped box from Sarah and erupted into shrieks.

"Oh my God! Mom, Dad, Laurie, look what I got from Sarah!" She pulled a blue-and-white hockey jersey free from its confines, displaying the name Brennan and number seventeen on the back. Her face transformed into pure euphoria. "Wow! It's an autographed jersey. And not just *any* jersey. It's Sarah's game-worn jersey!"

She looked at Sarah with a mix of disbelief and gratitude before flinging the jersey and its box down, and sprinting across the room. She threw her arms around her hero and pressed herself into her, happy tears and all. "Thank you, Sarah. I can't believe it! It's the best present ever, and I'm even going to sleep with it tonight!"

"Well, believe it, kiddo. My number one fan should have a game-worn jersey from me, so there. You're very welcome."

Claire exchanged a look with Matt and Laurie to try to tell them that the jersey was a complete surprise to her, too. It was inevitable now that the PlayStation from Matt and Laurie plus the new skates from Claire would be forgotten beneath the Christmas tree. Well, maybe not the skates, so there was consolation in that. She mouthed a silent "thank you" to Sarah; it was worth it to see Maddie so happy.

Sarah grinned back at her to acknowledge Claire's thanks, which ignited a furious burning in Claire's cheeks. Ignited something else, too, something exciting and pleasurable that surged through her chest. Its faint echo remained, but she refused to give it another thought because this was Maddie's moment. She averted her eyes, praying Sarah hadn't been able to read in her face this surprising exhilaration coursing through her body.

Laurie stood up. "Claire, how about I help you get everything on the table?"

"Yes, great, thank you."

"I can help, too," Sarah said, but Maddie immediately pestered her to come up to her room and look at her hockey card collection.

"I'll help, Claire," Matt supplied, grinning at Sarah. "I think Maddie's given you your marching orders."

Sarah saluted Maddie and chased her up the stairs, Maddie giggling all the way. In the kitchen, Matt said to Claire, "Man, that kid's got one wicked crush on Sarah."

"Poor Sarah," Laurie said on a laugh. "She won't know what hit her."

Claire shook her head. "Oh, I think she has by now. I have to admit, Sarah's being a really good sport about all of this."

"She's good, period." Laurie began dishing up the mashed potatoes into a large serving bowl. "Not a lot of people would go the extra mile for a stranger the way she has. Huh. What's her story? Is she single?"

Claire hadn't given much thought to whether Sarah might be involved with anyone—it had never come up in conversation between them—though she suspected she wasn't, because it was Christmas and she was here, spending it with them. "Why do you ask?" She wouldn't mind knowing the answer herself, but her own single status made her suspicious of people's motives. It sounded too much like matchmaking.

"No reason. I think she's great. And she'd make a great catch for someone instead of spending Christmas with all of us."

"Hey," Matt interjected. "We're not exactly chopped liver, you know."

Claire longed for a change in subject. Her love life, Sarah's too, was not going to be grist for idle conversation. Not in her house. "Well, regardless, it's just nice that she was free to join us tonight. Matt, do you remember where the carving set is?"

"Yep, got it."

Matt carved the turkey while Claire and Laurie finished getting the side dishes out. The conversation meandered to the trip to Disney World that Matt and Laurie planned to take Maddie on during her school break in early March.

Claire called up the stairs, "Dinner's ready, you two!" Poor Sarah, she was Maddie's hostage up there.

Minutes later, Sarah's eyes were taking in the table crammed with turkey, gravy, potatoes, cranberries, broccoli, stuffing, dinner rolls. "Wow, what a feast! Good thing I've been saving my appetite."

"Me, too," Maddie parroted.

All Claire would think was, *Oh, Sarah, my kid's going to smother you to death.* She was nothing less than a saint with Maddie, and Claire both loved and hated that it was so, falling into the downward pull of guilt. Guilt for treating Sarah so poorly early on, guilt for the occasional pangs of jealousy over the way Sarah so effortlessly connected with Maddie, and finally, guilt for feeling that maybe she'd like some of that attention for herself. Seeing Sarah in her home like this, with her family, made Claire embarrassed by her first impression of Sarah, embarrassed by her coldness, embarrassed that she'd tried so hard not to like Sarah. She couldn't let their friendship, or whatever it was, go on any longer without an apology. Even if Sarah wasn't expecting one, it was the right thing to do.

After dessert, Matt, Laurie, and Maddie disappeared upstairs to help her get ready for a few days' stay at their place. Matt's side of the family was celebrating Christmas tomorrow.

"You okay?" It was Sarah behind her, in the kitchen, her arms occupied with dirty dishes from the dining room table. She set them down on the counter, the shifting of muscles in her thick forearms clearly visible and clearly spectacular. *Damn these athletes and their damned hot bodies.* "You seem a bit quiet."

"I'm fine, thank you." Claire added more dishes to the soapy water and began scrubbing.

Sarah picked up a towel to dry. "Is it because Maddie's going to be away for a few days?"

"Maddie will be fine. She likes it at Matt and Laurie's, and Matt's family will spoil her the next couple of days."

"I see. And what about you? Will you be fine while she's away?"

"Yes, I will. We're pretty much used to this routine now. Maddie goes to stay with Matt and Laurie every other weekend, a month in the summer, plus March break. Christmas and birthdays are organic, we figure it out as we go." She looked forward to Maddie's time away, for the time it gave her alone, and yet when Maddie was gone, she missed her like crazy. But Sarah didn't need to hear about all that mom stuff.

"That sounds like a good way to do things."

"It is. It's evolved into working really well." The years seemed to condense as Claire remembered walking Maddie to school in the mornings, holding her tiny hand in hers, listening to the high-pitched, happy chatter about her little friends at school, or the latest thing her teacher had taught them. Sometimes the chatter was more condemning, like what bad word had come out of a schoolmate's mouth, and sometimes the chatter was full of wonder, like her friend Emily's painting of her family that depicted two moms. Claire was proud of her daughter's intelligent curiosity, remembering the time, at the age of six, when Maddie asked her why weather systems almost always came from west to east, and why the sun was opposite, moving from east to west. Now that she was older, every night at bedtime they read in quiet solidarity together in Maddie's room for about twenty minutes—Claire with her book, Maddie with hers ("I'm too old for you to read to me now, Mom.").

Her love for her daughter was immutable. Which meant there was absolutely no need to feel threatened by Maddie's bond with Sarah. She stopped rinsing a plate to look at Sarah. "I really want to thank you for everything you've done for Maddie. It's meant the world to her. Really. As you can plainly see." Claire masked her anxiety with laughter. "And, well, it makes me happy to see Maddie happy, that's all."

"She's a great kid, you know."

"I know. I'm lucky."

"I think maybe she's lucky, too."

Before Claire could ask Sarah what she meant, the gang burst into the kitchen.

"We're all ready, Mom."

"Have you got your new jersey packed?" Sarah asked.

"It's the first thing she packed," Matt said. "If she could fit you in her suitcase too, Sarah, I'm sure she'd do it."

"Oh, Dad!" Maddie rolled her eyes. "Okay, Mom, love you and miss you already."

Claire pulled Maddie in for a big hug. "I love you, too, alannah, and I miss you already, too. Have a great time and come back safe and sound."

"I will, Mom." She hugged Sarah next. "Bye, Sarah! I'm so glad you came for dinner. Mostly I'm super glad for the jersey, though."

"Wear it in good health, my friend."

Matt stepped up to Sarah and spontaneously gave her a hug, too. Sarah, just a couple of inches shorter than six feet, was dwarfed by Matt. "Thanks for being a friend to Maddie."

"My pleasure."

Once the three were out the door and the kitchen was no longer a shambles, Sarah reached for her coat in the hallway. "I should probably go, too."

"Do you have to?" It took a tremendous amount of courage for Claire to ask and almost as much again to wait for the answer.

CHAPTER FIFTEEN

Sarah hadn't expected to be asked to stay. She hesitated, unsure if Claire was being polite or really meant it. In the seconds before she answered, the nervous anticipation in Claire's face told her all she needed to know. "All right. Sure, that would be nice."

"Shall we have another glass of wine?"

"I wouldn't say no."

The flames from the gas fireplace threw a warm glow across the living room, which was where they settled with their glasses of sauvignon blanc on a long, comfortably worn leather sofa. A Christmas tree—a real one—stood in the corner, its blue and red and green lights twinkling their cheerful patterns across the high ceiling. It gave off a faint, piney scent.

"Thank you again for the gift of the Yeats book," Sarah said. "It's gorgeous. I love it. It means a lot, actually." Leather-bound, *The Collected Poems of W.B. Yeats* had been presented to her before dinner in a beautifully wrapped box with a big red bow. A gift from her and Maddie, Claire had said, and it was Sarah's favorite gift this Christmas by far. Her parents had e-transferred her money as a gift—useful but not heartfelt. Her brother's gift had been perhaps more thoughtful, though all wrong for her—a gift certificate for a beauty spa she felt sure she'd never use. The Yeats book, though. That she would keep forever. And the inscription inside was more than enough to make it extra special: *To Sarah, with gratitude and affection. Maddie and Claire.* She already knew that the book would enjoy a special place on a shelf in her bedroom.

"You're very welcome. It was our pleasure. Sarah?"

"Yes?"

Claire touched her glasses at the bridge of her nose, something Sarah had come to recognize as a nervous habit. Her eyes weren't quite meeting Sarah's. "Are you single?"

"Yes. Are you?"

"Yes."

Okay. That was weird. Interesting, but weird.

"I'm…Good. I'm glad I'm not keeping you from being somewhere else, that's all."

"And I'm glad there's nowhere else you don't have to be, either." Huh. Still weird. And she had no clue what to make of it. Was it some kind of progress in their friendship, openly discussing their status? And what about women? Did Claire ever date women? Was she open to it? Sarah wasn't yet brave enough to ask.

An awkward silence fell as they sipped their wine, but what Sarah suspected, was that talking without emotional barriers was difficult for Claire. At least until the ice between them was fully broken or maybe altogether melted, she wasn't sure which. But she wanted to know her better, wanted to know what went on in that gorgeous, very complex, brainy head of hers.

"Tell me more about Maddie." *There. A safe topic.* "What else does she like besides hockey?"

Claire's face visibly relaxed. She talked for several minutes about Maddie, about her smarts, about how she loved anything to do with puppies and dogs and how she kept pressuring her mother for one. She liked to be organized, she figured out her clothes the night before, she was especially a perfectionist when looking after her hockey gear, her sticks lined up like soldiers in her closet. "She's not perfect, though. Sorry. I talk like she's some sort of miniature superhero, and you should have shut me up."

It was touching how proud Claire was of her daughter. Jesus, this was so new to Sarah. She'd never had a close friend, never mind a *girl*friend, who had kids. But she liked kids, and now that she would soon be in her late thirties, she supposed it was only natural that many of her peers…well, okay, Claire was a little bit older…would have kids. She just hadn't quite caught up. "No way. I love hearing about Maddie." She smiled gently. "And you. Tell me what co-parenting has been like."

Matt seemed like a good guy. Solid. Reliable. Sarah liked him, and found herself hoping, in no small measure, that Claire wouldn't say something awful about him so that she'd be forced to change her opinion of him. But she was curious. What about him had attracted Claire? Made her want to marry him, have his child? Would she ever share that with her?

"He's a good dad, I can't complain about that. He tries to be there for Maddie as much as he can, but his business takes up a lot of his time. And he's got Laurie. I won't lie though, it's hard some days. Coming home from work exhausted, and there's no one to make you dinner or help your kid with her homework." Claire's worry lines smoothed into a trace of a smile. "I don't mean to sound so ungrateful or negative. My life is grand. I've a great kid, a job I love."

Sarah smiled, because she understood how much strength and determination it took to be independent. She also understood how lonely it could be, and she suspected Claire did as well. "You sound like me. Except for the kid part, of course. How did you and Matt meet?"

They met at university, she said, where Matt was a football star and she was earning her undergraduate degree in English literature. Like most university couplings, they met at a party that Claire's roommate had dragged her to. "I tried sitting in a corner by myself, but Matt made a project out of trying to get me to talk to him. He sat down on the floor beside me and said he wasn't leaving, not even to go to the bathroom, if I didn't tell him at least five things about myself." She smiled at the memory. Clearly there was a time they had loved each other. She went on to describe their early years together, the moving around because of Matt's football career at the expense of her postgraduate studies, the surprise pregnancy that was Maddie. And then one day she realized the marriage wasn't her safety net, her strength, but rather the thing that was holding her back.

"I lost myself in the marriage, in Matt's career. I'd had a lifetime, really, of my goals and wishes taking a back seat. And it was no life for a little kid, all that moving around and her dad away a lot. She needed stability."

Maddie needed stability or *you* needed it? Sarah wanted to ask, but she couldn't bring herself to. She had always imagined that if a couple truly loved one another, they would find their way through the kind of obstacles Claire described, especially considering that a pro athlete's career, while certainly all-consuming, wasn't forever. She told herself, after Ruth left, that the problem was that they hadn't loved one another enough, but the truth was, they'd led two separate lives, with two completely different sets of priorities. She understood Claire's predicament, though from a slightly different perspective, because she'd never been the one to wrap her life—her goals and desires—around someone else's. She'd never really tried.

"Did you love him? Were you in love with Matt?"

"I loved him, yes. But in love with him?" Claire lost herself staring at the dancing Christmas lights on the ceiling. She shook her head. "I don't think I ever truly was. We had some fun together, but the compatibility part was never there. See, the thing is, Sarah, I decided I loved myself more, and I loved my child more, than whatever amount of love I had for Matt. And that was all I needed to know, to make the decision I made. You can't always fit a square peg into a round hole, no matter how hard or how many times you try. Not unless you make it smaller. Believe me. I tried."

Sarah reached for the bottle on the coffee table and topped up their glasses. "You're very brave, you know." Seeing Claire like this, in her own home with her legs folded beneath her on the sofa—relaxed and at ease—made her feel at ease, too. It was nice, talking honestly, like real friends. Sarah didn't have many of those, outside of hockey.

"Thanks, but I don't think of myself as brave. I think somewhere along the way I finally figured out how to be a survivor. No, wait, that's not quite right, because there's a lot more to life than just surviving. Or there should be, anyway. We should all have—or strive for—the luxury to thrive, as human beings. And so that part's taken a bit longer for me, but it's gratifying, I'll admit, to be in charge of your own life, your own happiness."

Sarah thought about thriving and being happy. She thrived, her hockey career was testament to that. And she was mostly happy. But she could see how, living in the shadow of a pro athlete, Claire would not have thrived, and the thought alarmed her. Was coupledom less about all-consuming love and more about thriving as individuals within the union? Was it even possible to pursue your own goals, your own happiness, while the bond remained strong and nurtured? It hadn't been that way at all with Ruth, but Sarah was unqualified when it came to long relationships. She sipped her wine and thought about the question she'd been dying to ask Claire.

"Can I ask you one more thing?" Her palms were sweating; this was way harder than any breakaway she'd ever found herself on, even in the last Olympics when the game was tied and the puck ended up on her stick with ten seconds to spare. But dammit, she wanted to know. She swallowed another mouthful of liquid courage.

"All right."

"Have you…" False start. Deep breath. "Are you bisexual?"

A long look from over the rim of Claire's wineglass, then finally a blink. A shy smile broke the tension. "Yes. The Martina poster gave me away?"

"It did sort of ping my gaydar."

"To be fair, let me ask you the same thing. Are you bisexual?"

Sarah laughed, nearly spitting out her wine. "No. I'm not the least bit bi. Gay through and through."

"I see." Claire's face noticeably colored, even in the low light. "I wasn't, you know, sure if you were. I guess I kinda figured. I mean, not that…Never mind. I don't mean to make this awkward."

"You're not." Sarah reached over and patted Claire's knee and spoke with what she hoped was a conciliatory tone. "It's fine. I don't stand on rooftops broadcasting it, but people aren't surprised when they find out. I prefer to keep my life off the ice pretty private, although that doesn't always happen, I suppose."

"It doesn't hurt your hockey career? Being gay?"

"Nah. Half the players are gay or bi. But I won't lie, it wasn't always easy for those of us who didn't have some guy on our arm to wear as a badge of our heterosexuality." There were years where she had to keep that part of herself hidden, at least in public. She was long past that now. If people in the hockey world didn't appreciate what she brought to the game every time she stepped on the ice, well, their loss. She was done pretending so that others could feel more comfortable. "Nowadays it's different, thank God. On one of the teams, two of the players are married, and on another team, two of them are engaged."

"Maybe that's the ticket. Being a couple on the same team."

"How so?"

"One doesn't have to feel like they're following the other around, sacrificing their own career and all that."

"Maybe. But think of the *massive* egos involved." Sarah laughed at the thought. She could never imagine being with another player on her team. Too much togetherness, too much stress worrying about the other's success on the ice, and then there was the worry about trades, injuries. She had been on teams where teammates who were sleeping together dragged their private problems into the locker room. Not exactly great for team morale. Brett had the right idea, marrying someone who had nothing to do with the sport.

"Oh, right. I don't know much about hockey, but I could see how that could be a problem. Like, what if one got picked to go to the Olympics and the other didn't?"

Sarah laughed. "You get the picture. Would you ever date another professor or someone you worked with?"

"No, never with someone I work with. Workplace romances involve the kind of drama I don't want or need."

"I hear ya on that one. I have to confess, though, I don't think I know what the answer is to make a successful relationship. If I did…" Sarah laughed to make a joke of it. "I probably wouldn't be single and sitting in your living room right now."

"Right. And if I was an expert on relationships, you probably wouldn't be sitting in my living room, either, because we would each be at home with the person we're madly in love with."

"And speaking of which—sitting in your living room, not the madly in love part—I should get going." Sarah rose, collected her empty glass and brought it to the kitchen. Claire waited for her in the foyer. "Do you know how to skate, Claire?"

"Hmm. I know how to walk on the ice while wearing skates. But skating? I wouldn't exactly call it that."

Sarah bit back a smile to keep her enthusiasm in check. She didn't want to scare Claire off. "Can we do something tomorrow afternoon? Maddie's away, right? And my team is on break for a few days."

"Do you have something in mind?"

"I do. Pick you up at noon?"

She could tell Claire was unsure.

"It'll be fine," Sarah assured her. "You'll enjoy it, I promise." *And if she doesn't, she'll probably kill me.*

CHAPTER SIXTEEN

"I don't know about this, Sarah."

Claire tried to keep her fumbling fingers from messing up the laces of her rental skates. Sarah had picked her up and driven them downtown to Nathan Phillips Square, to the outdoor public ice rink that Claire had always thought of as romantic whenever she drove by and saw couples skating together. Until now. She hadn't been in skates in close to a decade. She did not expect this to go well. Part of her motivation for going along with it was so to have a good story to tell Maddie. Maddie would *die* if she saw her, and Claire loved the idea that she was actually doing something almost dangerous. Something completely out of character.

"I'll be right beside you the whole time."

"Holding me up, I hope."

"I can do that, but I suspect you will be just fine."

"Don't tell me you're one of those eternal optimists."

Sarah grinned. "Nah. I know a closeted athlete when I see one."

Claire's laughter bubbled up from deep in her belly. She was the antithesis of an athlete, and she was pretty sure Sarah knew it. "I think you'd better get your eyes checked."

Sarah raked her eyes over Claire, and Claire's heart leapt a little. There was an undeniable momentary thrill that this gorgeous athlete, who was five years younger to boot, might be checking her out and might even be liking what she was seeing. It gave her the jolt of confidence she needed as she stood up and grabbed onto Sarah's arm for support.

"My eyes are just fine, thank you very much."

"I hope your biceps are, too."

"My guns are ready to help you at any time. Would you like to feel them?"

Claire felt her eyes widen in surprise. When she looked at Sarah and her waggling eyebrows, she began to stumble and would have fallen, if not for the strong arm holding on to her. Jesus, the woman was lethal when she turned on the sexy teasing.

"Don't worry," Sarah assured without the teasing tone. "I've got you."

"You mean you and your biceps."

"Right. Me and my biceps are here at your service. If I have to use my whole body to keep you upright on the ice, I'm prepared to do it."

Claire needed to get a hold of herself. The butterflies in her belly brought on by the prospect of skating quickly migrated further south and transformed into something that was definitely not nervousness. If she wasn't careful, she was *that close* to being aroused. She cleared her throat. "We're doing this, so?"

"We're doing this. Maddie would be so proud."

"Promise me there will be no photos or a play-by-play description of this calamity."

"You have my word. There will be no evidence left behind."

"Hopefully not my blood, either."

"No blood will be shed, I promise."

Clutching onto Sarah, Claire gingerly walked the short distance to the ice surface, the skates confining and unfamiliar. The afternoon was mostly sunny, a few clouds skittering across the sky. It was cold but only a bit below freezing, nothing Claire couldn't handle. She wore warm socks, long underwear beneath her jeans, plus her Canada Goose parka. She was locked and loaded for this.

"Okay, here goes," she said, stepping one foot onto the ice, then the other, never letting go of Sarah's arm. And Sarah was right about being strong. Claire could feel the solidity of her muscles. She gripped a little harder, liking the feel of all that power beneath her mittened fingers.

"One step at a time," Sarah cautioned. "Or should I say, one glide at a time."

Off they went, slowly, Claire gliding on one skate at a time, Sarah not hurrying her at all, but staying right beside her, her free hand coming to rest over the hand that was gripping her forearm. Within minutes Claire gained more confidence, but not enough to let go of Sarah. They made it around an entire lap without Claire falling or embarrassing herself, which, in her mind, made the outing a success.

"There," Sarah assured her, "you're doing fantastic."

"That's a stretch, but you know what? It's actually not awful."

"Might just make a hockey player out of you yet, Professor Joyce."

"Ha. You have some magical powers I don't know about?"

"Maybe. Are you worried?"

The sun shining off Sarah's golden hair did make her look a little angelic, though it did not turn her into a miracle worker, Claire was quite sure. "I'd be more worried if you were serious about the hockey player part."

"Think of what Maddie would say if she could see you now. Are you going to tell her about this?"

"I will at some point." As fun as it would have been to have Maddie skating with them, Claire was glad it was just the two of them, their own private time that had nothing to do with Maddie and nothing to do with Irish literature, either. It felt oddly freeing. Here she was, in skates, doing something she never thought she'd do again, and doing it with someone she'd never expected to show up in her life. Making an exception to her personal no-fraternizing-with-students rule, if not some kind of divine intervention, had at least been the right decision on her part.

"Now, if I let you go, let's see if you can go some distance on your own, okay?"

Claire panicked at the idea. She couldn't imagine trying to skate without Sarah's sturdy presence beneath her fingers. She said no, she was not ready for that today.

"All right. No worries. I won't let go of you."

I won't let go of you. The words rolled around in Claire's mind, and she didn't doubt Sarah meant it. Every indication was that she was the type of woman who was dependable, solid, and Claire liked that about her. She was anything but the irresponsible, carefree, self-absorbed athlete type that Claire had wrongly pegged her as. It was time to clear the air, if Sarah would let her. She'd meant to apologize last night.

"I really, *really* owe you an apology, Sarah."

Sarah glided them over to a bench at the edge of the rink. They sat down and watched the other skaters go by. One girl, trying to do a figure skating twirl, fell over but got up right away, unscathed. Three teenaged boys chased one another in a game of tag. A young dad held his toddler up under the armpits and sped around the ice, the child's face to the sky, full of rosy-cheeked laughter.

"What could you possibly owe me an apology for?"

Two young girls, not much older than Maddie, stopped in front of them. One had a Sharpie clutched in her hand. "Excuse me, are you Sarah Brennan, the hockey player?"

"I am. And what are your names?"

The one with the Sharpie said her name was Becky, the other, so shy she could hardly speak, squeaked out that her name was Mika.

"It's very nice to meet you both," Sarah replied. "Do you girls play hockey?"

"Yes," they chimed and went on to answer a couple more questions from Sarah about hockey. Finally the one with the Sharpie asked for an autograph. "Oh, wait, I don't have a piece of paper or anything." Her face crumpled in disappointment.

"Don't worry about that. You're wearing your hockey skates. Why don't I autograph your skates?"

Both girls brightened immediately and grinned at Sarah like she was their savior. Claire watched the exchange with interest, appreciating Sarah's patience and generosity with these two young strangers. She bent over and scrawled her name on each girl's skates. They were so thrilled that they skated off in a trail of giggles, forgetting to thank her.

Claire stood up. "That was really nice of you, Sarah."

"Thanks. Sorry for the interruption. It happens occasionally."

"I don't mind. What you did was really nice." Claire chuckled. "It's not very private here, though, is it?" She wanted to be alone with Sarah because she wanted to properly apologize and she couldn't do it here with all the interruptions.

"You're not trying to get out of more skating, are you?" There was a smile on Sarah's lips even as her eyes narrowed in accusation.

"I wouldn't dream of it. But I do make a hell of a good cup of hot chocolate. Would you like to come back to my place?"

"Yes. I would like that. How about a couple more laps first?"

"You drive a hard bargain, lady."

CHAPTER SEVENTEEN

In the car, Sarah said, "You did really well back there. Seriously."

"You're being nice, but thank you. It was actually kind of fun once I stopped shaking and trusted my skates. And your arm."

"Next time I bet you won't even need my arm."

"Oh, I don't know about that. I think it'll be long time before I'm *that* comfortable."

Sarah glanced at Claire in the passenger seat, the blush on her cheeks from the fresh air, her blue eyes still sparkling from the sunshine. She might be mistaken, but she had the distinct impression that after the first few steps on the ice, Claire didn't really need to hold on to her arm, yet she continued to clutch it like a lifeline. At one point, for maybe a lap or less, they had held hands. Not bare hands, they both wore mittens, but Sarah enjoyed the physical contact, got a surprising thrill from skating hand in hand. It reminded her of the absence in her life of a special person, of how much she craved physical contact. She missed a woman's touch, and it didn't necessarily have to be sexual in nature. If she were brave, she would reach over and run her fingers through that dark hair beside her that looked so damned soft and luxurious, so caressable. But she wasn't that brave.

Sarah followed Claire into her house, where Claire quickly busied herself in the kitchen making the hot chocolate from scratch. Perhaps she'd forgotten about whatever it was she wanted to apologize for. Sarah could wait.

"Marshmallows on top?" Claire asked.

"I wouldn't dream of drinking hot chocolate without them."

"Exactly the answer I was hoping for."

They brought their cups into the living room. Claire switched on the gas fireplace; flames leapt to life and produced heat almost immediately. It had been a long time since Sarah had been alone with a woman like this. Not that this was like *that*. It was not a date. Claire was still her professor, and even if she wasn't, there was no reason to believe that she would want to date her or be anything more than casual friends. It was nice, spending the day with a woman who had no expectations of her, other than a little skating, a little conversation.

"Sarah, I started to apologize when we were skating. I need to finish doing that."

"Okay. Though you don't have to. Whatever it is."

"No. I would like to."

"Okay."

They sipped in silence before Claire set her mug down with a soft thunk. "I was an ass. And I'm sorry."

Sarah chuckled. "That sounds a bit harsh."

"It's deserved."

"Claire—"

"No, please." Claire shifted sideways on the sofa, tucking her legs under her. "I want to say that I'm so sorry for how I treated you that first day we met. And for, well, I'm sorry that my behavior toward you did not improve until…until I realized that you're nothing like what I assumed you were."

"And what did you assume I was?"

Claire's teeth worried her bottom lip. She pushed on her glasses at the bridge of her nose. She was so adorably nervous, and the display was such a contrast to her demeanor in class, that Sarah wanted to place her hand over hers and rub it soothingly.

"I, um, had you pegged as irresponsible. Cocky. You know, self-absorbed. I didn't expect you to take my course seriously."

It wasn't new to Sarah, the stereotyping of athletes. "If it makes you feel better, I have been known at times to be cocky and self-absorbed. Though I'm not irresponsible. And I do take your course seriously."

"I realize all that now. I mean…that you're not irresponsible and that you take my course seriously."

"Let me guess. I started off in your bad books because I was late to class that first day?"

"Guilty as charged. And then when I realized you were an athlete, it didn't exactly improve my impression of you."

Sarah took a long sip of her hot chocolate. Claire was right, she did make a killer mug of hot chocolate. "Is this athlete thing because of Matt?"

"Again, guilty. Being married to him wasn't a great time in my life. Don't get me wrong, he's a good guy, and he's a great dad to Maddie. But he wasn't a great husband back then. Those years were all about him, his career. Not that it should have surprised me. I knew playing pro football was his dream. But I was unprepared. And I guess the whole thing kind of…"

"Left you a bit damaged? Jaded?"

"Yes. And bitter about athletes. I took it out on you, and I'm so sorry. It wasn't fair. You didn't deserve it."

"All right. Thank you. I accept your apology." It was okay to laugh now, so she did. "I guess you can say we've come a long way since then. And since we're being honest, I think I was kind of scared of you. I might have been…pushing your buttons a bit."

Claire grinned. It was good to see her relax. "Really? You were scared of *me*?"

"Don't get yourself all flattered. I was only a tiny bit scared of you. Emphasis on tiny."

"God, you must have hated me."

"Hate's a strong word. I hate the player that intentionally took my knee out six years ago and caused me to miss most of a season, but no, I didn't hate you. Annoyed by you, yes, but there was never any hate. When did I finally start to change your mind?"

"When you stood up for yourself over that inadequate essay mark I gave you. That's when I knew you were serious about the course. But honestly, when first I saw the way you are with Maddie—so kind and patient—it really, basically—I knew you were different." Claire's voice grew thick with emotion. "It made me feel terrible about how I'd treated you."

"Thank you for being honest about this. I promise though, there's nothing to forgive." The need to touch Claire again ambushed Sarah. She inched a little closer to her on the sofa, close enough to feel Claire's heat. "You've got a great kid. I can tell you and Matt have been really good parents."

They sat not saying anything for a long moment, watching the fire, sipping their hot chocolate.

After a while, Claire said, "Since you're so good with kids, I've been wondering. Have you ever wanted any of your own?"

Sarah wanted to take her time with this one. She'd found the subject of kids to be a minefield with women. Ruth, most definitely. It came out in an argument over something completely unconnected that Ruth wanted kids one day and Sarah didn't. Claire, she suspected, would be on the Ruth side of the equation and would probably not think much of Sarah's reticence about kids.

"I like kids. I like their willingness to learn new things, their adventurous spirit, their honesty. But…" There was something about Claire that made her want to reveal herself without fear. It was a new feeling to get accustomed to, trusting someone she didn't yet know intimately. She studied Claire's eyes first and found the encouragement, the trust, to go on. "The thing is…I never wanted a child of my own."

"Okay. What was it you didn't like about the idea of being a mom? The baby years?"

"The baby years, yes. And please don't tell me they're fun."

"Don't worry, I won't."

"I guess I'm kind of intimidated about the whole parenting thing. Because it seems like failure would not be an option."

"Failure is inevitable, at times. It happens to everyone, including parents."

Sarah thought about that. Failure happened all the time in hockey, too, even to a player as good as she was. Hockey—all sports—was a game of failures. If no one ever made a mistake, there would never be any goals scored. Which would make for a pretty boring game.

"I suppose you're right. Maybe the problem is I don't like things that I have no idea if I'd be good at or not."

"Ah, so you're a scaredy-cat?"

Shock made Sarah's mouth fall open. "A *what*?" The sparkle of mischief in Claire's eyes, the little giggle from her, energized Sarah. "I'll show you scaredy-cat!" She dove for Claire and began tickling her, relentlessly, until Claire squealed with laughter, straining to catch her breath. She was no match for the stronger Sarah, didn't even try to fight her off.

Before she gave any thought to what came next, while the remnants of laughter remained on their lips, Sarah leaned closer to Claire and kissed her. Softly. Slowly. Tasting the trace of chocolate left behind, letting the joy bloom bigger and bigger in her chest until it almost hurt. She didn't dare deepen the kiss, she wasn't that brave, but she didn't hurry it either. Claire's lips were sensuous, responsive, everything she hoped they might be. The kiss felt like the most natural thing in the world.

What did not was the hand suddenly on her chest, unequivocally pushing her away.

CHAPTER EIGHTEEN

Claire fumbled with her pointer, dropped it, had to pick it up and start again. They were dissecting a short story by James Joyce, called "Giacomo Joyce." Her earlier choice to include the story in the class syllabus now horrified her so much that she almost called in sick. Could they—could Sarah—see the turmoil going on in her head right now? Were they somehow managing to connect the dots and conclude that she was a mess because she'd fooled around with one of her own students? Like the protagonist in "Giacomo Joyce" ached to do?

The hero of the story, believed to be James Joyce himself, possessed an erotic fascination, one might argue an obsession, with one of his young students (or several, it was unclear) whom he was teaching in Italy, Claire explained. "He admires and sympathizes with his student, patronizes and secretly mocks her. And yet…" Claire swallowed. "He clearly wants to have sex with her. Take a look at these passages."

She read more of the story to the class, ignoring the sweat between her shoulder blades. Feeling, the whole time, exposed and transparent. Naked. It was the first time seeing Sarah since their kiss. The kiss she continued to think about every day. The kiss that had taken her by surprise, and yet, nothing about it was surprising, because the wanting, quietly whispering for weeks, had made the kiss inevitable, she supposed. Sarah was the one who was better at math, but it was like some sort of force with tons of raging energy that finally combusts because it simply has to, with nowhere else for all that energy to go. Okay, that probably was physics not math, but in any case, the kiss was nothing like Claire had imagined, because, in her fantasies, she'd failed to imagine her own reaction.

The kiss…had almost made her come apart. It was every bit as overpowering, as explosive, as the first time she'd ever kissed a girl, which had scared her so much she didn't do it again for a couple of years. She had come so close to letting go with Sarah, to letting down all of her walls, to fully letting in the sublime pleasure the kiss promised. But she couldn't. She absolutely could not. "You're my student, Sarah. We can't. We *cannot* do this!"

She'd pushed Sarah away in her living room, a bit more firmly than she meant. The hurt in Sarah's eyes, even while she apologized and said she understood, remained imprinted in her memory. Sarah left shortly afterward. They hadn't talked since. What was there to say, really? They'd made a mistake. A momentously pleasurable one, but a mistake nonetheless. And given Claire's position of authority over Sarah, it was an embarrassing lapse in judgment on her part. It couldn't happen again. It wouldn't.

"The style of the piece itself," Claire continued, "combines the gritty realism of *Dubliners*, the lyricism and naturalism of *A Portrait of an Artist as a Young Man*, and the larger polysemic structures of *Ulysses*, which of course is one of the key early texts of modernism. This is really a free-form love poem that blurs the lines between poem and short fiction, don't you think?"

The students had been looking expectantly at her, trusting her to explain the piece to them. It was a rather difficult one—a lexically dense, multimodal mixture of several genres. They began to murmur, a couple of them raised their hands to speak, and the discussion was on. Claire let them take turns because her scrambled brain needed a moment.

"You can actually see that Joyce is working out some of his future writing style in this piece, in these textual fragments, before he wrote *A Portrait* or *Ulysses* at the time," said one of Claire's more eager students.

Another student raised his hand. "Do you think, in the story, that the girl rejects Giacomo because of their age difference?"

"Possibly," Claire answered. "She was seventeen, he was thirty-one. But in terms of context, this was around 1911 or 1912. Socially, I mean, even if Joyce never intended for this piece to be published, and undoubtedly this is true, the subject was a pretty taboo one."

Oh, Claire, it's still taboo. Sarah wasn't a child and Claire wasn't fourteen years older, but because it was a teacher-student relationship, Claire could potentially be suspended or demoted by the university. She simply could not jeopardize what she'd worked so hard to earn the last six years. Which was why she'd come to her senses and pushed Sarah away.

And yet, if she were being honest with herself, she'd been playing a mental game of blaming Sarah—for coming into their lives, for making herself so likeable, for tempting Claire into something that could be very costly. Conveniently, in her attraction to Sarah, she'd let herself off the hook.

Admit that you like her. Admit you miss her. There was the side of her that was appalled, frightened by the kiss and what could have happened beyond that. There was also the side of her that had wanted that kiss, that had *adored* that kiss. New Year's Eve—just the other night—Claire had sat up late, reading, after Maddie had gone to bed. She came so close to calling Sarah when midnight came along. Just to say hi. Just to say she was sorry for things being awkward. To say that she missed her. But she hadn't.

She looked out at the three dozen or so serious faces in front of her. Sarah, as was her custom, sat near the back. Her head was bent toward her iPad. She was taking notes, not looking at

Claire, not participating in the discussion. If she did look up, if their eyes were to meet, would the connection be so vibrant, so strong, that others would notice what was between them? See through the mist of blame and guilt and regret? Would they agree that she was no better than the teacher in "Giacomo Joyce," lusting after his student? Maybe that was exactly why Sarah wouldn't look at her.

She circled back to the story again. Did she want to sleep with Sarah? Did she have a crush on her? An obsession? No. No, she did not. She didn't go home and write love poems about her, didn't indulge in sexual fantasies about her, didn't dream about her. There was an attraction, yes, undeniably. But it was transient, like Maddie's obsession with hockey and with one of its biggest stars. It was the kind of thing that would pass. She was sure it would.

"All right, class." Already Claire felt better. She had everything under control. "As you know, the final exam for the course is in fifteen days. I want you all, in these fourteen days left, to read the Roddy Doyle novel *The Woman Who Walked into Doors*. In the exam, there will be three essay questions about the book." Claire smiled. "What those three questions are, you'll have to wait to find out."

CHAPTER NINETEEN

Sarah and Brett walked side by side to the arena's elevator, heading for the parking garage. The afternoon game against Chicago had finished two hours ago, a tough slog that they managed to win in overtime. Afterward came rubdowns and ice baths, then media interviews. Sarah was starving.

"Wanna hit that new Greek restaurant on the Danforth?" Brett asked.

"All right. Is Kelly going to meet us there? She's about done at the hospital, isn't she?" Kelly was a pediatrician at the Hospital for Sick Children. To locals, it was known as SickKids.

"She texted me to say she's working a couple of extra hours. The doc who was supposed to relieve her called in sick, so they're scrambling to figure things out. I'm afraid you're stuck with me."

"Oh. Okay."

"Don't get too excited about it."

"Sorry. I guess you will just have to do."

On the elevator ride down, Brett, same as she'd done a few times this week, asked Sarah if she was okay. She wasn't, not really, but she would lie about it for now.

"Sure. Everything's fine."

"It doesn't seem fine. Something is off with you. I actually have a brain, you know. You could tell me stuff and then I could tell you stuff back that might make you feel better."

"Yeah, yeah. And sometimes talking is overrated."

"That's not what my wife says. And I kinda agree with her."

They stepped off the elevator. Sarah had walked to the arena, since her condo was only a few blocks away. They'd have to take Brett's car to the restaurant. As she strolled toward the exit door, her cell phone rang. She was going to ignore it, it was probably spam, but it seemed particularly insistent. She glanced at the screen and stopped in her tracks. It was Claire. Claire never called her.

"Claire?"

There were tears in her voice. "It's Maddie. I didn't know who else to call. Matt is out of town on business and Laurie's working late."

"What's happened? What's wrong?" Brett halted beside her. Sarah's hand, the one holding the phone, trembled.

"I'm at the hospital."

"Which one?"

"SickKids."

"I'm on my way." Sarah put her phone away and jogged out the door, Brett hot on her heels. "Can you take us to SickKids? It's Claire's daughter. God, I hope Kelly is still working."

"Text her while I drive. By some miracle she might actually have time to text you back before we get there."

Brett drove as fast as she could, managing to zip along the streets without attracting attention from any cops, only refraining from zooming through red lights because Sarah ordered her not to. She frantically texted Kelly, explaining that they were on their way and that her friend Claire Joyce and her daughter, Maddie Hendry, were there, likely in the ER. Shit, she hadn't even asked Claire what the emergency was. A reply from Kelly came back: *I'm on the case. Kid will be okay.*

"Oh, thank God," Sarah said out loud.

"What?" Brett asked.

"Kelly drew the case. She didn't say much, just that Maddie will be okay."

"Oh, good. I know I'm biased, but my wife is one of the best pediatricians in the city."

"I know she is. And I know she'll do her best to make sure Maddie is okay. Whatever it is that's going on." Sarah kept her thoughts to herself for the rest of the drive. She worried about what had happened to Maddie, worried about Claire, too, because Claire had sounded almost inconsolable on the phone.

Brett knew her way around the ER. She told the triage nurse, who recognized her, that she needed to see Dr. West immediately. Within two minutes, Kelly appeared and shepherded them through a set of doors and down a hall on tiles that gleamed. They had to dodge two teenagers in wheelchairs, a toddler throwing up into his mother's empty coffee cup, and a baby crying while his parents tried to calm him.

"Claire!" Sarah rushed to her and wrapped her in a hug. Claire was stiff in her arms. When she pulled back, Sarah could see the tear tracks down her cheeks. "What's happened? Where's Maddie?"

Claire seemed frozen in place.

"She's in x-ray," Kelly answered. "She has a broken clavicle. I doubt it's going to require surgery, but when the x-rays are done, I'll have one of our orthopedic surgeons take a look to be sure."

Sarah let out a breath. "Okay. Good." To Claire, she said, "How did it happen?"

Claire's eyes were glacial, a look Sarah recognized from class. "Hockey. She fell into the boards at her game tonight. Or got knocked into the boards, I'm not sure which."

Oh, no. Of course it had to happen while Maddie was playing hockey. "I'm sorry, Claire. It sounds like she's going to be fine, though. Right, Kelly? Oops. I mean, Dr. West."

"She's going to be just fine." Kelly gave Claire a reassuring smile. "Although, no hockey for at least six weeks."

"Thank God," Claire uttered. The fear and worry rolled off her in waves of anger. Sarah could see that she was going to take every bit of her anger and worry and pin it right onto the game of hockey. Another strike against the sport that Sarah, and now Maddie, adored.

To change the subject, Sarah introduced Brett and Kelly to Claire. By the time they'd made some small talk that bordered on the uncomfortable, a transporter wheeled Maddie into the room. She was in a pediatric wheelchair.

"Sarah! What are you doing here?"

"I heard about your injury, and I wanted to make sure you're okay. How are you feeling? Are you all right?"

Maddie's face twisted. "It hurts. It really hurts."

"The pain meds we gave her should kick in very soon," Kelly said. "Now if you all will excuse me, I'm going to look at the x-rays and talk to one of our orthos." She winked at her wife. "Be back as soon as I can."

Brett stepped closer to Maddie and stuck out her hand. "I'm Brett Quincy. I hear you're a real good hockey player."

"You're on Sarah's team. Number fourteen, right?"

"Right. Good memory, kid."

"I'm really happy to meet you. But I'm not good yet. Not good like you guys."

"Give it time. Like they say, Rome wasn't built in a day." She lowered her voice. "Don't tell Sarah, but we weren't very good at your age, either."

Maddie laughed. "Mom, what does Rome not being built in a day mean?"

Claire explained the phrase to her daughter while she helped her back onto the narrow treatment bed. The room was awfully tight for three adults and a kid. Sarah could see that Claire was trying to stay calm for Maddie's sake.

"Guess what, Maddie?" Sarah discreetly nudged Brett. "We won our game this afternoon!"

"You did? Woohoo!"

The pain meds must be kicking in, Sarah thought, as she and Brett went into great detail about the game, Maddie hanging on every word.

"And you scored, right, Sarah?" Maddie asked.

"Actually I didn't this time. But Brett did."

"Garbage goal," Brett said with a laugh. "But a goal is a goal, right?"

"Right!" Maddie high-fived them both with her good arm.

"Boy, the goalie sure wasn't happy when I scored, though."

"What did she do?"

Sarah stood back and imitated the frustrated goalie, who slammed her stick so hard on the ice, it broke in half. Claire's frown said she wasn't amused, but Maddie, Brett, and Sarah had a good laugh over it. By the time their antics were over, Kelly was back in the room, and explained to Claire and Maggie that the injury did not need surgery and would heal just fine on its own over the next couple of months. She recommended a special chest strap to use overnight as well as when she was being active, to keep the bones aligned. "Even if they don't line up perfectly, they will heal just fine."

Sarah whispered to Brett that she would escort Claire and Maddie home. After her best friends disappeared out into the hall, Sarah said to Claire, "I'll come home with you and Maddie to make sure you guys are okay."

"You don't have to do that," Claire said, exhaustion heavy in her voice.

"Oh, can you please, Sarah?" Maddie whimpered a little, probably to bolster her case.

"Of course I can. I don't have my car, but I'll ride with you guys and catch a cab home later, all right?"

During the ride, Claire remained deep in her own thoughts while Maddie slept, the pain medication and all the excitement of the last few hours having caught up to her. She continued to sleep even as they pulled into the driveway.

"I've got her," Sarah said. Carefully, easing her arms under Maddie, she lifted her out of the car and carried her into the house.

"Are you sure you can handle her?"

"I'm sure."

Sarah continued up the stairs with Maddie in her arms, Claire racing ahead of them to open doors and switch on lights.

"I'll get her undressed and into bed," Claire said. "Thank you for helping us out tonight. Matt's out west at a homebuilder's conference. I was…Well, thank you."

"It's okay," Sarah whispered. "I'm glad you called me. I'll wait for you downstairs, okay?"

"You don't need—"

"I'll see you downstairs." She knew Claire well enough. Knew the stoic demeanor had more than a few cracks in it.

"Can I get you anything?" Sarah said to Claire moments later.

"Thanks, but I'm fine."

"Actually, I think you could use a glass of wine."

Claire didn't protest. Sarah found a chilled half-bottle of white in the fridge, poured them each a glass. She found Claire in the living room on the sofa, chin tucked tight against her fist, the light from a single Tiffany lamp casting a muted but colorful glow.

"You're upset." Sarah handed a glass to Claire and sat down beside her.

"Damned right I am. That sport is violent. It's not safe for Maddie."

"Okay, hold on a minute. She's just been injured. I understand that it's hard to watch someone you love in pain. But you'll feel differently in a few days or a few weeks."

"I won't."

Sarah sipped from her glass, giving Claire's anger time to spend itself. Gently, she said, "Injuries can happen in any sport, Claire. Soccer, lacrosse, baseball, even just running or playing in the backyard. What's important is that Maddie wasn't seriously injured. She's going to be okay."

"What if it's serious next time?"

Sarah had never been much of a talker. She was an athlete, someone who responded with movement, with *doing*, and not with thoughts, debates. She identified a problem and then tried to fix it. Quickly. She didn't know how to fix this, but she did know a lot about being an athlete. And she understood that Claire needed to talk about it.

"Claire, is this more about Maddie or about you?"

"Me? What do you mean?"

"Does this have anything to do with Matt's past career? With his football injuries?"

Claire rolled her eyes. "Please. Matt and his football career happened a long time ago. It feels like a lifetime ago, and it's one I don't want to revisit."

"I get that. But the scars we acquire, and I don't just mean physical scars, can take a lifetime to disappear. I just…"

It wasn't her business, not Claire's former marriage nor the raising of her daughter. But she hated seeing Claire like this, hated to think that she might try and stop Maddie from playing a sport she loved so much.

"I would hate to see you make a huge deal out of this, for your sake and for Maddie's."

"You don't understand."

"I might, if you give me a chance."

It was a standoff—Claire as tight as a tuning fork, Sarah refusing to absorb her misplaced anger. There was only one way through this. Instinctively, Sarah held out her arms, and in a whisper, urged, "Come here. Let someone else take the reins for a while. Let *me* take the reins."

Sarah expected resistance, but to her surprise, Claire collapsed into her arms, her body quivering, her mouth choking out quiet sobs.

"Shh, shh. It's going to be all right." She caressed small circles on Claire's back, pressed her cheek against the thick waves of her hair, softly inhaling the citrus scent of her shampoo, wanting to remember every second of this. Wanting to live inside of this very moment.

CHAPTER TWENTY

Claire lost track of the time in Sarah's arms, even though it'd probably been only a few minutes. She hadn't felt this weak, this emotionally exposed, since her divorce. Out of habit, she typically resisted others' attempts to soothe or placate her, but something about Sarah's words, *let someone else take the reins for a while*, had blown out the flame of her indignation, her anger. She let Sarah console her in the silence, let herself surrender a few moments of control, because in Sarah's arms, strong arms that were also yielding, soft, Claire felt safe. And seen. And these were not small things in her world.

If only she could stay swept away like this, but her need to exert her own strength won out. Claire was used to saving herself; she'd had a lifetime of practice. "Are you always this capable?" she mumbled into Sarah's shoulder.

"Mostly. Except when I'm looking for a particular building on campus."

Claire burst out laughing, and it felt wonderful, the releasing of the pressure valve. "As I recall, you did have quite a bit of trouble with that."

"As I recall, you didn't cut me much of a break."

Claire pulled back to look into Sarah's eyes, moist from the remnants of their shared laughter. She was still smiling. God, she was beautiful. And strong. And not only because of the effortless way she'd carried Maddie into the house and up the stairs, which had been impressive. Had Claire not been so upset, she would have spent more time admiring Sarah and her muscles, but she did have time now to appreciate that there was strength in Sarah that went so much deeper than her muscles.

"Well, it's true that I don't cut freshmen much slack. Let's just say that I didn't fully appreciate your true self that day. Annnnd…I've already apologized."

"I know, and I'm over it, I promise. So, um, you're appreciating my true self now?"

Claire did, absolutely. "Yes." There was more she wanted to say, but she lost herself in those hazel-green eyes, becoming only dimly aware of Sarah gently removing her glasses and setting them on the coffee table. The kiss came like a warm summer breeze against her lips. She didn't push Sarah away like last time, even though she understood what they were doing was forbidden. She needed the kiss, needed more tactile connection with the woman who had dropped everything to come to her when she needed her.

The kiss deepened before Sarah, with what Claire could only imagine was great effort, pulled back to look into her eyes. She felt the absence of Sarah's lips in the worst way.

"Claire, I want to see you. And I don't mean in a classroom or in a hockey arena. I want to *see* you."

"Oh, Sarah. You don't really—"

"I do."

Claire was stunned. She hadn't seen this coming, not really, even though the possibility of being with Sarah had lurked not too far below the surface of her imagination. It was disbelief that such an attractive younger woman, who was also a gifted athlete, smart, capable, and kind, too, wanted to date her. Was she nuts? She could date anyone she wanted, especially someone without Claire's baggage. "Look, I'm…I have a kid, I'm divorced, I—"

"I don't care about any of that. I do, but not in the way you think."

"I'm still your profess—"

"For three more days. Or, okay, the exam is in three more days, so I guess technically you're my professor until my final grade has been submitted which should be, oh, in about a week or so? Am I right?"

Claire leaned back, took a timely sip of wine, and indulged herself in a brief fantasy of what dating Sarah might be like. It'd been a long time since she'd dated anyone. After she and Matt split, she didn't have time to date at first. In the years since, she'd been on a total of three dates, all of which went exactly nowhere because there'd been no spark felt on her part, no desire to take things further. No one had gotten through or around her walls.

Sarah was different. She was the only person since her marriage that Claire could see herself doing *couple* things with— going out for dinner or a show, driving somewhere out in the country for a picnic, spending quiet nights together cooking or just hanging out. And kissing. And sex. Jesus, she couldn't allow herself to think of those things, not when Sarah was still her student and not when Maddie was upstairs sleeping. Maddie. She'd be over the moon if her mother and Sarah began dating, but reality finally smothered the fantasy. There was too much to consider, too much that could go wrong. And had Sarah forgotten that Claire had sworn off relationships with athletes?

"Sarah, I think it would be an awfully big step right now."

The yearning in Sarah's eyes flamed out. "I think I get it. You won't date athletes ever again."

"It's not that simple. I know you're not Matt. And—"

"And you're not the same person you were when you were with Matt."

That was true. Sarah wasn't Matt, and Claire wasn't the Claire of fifteen years ago, but it was so hard to let go of those events, those years that had come to define her. "I know it's completely unfair to say I'd never date you because you're an athlete. I'm sorry, Sarah, but it *is* a factor for me, a huge factor. It's…I also have a daughter, and I don't want to do anything that could hurt her." Claire hated how defensive she sounded, how wounded.

"I know you have a daughter. You think dating me would hurt her somehow?"

Sarah was growing more hurt by the minute, and Claire couldn't see her way out of the spiraling. What she needed was time to process things, to consider the reality of what dating Sarah might be like. It was impossible to do in minutes. "I don't, no. In fact she would love it if we were dating. But she's so attached to you already. She adores you. She wouldn't handle it well if things went south between us."

"I adore her, too. She's a great kid. It's not like I would enter into this lightly, that I would ever be cavalier about hurting her. Or you. I never go into something thinking it is going to fail."

Claire reached for Sarah's hand and held it tightly, looked her square in the eye. "I do know that about you. I know you're a woman of integrity."

"Just not your type, huh?" A quirk of an eyebrow, a slow smile that wobbled between cocky and devastated. Sarah knew damned well that Claire was attracted to her. The chemistry that ran hotly between them was too obvious to ignore, but Sarah was worried, she could see, about things falling apart between them before they'd even gotten off the ground. And they *were* teetering on a precipice. If she pulled away from Sarah now, it would be the end of…whatever they had between them.

She closed her eyes. This was going to require a boldness she rarely possessed, but she leaned in anyway and kissed Sarah firmly on the mouth. "I think that answers that question."

"Then date me."

"Looking for an A-plus on your exam?"

"I'll settle for an F as long as you agree to date me."

Claire laughed. "You're persistent."

Sarah held her in her arms, kissed her again. "I'm persistent when it's something important. And so worthwhile."

"How can you be so sure?"

Sarah held her tighter. "Some things you just know."

"I admire how deeply you know what you want in life, Sarah."

"But you don't know if you want this."

"The only thing I know is that I don't want complicated and I don't want myself or my daughter to get hurt. You can't promise me any of those things, can you?" It was a fact, not a criticism.

"You want to know the ending of the book before you start reading it."

Claire froze. She hadn't thought of it like that before, but Sarah was right. She was scared of the outcome. "Sarah, I need time to process this and what a deeper relationship between us might mean, for me and for Maddie, too. I need time. I don't want to be pressured. This is too important."

"All right, I understand. I'm going to call an Uber, okay? And I want you to know that I'm going to earn at least an A on your exam, even if it kills me. And I'm not going to pressure you or bug you. But I am going to leave you with this."

Sarah pressed her mouth to Claire's and kissed her with such feeling that Claire forgot to breathe. When the kiss ended, she was so light-headed she nearly toppled off the couch. "My God," she mumbled. How was it possible that kisses from Sarah Brennan had the power to flatten her this way?

Sarah rose and called for an Uber. At the door, she said, "Are you okay? About Maddie getting hurt at hockey?"

"No, but I will be."

"I'll call in the morning to check on her."

"She'd love that."

Sarah lingered a moment, a smile turning the corners of her mouth. And then she was gone into the night.

CHAPTER TWENTY-ONE

Sarah popped the cork, finishing with an exaggerated flourish.

"Careful," Brett said. "Or somebody could lose an eye."

Kelly held out her champagne glass. "Not that I'm complaining, but what are we celebrating?"

"Me," said Sarah. "Or rather, my A in my Irish literature course. I just got my final grade emailed to me this morning."

Brett slid her empty coupe glass along the marble-topped island next to her wife's. "Ah, so you provided the professor with some special motivation, did you?"

"You know, I do actually have a brain." Sarah filled the three glasses.

"So it's been rumored."

Kelly rolled her eyes. "Oh, you two. Give it up already. I swear you guys were separated at birth."

"Sorry," they replied in unison, which only proved Kelly's point.

Brett made it known she was starving and began tearing open the cartons of Thai food Sarah had brought over—pho for the three of them and an order of pad thai that could probably feed the entire hockey team.

"How was that book you had to read for your final?" Kelly asked. She was a reader; Brett was not.

"*The Woman Who Walked into Doors*? It was really well written, though the scenes of violence—the parts featuring her jerk of a husband—were tough to read at times."

"What did you have to do for the final exam?"

"We had to choose to answer two out of three essay questions about the book. I chose to write about why the main character is an unreliable narrator and whether it was inappropriate for the author, being a male, to write from the perspective of a battered woman."

"And what did you conclude?"

Brett grew whiny between bites of pad thai. "Can we skip the book club meeting and go back to talking about hockey? Or women, or something?"

"Okay, have it your way," Sarah huffed. "We're playing like shit lately. All of us. We lost last night because we collectively sucked. But I've filed it all under G for garbage, and I'm not interested in hashing it out again. The A in my lit class is much more fun to talk about."

"Fine. Let's talk about your professor. Or rather, she's not your professor anymore, is she?" Brett's eyebrows went for an acrobatic dance.

"Hold on," Kelly interrupted. "How's Maddie doing?"

"Good, I think. I haven't heard anything for a few days. Claire and I have hit the pause button until this course is wrapped up. Or at least, I hope it's only until the course is wrapped up." They hadn't made plans for when they would talk again.

Brett said, "Sounds like it's wrapped up now, since you have your mark."

"Maybe. I don't know how it works." Was she supposed to reach out first? Or was it up to Claire? Probably Claire. So why hadn't she? Did she need a few more days to do whatever professors had to do to close the books on one semester before starting the next? Nothing about her and Claire could be drawn in a straight line. Getting from A to B seemed to entail a hell of a lot of detours.

Gently, Kelly asked, "How serious are you about Claire?"

Sarah knew her friends cared about her and wanted her to be happy, but it wasn't easy trying to come up with an answer that would fit nicely in their little box of expectations. "I like her. She's smart, gorgeous, she's a great mom. There's something about her that intrigues me, something I can't quite put my finger on."

"Her vulnerable side?" Kelly asked between bites of pad thai. "I mean, it's pretty attractive when someone is tough or rigid or has a super confident demeanor on the outside and then on the inside they have this whole other side to them. A soft side. It's kinda like unwrapping a present and finding out it's something completely different than you thought."

"Different and spectacular," Brett interjected, taking a moment to nuzzle her wife.

Sarah thought about it. She loved the contradiction that was Claire: her toughness and independence, her softness, her fears. With Maddie, she was a loving, affectionate mom, but with others, Sarah could see that she held back emotionally. "She's been hurt before, and it makes me ache inside at the thought of it."

"From her first marriage?" Brett asked. "Is her ex, Matt, an asshole?"

"No, he's not. But yes, I think the failed marriage hurt her. Who wouldn't be affected by divorce?"

"Is there something else?" Kelly asked.

For Sarah, it was the million-dollar question and one to which she might never know the answer. But there were scars on Claire's heart that she felt sure weren't entirely from Matt. "I'm not sure. I do sense there is, but I don't know what."

Brett asked, "Is she relationship-phobic?"

The more they discussed Claire, the more Sarah's mood dropped.

"I hope not, but I suspect she is. I don't know if this thing about her being my professor is a convenient excuse or what. I mean, she told me she doesn't want to get hurt and she doesn't want Maddie to get hurt, but in my experience, when people say that stuff, they're really just looking for reasons not to get involved."

And yet, she reasoned, she had been the first person Claire called when Maddie got hurt, and Claire had responded so sensually to their kiss afterward. She'd kissed Sarah back with the kind of fervor that could have easily led to more, if circumstances were different. The signals were all over the place. What Sarah needed to decide was if it was worth her time and effort—and her heart—to keep trying to unravel the mystery that was Claire Joyce.

"Speaking of Maddie," Kelly said. "How do you feel about getting involved with somebody who has a kid? That's new territory for you."

"It is. And it scares me a little, to be honest." Claire called her a scaredy-cat when she admitted the idea of parenting intimidated her. Sarah smiled at the memory of what had led to their first kiss.

"Why?" Brett asked. "You're great with kids. And they're always drawn to you. Of anyone on the team, you always have the biggest lineup of kids waiting to get your autograph or to get a selfie."

Sarah shrugged. "That's a lot different than being a stepmom or co-parent or whatever."

"Sounds to me," Kelly offered, "like you just need to get your confidence up. And that kid adores you. I could see that for myself, the way she lit up when she saw you waiting for her at the hospital. Don't let your fears keep you from trying something new. Take things as they come. You might be surprised."

Kelly was right. Fear wasn't normally something Sarah let paralyze her. "I don't always know what I'm supposed to say or do around Maddie. I feel so awkward sometimes. Like, I know she hero-worships me, and I don't want to disappoint her." She wondered how much of seemingly normal adult life was simply going through the motions and pretending you knew what you were doing.

"She won't be disappointed," Brett said.

"She might be. I can't be a hero twenty-four hours a day. Nobody can."

"So be yourself." Kelly gave her a pat on the shoulder as she stood to remove their plates. "That will be enough."

Sarah continued to stew. What the hell she was thinking, getting so serious (in her head, anyway) about a woman with a kid? She could never be enough for someone like Claire and Maddie. She was a professional athlete with a career that would come to a close in the next few years—her aching knees reminded her of that every single day. What did she have to offer them? What did she know about relationships? About raising a kid? About anything outside of hockey? And as for her post hockey career plans, they amounted to zero so far. All of which would only remind Claire that the one time she had fallen for a pro athlete, it was a fail. "I don't know, you guys."

"Don't give up yet, Sar." Brett glanced at Kelly, who gave her a nearly imperceptible nod. "I've got an idea. Why don't you ask Claire and Maddie to come to Detroit for the All-Star game? Just to hang out as your guests? That way, there's no pressure that it's a date or anything."

The idea was a good one, but Sarah doubted Claire would go for it. "I don't know. That's only nine days away."

"It's a three-day weekend, so it shouldn't interfere much with her work. Maddie will be in absolute heaven. And besides, if Maddie gets sick of all the hockey, she can hang out with Kelly's nieces."

"You're bringing Jane and Hillary?"

Brett and Kelly were practically surrogate moms to Kelly's two nieces, who were nine and seven. Close enough in age to Maddie. The kids were adorable and a lot like their aunt—smart and empathetic.

"They can't wait," Kelly said. "And I know they will love Maddie. Why don't you give it a try?"

"Yeah," Brett added. "Either you or Claire better get off your butt and get this train out of the station."

There was probably no point, but what the hell. It was an excuse to contact Claire. "All right. I'll call her tomorrow and ask."

"Attagirl."

Brett high-fived her, which Sarah returned without much enthusiasm. She had the sinking feeling she was setting herself up for a fall.

CHAPTER TWENTY-TWO

Maddie seat-danced in the car beside Claire, singing along with the radio to "Life Is a Highway." Maddie loved the old tunes as much as Claire, and it had been her own initiative to learn the words to the songs of many of her mother's favorite artists—The Indigo Girls, Tina Turner, The Cranberries. In return, Claire made a project of learning the words to Maddie's favorite Taylor Swift songs.

"Mom, I can hear their accent in your voice when I listen to The Cranberries," she'd once said, and Claire went on to describe the city of Limerick, where the band members hailed from, how it wasn't far from the town Claire grew up in. She painted a verbal picture of the River Shannon meandering through the city's center along with the famous King John's Castle jutting into the horizon. She'd taken Maddie to Ireland once, but she was too young to remember much about it. "We haven't been on a road trip in a long while, alannah."

Maddie's grin hadn't left her face, and they were almost at their destination. "We should do this more often, Mom."

"I agree."

"Like, we should go to all of Sarah's road games! Can we?"

"Um, there's this thing called work and school. So, no."

"Then how about season tickets next year for all her home games?"

Claire was about to say no but closed her mouth. Why shouldn't they get season tickets next year? Maddie would love it, and for Claire, watching Sarah play hockey in the flesh once a week or so sounded...well, sublime. All that strength and grace and athleticism on display was sexy as hell. Maddie could admire the hockey and Claire could admire Sarah.

"Hmmm, maybe we will. Let's talk about it over the summer, okay?"

"Okay. But I'm going to keep bugging you about it."

"I know. Believe me, I know."

There had been no letup in Maddie's obsession with hockey, even though her broken collarbone meant she couldn't get on the ice for a few more weeks yet. Asking her if she wanted to go to the All-Star game was like time-traveling back to all the excitement of Christmas again. Of course Maddie wanted to go. Claire did too. And the way Sarah had invited them left no room to say no. It came via a courier who delivered a small box to her office. Inside was a plain black hockey puck with a message written on its front and back in silver Sharpie: *Will you and Maddie join me as my guests at the All-Star game in Detroit? Pretty please? Call me.* ☺ Before she had a chance to think too much about it, Claire called immediately and said yes. Sarah was speechless on the other end, as though she'd never expected her idea to work.

Thinking of Sarah, the prospect of seeing her again, brought a secret pleasure to Claire. But with those secret thoughts came a ribbon of doubt, a lack of certainty about what she was doing, driving four hours, taking the day off work, and pulling Maddie out of school. It wasn't like her to wade into unknown territory. And with Sarah, there was no map, no manual on how they were supposed to do any of this. The things at stake—her daughter, for one, her own heart, for another—kept her awake at night. To pursue this thing with Sarah required some selfishness on her part, a temporary shedding of being a responsible adult. And to be selfish meant behaving exactly as her parents had behaved when she was a kid, living their lives as if they were childless—trips, parties, all sorts of things that excluded Claire, their only child, left with babysitters or to sit silently at the top of the stairs listening to the rise and fall of all the adult voices below. She would never do that to Maddie, had always, as a matter of principle, placed her first.

Maddie had no idea of the romantic current running fast and furious between her and Sarah, which was exactly the way Claire wanted it. She'd always played the part of whatever Maddie needed—strong and reliable, loving her unconditionally. Maddie wasn't little anymore, though, and Claire knew she couldn't forever shield her from seeing her mother's doubts, her fears, her weaknesses. One day, she was going to have to let Maddie see that she wasn't just a mom. That she was a woman, too, a person who made mistakes like everyone else. And a woman who had needs. Today wasn't that day, though.

Claire pulled into the hotel parking lot. Trunk raised, she was about to retrieve their luggage when Sarah jogged up to them.

She hugged Maddie first, lifting her off the ground, twirling her around. She hugged Claire much less dramatically, whispering into her ear, "I wanted to hug you like that too, but, well, you're not a hockey player, so I figured you might break."

"Smart aleck. Perhaps one day I will show you exactly how strong I am."

"Oh, I don't doubt you will."

Sarah's eyes sparkled with delight, her cheeks flushed in that bashful way that was reserved for few to see, Claire was sure. She wondered if her own face revealed her joy at being with her again, and this time, without the shackles of a teacher-student relationship. There were no outside forces to keep them apart anymore. In theory, anyway.

"Maddie," Sarah said, "how are you feeling, buddy? How's the collarbone?"

"It's okay, I guess. I want to skate again, but Mom won't let me yet."

"Your mom's a smart lady."

Maddie shrugged. "Yeah, I guess."

"Here, let me help carry these bags in. Brett and Kelly and their nieces are waiting for us in the lobby. Do you remember Dr. West from the hospital?"

"Yup. She was a nice lady. And Brett, too."

"You're going to love their nieces, Jane and Hillary. They're almost as enthusiastic about hockey as you are."

"Really? They play hockey, too?"

"They do. And you can ask them all about it this weekend."

Sarah set down the two suitcases inside the lobby as they met up with Brett and Kelly, and Kelly introduced her nieces. The younger one, Hillary, was shy, but Jane, just a few months younger than Maddie, made up for it with a constant stream of friendly chatter. Already she was pulling a set of hockey cards from her pocket.

To Claire, Sarah said, "How about you and I take these suitcases up to your room, and then we'll come down and talk about the plans for tonight, okay?"

"All right. Maddie, honey, Sarah and I will be right back."

"Okay, Mom." Maddie turned back to her new friends.

In the elevator, her tension made Claire blather on about nothing and everything, while Sarah, calm but with eyes that suggested restlessness, listened. In the hall she fumbled with her key card; it was Sarah who slid it in seamlessly and opened the door, then set the bags on the floor. She felt like a teenager about to do something naughty.

"You," Sarah said in a ragged whisper, "look fantastic. I've missed you."

"I...I missed you, too." Saying it lifted a weight off Claire's shoulders. "And you look like an oasis after a long drive in the desert."

Sarah came closer. "Do you mean it?"

"I do." She wanted Sarah's arms around her, and, as if reading her mind, or perhaps because they were somehow so weirdly in sync, Sarah took her into her arms. The warmth and sturdiness of the embrace sent a tingle of excitement down her spine and into her legs. She'd be wobbly if not for the strength of Sarah's arms.

"I'm so glad you're here," Sarah said, her breath ruffling Claire's hair. "I feel like I can't stop looking at you."

Claire breathed in the unique scent that was Sarah as they pulled back enough to look at one another. "Sarah." She didn't know what to say, now that they were together. And alone.

"I want to kiss you. May I?"

Claire drew breath. She wanted to kiss Sarah, too. She wanted to kiss her and then not think about it, just sink right into it and enjoy the hell out of it. "I want you to kiss me." Her pulse quickened. She wanted Sarah to do things to her, so many things, none of which she would assign a word to, because that would make the longing somehow more real. But the feeling of giving herself to Sarah, giving *in* to Sarah, *that* she would hold on to and think about in her alone moments.

There was no hesitation from Sarah. She cupped Claire's cheek, and then her lips were on Claire's. It was an exquisite kiss, delicate yet full of meaning. A kiss that said "I want you but I can wait." The problem was, could Claire wait? She took a step back, cleared her throat, attempted to restore her equanimity.

"Well," she said. "Hello, Sarah Brennan."

"Hello, Claire Joyce. Are you hungry?"

She was. She was hungry for a lot of things. "A little. What's the plan for tonight?"

"The big skills competition is at seven-thirty. Kelly has the tickets. You'll be sitting with them. Brett and I have already eaten, and we have to head to the arena shortly. I'm sorry about that. The schedule is a bit tight. Anyway, Kelly and you and the girls should go have dinner."

"All right."

"And then, afterward. Later tonight..." There was that little sparkle again in Sarah's eyes. Claire knew it well by now. "I thought, just the two of us, could have a glass of wine and a snack downstairs in the lounge."

The idea was enticing, but Claire's thoughts drifted to her daughter. "I can't leave Maddie alone in here." She wanted some time alone with Sarah this weekend, but she could already see it wouldn't be easy. Other people, the duties Sarah had to fulfill, Maddie's presence. Claire sighed. The reality was that they would hardly see each other. "But yes, I do want to see you tonight. Later, I mean. If we can swing it."

"Don't worry," Sarah said. "We'll figure something out. And since my room is right across from yours, if we have to, we can order room service. And keep the doors open in case Maddie wakes."

With the door open, did that mean no more kissing? Claire hoped not. "All right, sounds like a plan."

CHAPTER TWENTY-THREE

It was so much more satisfying on the ice when Sarah knew she had people in the crowd cheering for her—people who cared about Sarah Brennan the person and not just Sarah Brennan the hockey player. She thought of Claire and Maddie as her blades dug grooves into the ice, when she glided tightly around the corners—it was as if she had them on her back, carrying them along on the ice as she flew around. The league's All-Star game meant more to Sarah than an obligation, because she didn't know how many more seasons she had in her, whether she'd ever have the honor of being called to another All-Star game. She looked around the packed arena, at the nearly twenty thousand people yelling, clapping, waving signs, wearing jerseys or shirts with her team's name or with the names of the other seven teams in the league. Music, hard and driving, blared from speakers in the rafters. It was deafening, even though tonight's event was not the main event, but rather a showcasing of skills. She soaked it all in, letting the presence of the crowd wash over her in one massive tidal wave of euphoria.

Brett skated up to her and propositioned her with a fifty-dollar bet for the first of the skills, which involved hitting four small targets at each corner of the net. The player to hit all four targets in the fastest time would win. Sarah nodded; she'd take that bet, having one of the most accurate shots of anyone in the league. Brett went first, taking twenty-eight seconds to hit all four targets. Next up was Hannah Tyler, a member of the New York team, who was third overall in league scoring. She'd be tough competition in this one. Sure enough, she hit all four targets in just seventeen seconds. The crowd loved it, sensing how tight the contest was. Another player, this one from the Montreal team, took nineteen seconds to complete the task.

Last came Sarah. She'd need to beat Tyler's time, but it wouldn't be easy. Her eyes lasered in on each of the four corners and their small foam targets, mentally drawing the angles she'd need, figuring out exactly how much time she had—about four seconds per target—and calculated the velocity of each shot she would have to get off. Stick on the ice, she set herself, nodded at the first passer for the puck. Her first shot went wide, ricocheting off the backboards. She'd need to bear down and not miss her next four. Her next shot hit the target in the top right corner, then she hit the target in the corner below it. As a leftie shot, the targets on the left side of the net were hardest, but she nailed them both. She did a little fist pump when her time was announced—sixteen seconds. She'd won by a second.

"Okay, okay, so it was a bad bet on my part," Brett whined.

"Nah, the opportunity to take fifty bucks off you was just the motivation I needed."

"Fine, but I'm winning it back for the hardest shot."

And Brett did. She had a boomer of a slapshot. They both skipped the fastest skater segment—the younger players whooped and hollered for each other until a winner was named. The last contest was stickhandling around an obstacle course. The competition was stiff, there were so many good skaters and stickhandlers, but Sarah wanted to win this one most of all, because it was what she most enjoyed doing. That and setting up another player with a good pass.

Emily Kane, who played for Chicago, was every bit as good as Sarah at stickhandling, deking, passing. And she was five years younger. Sarah watched her deftly skate around the pylons, the puck looking like it was glued to her stick. She wove her way around, skating forward, backward around another set of pylons, laterally too, before she took a shot, which hit the net. Pretty much perfect. It was Sarah's turn next, and Brett gave her a whistle of encouragement. She took a deep breath and steadied her nerves, because while the competition was meaningless in the grand scheme of things, it gave her something to prove. Namely, that she was not done with the game of hockey yet.

Sarah skated around the first pylons, careful to not go too fast and lose the puck. She kept her angles tight, because efficiency at skating went a long way to make up for any lack of speed. And she was slower this year than a year or two before, she could tell. It might only be a half step, not even, but it was there, reminding her that her body was in the driver's seat and not her wishes and desires. In the switch from forward to backward, she felt a little pinch in her knee. Nothing that she hadn't been feeling all season, but it wasn't improving. Her lungs began to burn as she took her shot into the empty net. She'd made it around the course without a mistake, but three seconds behind Emily. The two players gave each other a high-five.

"I'm starving," Brett said to her as the festivities began to wind down. "Why don't the four of us adults have a bite while we set the kids up in one of our rooms with a movie or something?"

"Actually, I've got a better idea." Sarah's smile bloomed in her chest before it worked its way to her mouth. "How about you and Kelly hang out with the kids and watch a movie while Claire and I have a little date? I'll even spring for room service for you guys."

Brett's eyes widened. "Oooh, nice. In that case, it's a deal."

"Thanks. I owe you guys."

It was rare for Brett to turn off the sarcasm, but as they walked through the tunnel to the dressing room, she said, "Sar, I just want you to be happy. And for the record, I think Claire makes you happy."

Sarah thought about that. As an athlete she was keenly aware of her body at any given time—her heart rate, her breathing, pain, her energy level. Around Claire, her body reacted the same every time. Her breathing and pulse picked up, a nervous energy swirled in her stomach, anticipation tickled the back of her throat. "I think she does, too."

After they'd showered and changed, Claire, Kelly, and the girls were waiting for them. Brett and Sarah presented each of the girls with a wooden hockey stick, signed by all the players. It was Kelly who'd thought it would be a nice gesture. The sticks were a huge hit, Maddie declaring that she didn't want to lose sight of it all weekend, "In case somebody tries to steal it."

"They'll have to go through me first," Sarah promised her.

It was late by the time they got back to the hotel, the girls yawning. There'd probably be no need for a movie to keep them occupied, but Kelly and Brett made good on their promise to babysit.

"Are you sure?" Claire asked.

"We are," Kelly said with a smile. "Now, go have a good time, you two."

Minutes later, in the elevator down to the lounge, Claire said to Sarah, "You sure have some very nice friends."

"They're the best. But let's not talk about them anymore." Sarah opened the door for Claire to the lounge. "I can think of a couple of other people to talk about."

"Oh?" Claire laughed. "And who would that be?"

"Us."

"In that case, I'm all ears."

All lips would be better, but Sarah could wait until they were alone together.

CHAPTER TWENTY-FOUR

"You were so impressive out there," Claire said, gushing. It was true that she didn't yet know a slap shot from a snap shot, but she was learning ever so slowly. And she didn't need to understand the game to let herself feel the immense pride at seeing Sarah—*her* Sarah—dashing around the ice, making it all look so easy.

Sarah shrugged. "Thank you, but I'm just happy I can almost keep up to the younger ones."

"Oh, you more than kept up, trust me."

They'd killed half a bottle of chardonnay, and the server was asking if they wanted dessert or coffee. It was too late in the evening for either, so they declined and decided to take their time with the rest of the wine.

There was a question on Claire's mind that wasn't really her business, but it persisted like an impossible-to-reach itch. She pushed her glasses up higher on her nose.

"What is it?" Sarah asked.

"What do you mean?"

"When you're thinking about something serious, you always fiddle with your glasses."

"I do?" Stall tactic, but she wasn't about to admit it.

"You do." Sarah's gaze was soft, patient. "Is there something on your mind?"

Oh, there were many things on Claire's mind, but she wasn't used to spilling whatever was on it; it wasn't her style. The hard stuff she usually relegated to introspection. But perhaps such emotional guardedness hadn't served her so well. There was her failed marriage, her extremely distant connection with her parents. Both sets of relationships had withered from lack of nurturing, from lack of communication, because it seemed easier sometimes to let a thing die than to work at fixing it. She understood that she sometimes kept too much inside. Breaking old habits wasn't easy, but she needed to try.

"I'm just wondering," Claire finally said.

"Claire, you can ask me anything. Honestly."

Sarah was so calm, so open, so brave. It was obvious she would not shrink from anything Claire might say, would not run away. "All right. Have you thought about...the end of your hockey career and what that might look like? And when that might come?"

A small groove appeared between Sarah's eyes. It was probably not the question she was expecting, particularly on a night like this where she'd really shone at the All-Star skills event and proven that she still belonged among the game's elite. Claire regretted her question immediately, and yet the subject had begun taking up all sorts of space in her mind after that first kiss. Because it wasn't just a kiss. Sarah meant something to her. And if they were going to have a future together, they were going to have to discuss Sarah's career.

"I try not to think about it too much. One thing I for sure don't see myself doing is sitting behind a desk all day."

"You're at the top of your game, Sarah. Even I can see that. I didn't mean to imply that retirement was imminent. I'm sorry."

"Don't be." Sarah took a sip of wine. "It's only natural you would ask...having been married to a pro athlete. I know that time comes for us all. It's just…hard to think of a life without hockey when you're still so immersed in the sport."

Claire wanted to reach across the table and take Sarah's hand, but she worried she would not appreciate the gesture. Such a fiercely driven athlete didn't need consoling from her, even though she had a pretty good understanding of pro athletes. Though transitioning from one career to something entirely different was not familiar territory for her. It was a touchy topic, and maybe now wasn't the time for it. She went for a change in subject.

"That signed stick you gave Maddie, she's over the moon with it. Almost as over the moon with it as the game-worn jersey you gave her at Christmas."

"I'm so glad."

"You don't have to impress me through my kid, though."

Sarah's face fell. "Is that what you think I'm doing?"

"I keep putting my foot in it, don't I?"

Sarah shook her head. "No, you don't. You're just being honest. It's me who seems to be overly sensitive to everything you're saying tonight. I'm sorry."

"Don't apologize. I'm asking things that are personal, and I have no right—"

"You do have a right to ask those questions. Come on. Why don't we take the rest of this bottle up to my room."

"You don't think our babysitters will mind?"

"I'll text, but I'm sure they will be fine with giving us a little more time together."

In the elevator, Claire held the bottle of wine while Sarah texted Brett.

"Brett says it's all good. The kids are fast asleep and she and Kelly are having some alone time in front of the television."

Claire took a deep breath at the threshold of Sarah's room. She knew Sarah wouldn't jump her bones, that nothing would happen that she didn't want to happen. There would be no pressure, nothing to regret later. Yet she felt oddly nervous, wavering between wanting something to happen with her and not wanting something to happen with her. Adult that she was, she made herself relax and hunted for glassware for their wine.

After pouring them each a glass, she made herself comfortable on the love seat. It was the only furniture in the room, other than the king bed, and she was not about to sit on *that*. Sarah sat down beside her. There was almost no space between them, and the length of their legs easily touched.

"I...Sorry. A few minutes ago," Sarah said, "when you said I didn't have to impress you through Maddie—"

"That sounded terrible and I didn't mean it that way. Forgive me?"

"There's nothing to forgive. And I wasn't offended. But... if there's anything that worries you, if you're unsure about anything...with us...we need to talk about it openly."

Claire winced. "I know. I'm severely out of practice with... all of that."

"I know. It's fine, honestly. I...Claire, the thing is, I have to know. What is it that we're doing, exactly?"

"I was hoping you knew."

"I'm serious."

"And I'm seriously...scared."

"Of what?"

Claire didn't speak for a moment. It wasn't Sarah who scared her. It was her own reaction to Sarah that scared her. And not simply her desire for Sarah, but her need for her, because needing something or someone meant that there was also a chance of losing them. She had to push past the dryness in her mouth to get her words out. "I'm scared of things not working out. I'm scared of getting hurt, of Maddie getting hurt."

Sarah's eyes were big and moist in the low light. "What if we didn't prioritize failure over success? What if we actually banked on this working?"

Claire understood immediately. As a pro athlete, Sarah couldn't afford to spend her emotional energy on worrying about failing. If she weren't an optimist, she wouldn't be where she was. "All right. You're right. I get ahead of myself with the overthinking. A lot."

Sarah took both her hands and held them in hers. "Claire, I'm asking you to take a chance on me. On us. That's it, just a chance. No promises, no guarantees. Just…some time. To see how it feels. Are you willing to do that?"

She swallowed. This was Sarah's version of an ultimatum, her way of saying she wanted clarity, direction, a yes or a no. What Claire wanted was to leap without the weight of her own baggage pulling her down, keeping her back. Emotion gripped her, but she fought to stay level. "I want to take a chance, Sarah. I'm not sure I know how, but I would like to."

Gently, Sarah reached over and removed Claire's glasses. "I want to kiss every inch of your face right now. Starting with your mouth."

Claire sank into the kiss. She let something unspool in herself, something that she'd been clutching so tightly for so long. Sarah's arms were around her, soft but firm, safe but not stifling. She nestled further into the embrace, let the kisses steal her sense of time. Finally, as Sarah's lips lightly fluttered over Claire's eyelids, Claire said, "Does this mean we're dating now?"

Sarah laughed, kept her arms around Claire. "I think it does. Shall we consider this our first date?"

Claire thought about that. An ideal first date probably didn't involve a group of kids and friends and a hockey game, but what the hell. Dinner alone, and now an insane amount of kissing? Yes. It was a date, all right. "I don't think I can consider it a first date without at least another ten minutes of kissing."

"Hmmm." Sarah's eyes were playful. "I'm pretty sure I'm up to the challenge."

"Oh, I *know* you are. Though…should you be saving your energy for tomorrow's All-Star game?"

Between kisses, Sarah said, "I could play that game in my sleep. Besides, this is more fun."

Claire believed her on both counts.

CHAPTER TWENTY-FIVE

Sarah clutched a bouquet of flowers in each hand—one for her date and one for her date's daughter. It might be a little unorthodox that Maddie would be with them for at least part of tonight's date, but Claire and Maddie were a package deal. Dating Claire meant an instant family, and while the idea didn't scare Sarah so much anymore, it was new and she didn't want to screw up. Relating to a kid whose mom she was dating couldn't possibly be the same as talking to kids after a game, signing autographs, giving them hockey tips. Could it? Claire made it look easy, and Maddie was a great kid. With their help and a little time, she'd figure it out.

"Hi," Claire said at the door. "Come in." They kissed on the cheek, Sarah taking the hint that any PDAs would need to be mild while Maddie stood quietly in the front hallway, looking everywhere but at Sarah.

"Thank you, and hi." Her words came out breathy, because she couldn't entirely contain her emotions from seeing Claire again for what would be their second official date. The days between tonight and last weekend's All-Star events had dragged interminably. She'd read two novels, which did little to ease her boredom. Just yesterday she fantasized about going to campus and sneaking into one of Claire's classes, just to see her and to listen to her teach. "These are for you." She handed the largest bouquet to Claire and the second one to Maddie, who still hadn't raised her eyes.

Uh-oh. Something was up with Maddie. Sarah exchanged a look with Claire, who gave her a slight nod and a shrug. Sarah cleared her throat. "So, Maddie, is your collarbone continuing to heal up?"

"Yes. It feels a bit better now."

"Good. You'll be back on the ice in the next month?"

"Yes." She glanced at her mother for confirmation.

Sarah had never seen Maddie so reticent, so aloof with her, and her heart sank a little.

"Let's get these flowers in some water," Claire suggested, leading the way to the kitchen. She retrieved two vases from a cupboard, filled them with water, placed the flowers in them. "Maddie, honey, why don't you and Sarah go find a couple of nice spots to place these flowers while I check the stew and give the mashed potatoes a stir, okay?"

"'Kay."

Sarah wordlessly took the two vases from Claire and followed Maddie out of the kitchen.

"So," she said to Maddie, "what do you think, should we put one of these on the mantle? Would that look nice?"

Maddie nodded.

"And the second one? What about that one?"

Maddie looked around, then pointed to the table in the adjoining dining room.

"Oh, good idea." Sarah handed the vase to Maddie. "How about you place it on the table?"

Maddie did as she was told.

"Umm. So…" This was so not Sarah's comfort zone, talking to a kid about a problem. Signing autographs, talking about hockey, those were easy. This was not. Claire was still in the kitchen and couldn't bail her out, so she decided to drive straight to the point, because she really had no idea what else to do. "I'm guessing your mom told you that she and I are dating now?"

"Yes."

"Then I owe you a big apology, Maddie."

Maddie's eyes widened. "You do?"

"I do. Because you know what? I should have asked you first if you would mind if I dated your mom."

"Like, ask me for permission? Like they sometimes do in the old movies my mom watches?"

"Yes, exactly like that." Sarah waited until Maddie met her gaze. "So what do you say? Is it all right if I date your mom?"

Maddie broke into a grin so wide that it swallowed her eyes. Sarah held out her arms and Maddie rushed into them.

Sarah laughed. "I take it that's a yes."

"That's a yes times five."

"Only five?" Sarah teased.

Claire found them like this, laughing in a loose hug. There was delight in her eyes. Gratitude, too.

"All right, a hundred times yes," Maddie joked.

Claire came in and ruffled her daughter's hair, as if her fingers had a mind of their own, before settling her arm around her shoulders. It looked so easy, so natural, like mother and daughter were an extension of one another. It was almost magical, in Sarah's mind, because it was nothing like her own experience growing up. Her parents loved her, but their affection never manifested itself in a physical way like this. She and her brother would notice other families being affectionate, but they learned to shrug it off, to accept the kind of love their parents were prepared to give as, if not entirely normal, normal to them. She envied the bond between Claire and Maddie. She followed them into the kitchen.

"Are you okay?" Claire whispered to her while Maddie stirred the Irish stew simmering on the stove.

Sarah nodded, basking in the warmth of the kitchen and all its mouth-watering smells. "God, this smells good. Is this your mom's recipe or something?"

Claire shook her head. "She wasn't much of a cook. I'm afraid any warm and fuzzy Irish stew memories are entirely self-made."

"Then I hope tonight will be another warm and fuzzy Irish stew memory."

Claire gave her a smile that made Sarah's chest hurt. She was falling for this woman, this woman who was so smart and independent, but a mom too. She was fierce and yet there was a soft and loving side to her that Sarah respected so much. She watched Claire rub Maddie's back while gently reminding her to set the table. Patience, guidance, correction, affection. These seemed to be the things that made up being a parent. Sarah possessed those things. She would be okay.

The traditional Irish fare was a gastronomic treat. Claire had made soda bread, too, and she explained how the mound of mashed potatoes went into the bowl first, and then the stew was poured over it. It was delightfully creamy and tasty, and Sarah joked that she needed to get to Ireland one of these days, how maybe they'd adopt her as their own since her last name was Brennan, and oh, could you be my tour guide over there, Claire? But Claire's jaw tightened and she changed the subject. There was something puzzling about her relationship with her home country, but clearly the subject was off-limits.

"Let's do a game," Claire suggested. "It's a game of favorites. We go around the table and answer quickly, no time to think, okay?"

Sarah was up for it.

"Ooh, my favorite game!" Maddie said.

"Wait," Sarah teased. "You mean you like this game better than hockey?"

Maddie gave her a look of outrage. "Are you kidding me? Nothing beats hockey."

Sarah reached across the table for a high-five. "Good answer, kiddo."

"All right." Claire clapped her hands once, the teacher in her emerging. "We're going clockwise. Be quick about it, now. Favorite singer?"

"Taylor Swift," Maddie said.

"Pink," Sarah answered.

It was Maddie's turn to ask a question. "Favorite hockey player?"

Sarah's answer was her friend Brett. Before Claire gave her answer, the tip of her tongue darted out to touch her bottom lip. It was adorable, and oh, Sarah was in trouble with this woman. Claire looked at her with smiling eyes and said that she was her favorite hockey player, and Sarah wanted to swoon. Except she remembered Maddie was there.

"My turn," Sarah said. "Favorite musical instrument to listen to?"

"Cello," Claire said.

Maddie gave her mother a face. "Cello? You're old, Mom. Mine is guitar."

"Guitar is pretty good," Sarah interjected. "But there's something gorgeous, almost sweetly haunting, about a cello."

The doorbell rang. As Maddie left to answer, Claire gave Sarah a quick kiss on the lips. "You're doing great."

Relief swamped Sarah. Claire had read her anxiety perfectly. "You really think so?"

"I know so." She looked at her watch. "That'll be the neighbor who's going to stay with Maddie. We should get going."

Sarah had no idea what Claire had planned for them. "You're not taking me to a tattoo parlor, are you?"

Claire laughed. "Are you worried?"

"Nope, but just remember, I get to pick the itinerary for our next date."

Claire grinned. "I trust you implicitly with any date plans. I think you'll be okay with this, though it is kind of on the geeky side."

"I can do geeky."

"I know you can. You took my class, remember?"

CHAPTER TWENTY-SIX

Claire's hand slipped into Sarah's as they walked up the sidewalk leading to the library. The pressure from Sarah's fingers answering back felt warm and tingly, the kind that fluttered all the way up to Claire's heart.

"Hmm, a library for a second date. I'm digging it."

"You are?" Claire had worried Sarah wouldn't be thrilled with tonight's literary event, but then again Sarah wasn't most dates. Her worrying had been pointless, Claire realized now. Sarah loved books almost as much as she did.

"And if I'm guessing correctly, you're taking me to some kind of a book reading."

"You did guess correctly. Damn, I wanted it to be a surprise."

Sarah halted their progress long enough to look into Claire's eyes. "Anything you want to do for a date is fine with me. Because being with you is what matters to me. So I'm good with whatever you want to do. Except for downhill skiing, that is. Did that once, still have the scar on my wrist."

"You broke your wrist skiing?"

"Yup. When I was fourteen. It was on a school trip. First and last time I ever skied."

"I didn't think something like a broken wrist would stop you from doing a sport again."

"Oh, it wasn't the broken bone. The problem was the three months of hockey I had to miss. So, no. This body doesn't do anything that might interfere with hockey."

This wasn't new territory for Claire, being with an athlete committed to their sport to the exclusion of almost everything else, but there were layers to Sarah. So many layers Claire had yet to uncover. And speaking of layers, just inside the main foyer, she dragged her eyes over Sarah's body as she slid her parka off. She was so perfect with her sculpted shoulders and arms, her slim but tight torso, legs and ass thickly muscled from all that skating and working out. She wanted to know how Sarah's body would feel on top of her. Beneath her. Spooning her. *Oh, my.* Her cheeks were on fire. It took considerable effort to force the fantasy from her mind. "Well, I promise tonight isn't going to affect your ability to play hockey."

Sarah moved closer and spoke in a low whisper that went straight to Claire's toes. "Kissing definitely won't affect my ability to play hockey. Please tell me there's going to be kissing later."

Heat rolled through Claire again. "Oh, there will be kissing later."

"Promise?"

"Absolutely." Kissing Sarah was the highlight of her year. Maybe even her life.

They took their seats in the auditorium. The guest of honor was an up-and-coming Irish author named Rebecca Connor. Claire had read the reviews of her debut novel—a gritty crime tale set in Dublin—that had been short-listed for the Dublin Literary Award and long-listed for the Booker Prize.

"I'm not normally a crime novel reader," Claire whispered. "But her writing is so good. It's more literary than detective."

"I don't mind a good crime novel once in a while," Sarah whispered back. "Have you read *Old God's Time?*"

Another book that was doing well on the awards circuit, by Sebastian Barry. He was one of Claire's favorite writers. "I have. It was so good. I like the way he—"

The emcee called the audience to attention and began introducing the author, a young woman with a pleasing smile and a soft Irish accent that immediately transported Claire back to Éire. Closing her eyes, she could almost smell the peat, feel the salty dampness from the ocean kissing her skin. She listened as Rebecca Connor read a few pages from her novel, talked about what inspired her to write it, then answered questions from the floor. Afterward, the emcee directed everyone to a room upstairs where wineglasses were handed out and a table was bedecked with plates of cheese and crackers, spicy sausages, and dips of all kinds.

Claire spent a couple of minutes talking to the head librarian about the novel potentially becoming part of her course curriculum at the university, and within minutes, she brought Claire and Sarah over to the author.

"I'm humbled and extremely flattered," Rebecca Connor said to Claire. "A university professor of Irish literature wants to include my work. That would be brilliant, thank you. You're from the west? I think I hear the west in your accent."

"I grew up mostly in Nenagh." Claire sensed that Sarah was listening raptly by her side. Nenagh wasn't known for much except as the home of Shane MacGowan, lead singer of The Pogues, and she didn't want to talk about any of it. She changed the subject, asking Rebecca what she was working on currently.

Moments later, alone in a corner, their glasses of wine almost drunk, Sarah said, "How come you don't talk much about Ireland?"

It was an innocent question and one that Sarah had every right to ask. They were dating, after all. But Claire didn't want to risk her mood plummeting and the evening devolving into something unpleasant.

"Another time."

There, case closed, and while Sarah nodded that it was okay, Claire could see the inquisitiveness remained in her gaze.

"What do you think about blowing this joint? I think there was something said earlier about kissing?"

"Music to my ears." Sarah took their empty glasses back to the bar, returned, and took Claire's elbow.

"Are you sure you didn't mind this event?" Claire asked on the drive back to her house. Sarah had seemed interested, engaged, enthusiastic, even. But Claire's tiny streak of insecurity made her ask. A library reading was the polar opposite to the excitement of hockey.

"I loved it, Claire. And like I said, I don't care what we do. I just enjoy spending time with you."

Claire relaxed in the passenger seat. She needed to stop worrying so much, but it was hard. She was a worrier by nature, and this was all such new territory. Not being with a woman, that wasn't new, though it had been almost twenty years. What was new was being in a relationship. She would need to feel her way through, as if being in a blackened room that was familiar yet not familiar.

"You did really well with Maddie earlier, by the way. Are you sure you're not secretly a mom?"

Sarah grinned. "I'm definitely not a mom and never thought I would be. Or wanted to be. But that kid of yours is awesome. She makes it all seem so easy."

"She is a good kid. But she didn't come out of the delivery room like that."

"Oh, you mean you might have had something to do with how she turned out?" Sarah reached over and took her hand, letting their joined hands rest on Claire's thigh. "I think you're a fantastic mom. And I'm so glad you think I'm doing okay. For a newbie, that is."

"So you're not turned off by dating someone with a kid?"

"Are you kidding me? I feel like I only know how to fake it with kids, because sometimes it scares the hell out of me, but I really want to try. Is that okay with you?"

"Yes. It's more than okay." Claire could relax now. Sarah wasn't going to suddenly get cold feet because of Maddie. It had happened once before, when Nora tried to set her up with a cousin of hers. It had sounded promising until Mr. Blind Date found out Claire had a kid. Bullet successfully dodged.

Sarah pulled to the curb in front of Claire's house. They'd already decided she wouldn't come in, in case Maddie was still awake or if the neighbor lingered. Their hands were still joined on Claire's lap.

"Being a parent, it sure shifts your priorities. But I wouldn't trade it for anything, and I wouldn't jeopardize it for anything. Maddie has been the best thing that's ever happened to me."

Claire would do anything to protect her daughter from life's curveballs; she cared more about that than protecting herself. She'd made a good life for the two of them, and she liked it—the routine of it, the security of it, the mostly peacefulness of it. Letting someone else in was...different. Exciting, but there were so many unknowns, so many things about it that were beyond her control. She'd have to take it slow with Sarah, not let things become too serious, not turn everything she'd built upside down. They were having fun, she looked forward to seeing Sarah, enjoyed the spark of heat and attraction that was nice as long as it didn't become an inferno. Maddie adored her. But there was no forgetting that she was a pro athlete, which meant her roots probably didn't run too deeply. Claire had certainly learned the hard way that athletes placed their sport above anything or anyone else. All of which meant she needed to protect herself and Maddie a little.

"Oh, Claire." Sarah's eyes were full. She'd understood perfectly what was on her mind. "I respect you and admire you for the mom you are. And I would never intentionally do anything to hurt Maddie. Or you. I hope you believe that."

"I do. It's just..."

"We talked about this, about how you like to know the ending before you jump into something." Sarah's voice was gentle. "I know you have trust issues, but I will do everything in my power to never give you cause to mistrust me. Okay?"

Part of her wanted a promise or a guarantee from Sarah, which was something she couldn't humanly make. She understood that, but it didn't make all of the uncertainty any more comfortable. "I'm working on it, Sarah."

Sarah brought their joined hands to her lips for a kiss. "That's good enough for me. But talk to me, okay? If you're, you know, ever worried or scared. Or anything at all."

Claire smiled at the woman who was so much more than a great hockey player. "Now, I think I promised you there would be kissing tonight. Real kissing." She lifted her eyebrows in a teasing gesture. She was not immune to the delights of kissing Sarah.

Sarah was swift in moving in and capturing Claire's mouth in a greedy kiss. It was exactly what Claire wanted—kissing that would ravage her, make her forget her fears and insecurities and everything else that wasn't right here in this car with them. Sarah seemed to understand. She kissed her deeply, thoroughly, with abandon, and Claire's body responded. Heat gathered in her chest and shot straight south. She was throbbing and wet, and it shocked her. The sensory overload made her hungry for more. So hungry. She heard herself moaning, a distant murmur that sounded outside of herself, as Sarah's hand softly cupped her cheek. This woman was literally melting her.

"Oh," she uttered, when Sarah's lips traveled to her jaw, her neck. "You're good at this." Stupid thing to say, she chastised herself, but she *was* good at this. She was a genius, brilliant. Claire, not so much.

"I'm only good at it because you're so hot," Sarah said, all smoke and heat in her voice.

Claire couldn't speak, so complete was her hormone-infused daze. She gave in to more kissing, because…how could she not? Thoughts of neighbors spying on them, or Maddie looking out the window, flitted from her mind as though carried away on a breeze. Sarah and her mouth were all that mattered. The hands framing her face were all that mattered. She had no idea how many minutes passed before Sarah pulled back, her eyes, heavy-lidded, landing directly on Claire's.

"I just want to make sure we're not going too fast. Everything okay?"

"Yes. Thank you for asking." She took a moment to collect herself, regain her breath. Sarah, elite athlete that she was, looked no worse for wear. She could probably kiss all night and look as fresh as the first kiss. "I kind of lost myself there."

"Me, too. Have I passed muster to go on another date with you?"

Claire quirked an eyebrow. "Um, I would say that's a yes." Especially if it ended with an avalanche of kissing, like this one did.

"A solid yes or a so-so yes?"

Claire laughed, reached for the door handle. "That's a solid yes."

"I have a game tomorrow night, but the night after that?"

"Perfect. Maddie will be at her dad's."

"Pick you up at six?"

"Going to tell me where you're taking me?"

"Nope. It'll be a surprise, like tonight. But it's kind of on the dressy side."

"I think I can handle that. As long as you're not taking me ice-skating again. I don't want a matching scar on my wrist like yours."

"Duly noted."

Sarah got out and walked her to the door. She left her with a chaste kiss, and Claire couldn't help but linger there, watching Sarah stride back to her car, where she gave her a little wave and a smile before she drove off.

With her back against the door, Claire asked herself for the millionth time what the hell she was doing. Then she smiled. *I'm having some fun, dammit.*

CHAPTER TWENTY-SEVEN

Sarah couldn't keep her eyes off Claire, seated in the banquette across from her at the Royal York Hotel's restaurant. Her luscious dark hair was swept up, exposing pearl earrings and a matching pearl choker at her throat. Her dress, emerald green, was cut low enough to keep Sarah's eyes drifting downward—the view so tempting that it made remembering to eat her salmon difficult. "How's the duck breast?" she asked Claire, but the word *breast* stuck in her throat. She hoped Claire hadn't noticed the tiny wince of embarrassment.

"Divine, thank you. How's the salmon?"

"It's delicious. Though not as delicious as looking at you." A cliché if ever there was one, but it was how Sarah felt, and she enjoyed the corresponding blush her words produced. Claire always looked beautiful, but tonight she looked special. And it was all for Sarah's sake.

Claire sipped her wine, a French cabernet. It would be an expensive evening, but Sarah didn't care. It was already worth every penny. Between bites, Claire teased, "So, am I going to have to bribe you to tell me what else is in store for the evening?"

"Ooh, that might be fun." Sarah had no problem rising to the challenge. "What have you got in mind? As a bribe, I mean."

The blush in Claire's cheeks deepened. She smiled around her fork, then licked the tines in a way that made Sarah blush. Game on.

"Let's see," Claire said benignly. "How about two tickets to a Leafs game?"

"I can get that anytime I want."

"A Raptors game?"

"Same. Afraid you're going to have to do better."

Claire's eyes narrowed playfully. "My last offer in the bribe department. How about dinner at my place next weekend? Maddie will be at her dad's again. It's usually every other weekend, but we had to double up because he's busy the two weekends after that."

"Now you're talking. It's a bye weekend for my team, so no games." They hadn't talked about sex, yet Claire's invitation dripped with the promise of it. It was a discussion they were going to have to have, and they were going to have to talk about other things, too. She washed down the last of her meal with a sip of wine.

"Claire, I want you to know how happy it makes me being out with you like this. I..." *Say it, you coward.* "I'm very attracted to you, in case you haven't figured it out. I mean..." She leaned over the table and dropped her voice, praying she didn't sound as nervous as she felt. "There are so many things I want to do to you. It's all I can do to keep my hands off you, to be perfectly honest. But..." She straightened up. "I also want you to know that it's much more than that for me." Sex she could get anywhere. "None of this..." She spread her arms to encompass the room. "Is about trying to get you in bed. Just so you know."

"I know, Sarah. But thank you for saying that. I feel things for you, too."

Sarah absorbed the fog of Claire's words. The vagueness, the curtain that had come down over Claire's face, the disappearance of the playfulness that had been there seconds ago, alarmed her. She wanted more from her. She wanted to know her feelings, all of them, even the ones that didn't sync with hers. They needed to talk. God, where was her desire for this kind of honest communication before? It sure wasn't there when she was with Ruth. Maybe it would have saved them. Or not. Probably not. With Claire, though, she wanted things to be different. *She* wanted to be different.

All right, Sarah thought, deciding she wouldn't press Claire for more, not here. "Can I talk you into dessert? A glass of ice wine?"

"If I have dessert," Claire said, spearing the last roasted potato on her plate and popping it into her mouth, "this dress will no longer fit."

Sarah bit her tongue to keep from uttering a sexual remark. She didn't want to spook Claire, not until they could fully talk about this sex stuff. "Ready for the second part of our date?"

"Still not telling me where we're going?"

"You'll see soon enough."

Sarah took Claire's arm and hailed a cab to take them the few blocks to the Four Seasons Centre on Queen Street West. She loved the way Claire's eyes lit up in the cab when she instructed their driver where to take them. They were seeing *Giselle* at the national ballet, a psychological romantic drama that had been hailed as "the ballerina's *Hamlet*." She had worried Claire wasn't a fan of ballet, but she needn't have. Claire, on the arm of Sarah in her bespoke dark-blue suit, nearly bounced in her heels during the walk in. Sarah was not quite as limber.

"You're limping a little," Claire said, concern in her eyes. "Are you okay? What's going on?"

"Just a little tweak in my knee from the game the night before last. Happens all the time." The tweaks with her knee were happening much more frequently lately. More than they should. There was cartilage damage, but surgery was risky for her career and there was no time for it anyway, not while the season was still going strong. She'd have the summer to rehab it.

Their seats were in the tenth row, close enough to the stage for the tickets to be considered hard-to-get. Claire gave her an open-mouthed gape when she saw where they were to sit.

"Wow, you don't just have connections to sporting events. I'm super impressed."

"Don't be. They're season tickets from one of Kelly's colleagues at the hospital."

"You have nice friends." Claire blushed. "I know I said that to you before, but they're still nice."

"They are." Sarah reached for Claire's hand, and as it slid into hers, she realized that this was the highlight of the show for her, regardless of what happened on the stage. She could sit here all night holding Claire's hand and watch the worst show in the world, and it wouldn't matter.

Claire cried during "The Dance of the Willis" because it was so beautiful with all the ballerinas in white rushing simultaneously onto the stage, though she kept whispering her apologies, which Sarah found charming. She spent the rest of the show watching Claire, because everything that happened on stage played out in the expressions on her face—joy, alarm, sadness, hope. It was beautiful.

"I love the story of *Giselle*, but why must they always end so tragically?" Claire said later as she unlocked the door to her house and began switching on lights. She'd promised Sarah a drink after the show, and Sarah couldn't wait. The anticipation of what might or might not happen the rest of the night was killing her, and a drink was the salve she needed.

"Those tragic endings shouldn't be new to you, my lovely literature professor." Sarah slid off her overcoat and suit jacket and hung them on the antique wooden coat stand in the foyer. "Perhaps people from past decades, centuries, came to expect unhappy endings more often than not."

"Oh, there's more than enough misery to go around in literature, art, films. But enough of that. It was beautiful, Sarah. Thank you, I loved it. Let's have a drink and talk of happier things."

"I'm all for that." In the kitchen, Claire handed Sarah a chilled bottle of prosecco to open, which she did in one fluid motion and then filled the two flutes on the counter.

"Slainté." Claire clinked her glass against Sarah's. "Shall we take these to the living room?"

"Earlier tonight," Claire said, removing her spectacles and placing them on the coffee table in front of them. "When you said that this—us dating—is about much more just sex, I...I kind of froze. I'm sorry. It's confusing for me. A little scary. Okay, a lot scary."

Thank God they were finally talking about it. "I promise you sex with me would not be scary."

Claire laughed, leaned back against the sofa. "Oh, Sarah. Why do I have the distinct feeling that sex with you would be the best night of my life?"

"Mmm, probably because it would be?" She gave Claire a smile that she hoped wasn't too cocky, then leaned back too, running her fingertips loosely up the back of Claire's hand and wrist. "Claire, I would go to bed with you in about two seconds flat. Just so you know. So now that we agree the sex part wouldn't be scary, I want to know what *is* scary to you about us dating?"

Claire took a contemplative sip of her sparkling wine. "I know one thing, Sarah. I don't want to be scared. Not with you."

"Then don't be."

Sarah knew this wasn't the time to get physical, yet she angled herself to face Claire and cupped her cheek, because she couldn't sit this close to her and not touch her with such intention. Warm liquid shot through her as Claire pressed her cheek into her hand, closed her eyes, leaned further toward her. She pressed her lips against the side of Claire's mouth, a tender kiss intended to send a signal that her mouth was right here, waiting to be kissed.

Claire didn't make her wait. Her mouth captured Sarah's in a searing kiss that was dangerous, exciting, fucking irresistible. Within seconds Claire began unbuttoning the top of Sarah's dress shirt—when had she slipped her hand between their bodies?—one button, two, three before Sarah placed her hand on Claire's wrist to halt her progress.

"Claire—"

"I want to touch you, Sarah. I want to touch your skin." Breathless, the heat visible on her face, Claire was the very picture of arousal. "I can't help it, I want you. I don't want to wait."

Whoa. What had gotten into her? She was so hot, so fucking sexy, and she was clearly as turned on as Sarah. She was into this…and yet. Sarah couldn't possibly leap into bed with her until her feelings caught up, because she intuited that Claire was the kind of woman who needed the emotional side to factor into the sex equation. Same as Sarah. *Ah, hell.* She kissed her again, felt a soft moan ripple beneath her fingertips on Claire's throat. The moan did it, nearly made her come right there. If they didn't stop soon…

The thought evaporated. She tried to get it back, the cautionary part of her brain, but it was gone. Her hand found Claire's waist. There would be a zipper in the back; she could have her out of her dress in seconds. She slid her hand up until it found the swell of Claire's breast. Moved up a little more to the pebble that was her erect nipple. Oh, Jesus, it felt divine. Claire moaned loudly at the contact, a sharp reminder that things were happening fast. Too fast. She skimmed her hand back down to Claire's waist. It took her another moment before she withdrew from the kiss, the taste of wine lingering on Claire's lips.

"Claire. I want you so much. But not like this. Not until we figure things out a little more, okay? I want to do this the right way." *I want us to be in love first* was the thought that pushed itself ahead of all the other thoughts crowding her head.

Claire took a deep breath, let it out slowly, pushed away the hair that had fallen over her forehead. In seconds she composed herself, her control firmly back in place. "You're right, I know. I'm sorry."

"Don't be sorry. Please, be anything but sorry right now."

Claire returned a smile so full of meaning, it made Sarah's heart hurt. "You're right," she said before her gaze slid over the length of Sarah. "When we're alone and this close together, I lose my mind. And I'm not sorry. For the record, I'm just sorry about the waiting."

"I know. Me too." Sarah stood, leaving the rest of her drink untouched. "I should go."

"Call me tomorrow?"

"You bet."

At the door, she kissed Claire one more time, not rushing it, wondering if she was crazy to leave.

CHAPTER TWENTY-EIGHT

Claire sleep-walked her way through her routine the next morning, her thoughts in an endless loop since her date with Sarah. Her inability to focus was making her shortchange her class, a discussion about Irish literature's treatment of the Catholic Church. She meandered through her lesson plan, falling far short of what she wanted to accomplish. She'd need to be sharper for this afternoon's postgraduate class on fiction's portrayal of urban versus rural Ireland, but in the meantime, she had a couple of hours to kill. A couple of hours to feast on thoughts of Sarah.

Claire's phone pinged with a text. It was Sarah, as if their minds were in sync. *Need to see u right away. Be there in ten minutes.*

There was no reason for Claire to be concerned, not when she was so giddy with desire. Memories of Sarah's hands moving up her body, cupping her breast, brushing her nipple through the fabric of her dress, consumed her. It wasn't a stretch to think—hope—that Sarah might take her right here in her office—perhaps on the floor or on the desk. Or up against the wall? Ooh, that would be delicious. Perhaps not the most romantic fantasy, but its reckless promise set off a firestorm in Claire's veins. She couldn't remember a time, ever, of wanting to get it on with someone so badly that it obliterated every other thought in her head.

If someone had told her, after her first encounter with Sarah that late September afternoon, that she would become so swept away by her, it would have been the craziest suggestion ever— the absolute last thought that ever would have occurred to her. Yet here they were, on the brink of...something. Something much deeper than sexual desire. In Sarah's eyes, her smile, and in the words that didn't quite make it out of her mouth, Claire understood that she wanted to be with her, that she had a destination in mind. And Claire...didn't quite. At least, not that she'd shared with Sarah. It was an omission based purely on cowardice, because she did want Sarah in her life. Every day. And she wanted to share her bed with Sarah. Every night. What began as fuzzy images at the edges of her mind had gently, slowly crystallized into a clearer picture of what she wanted. She might not move as fast as Sarah when it came to her heart, but they were at least moving in the same direction. Together.

Sarah would be here in minutes. Perhaps it was time to confess her feelings, tell her that she was falling for her, that she wanted them to be exclusive, committed, and yes, have a destination in mind, no matter how long it took them to get there. She wanted to put her past failures behind her, her fears, and take that next step with Sarah. She wasn't sure where it would lead, but she wanted to try.

"Ah, there you are." It was Nora, peeking her head around the open door. "Your Sarah is here, I just saw her coming up the stairs." Her eyes were mirthful as she waved ta-ta and disappeared down the hall.

A small thrill tugged at Claire's heart. Nora had said *your* Sarah, and it sounded exactly right. Sarah was hers, and she would tell her so, right now. Except... As Sarah rounded into view, Claire nearly jumped at the sight of her—her face was sheet white, her eyes red-rimmed from crying. Something was desperately wrong. A chill shot up Claire's spine, and it was as though something inside her was tumbling down, down, down. "Oh my god, Sarah, what is it? What's wrong?"

Sarah shook her head once, her mouth a slash. Claire scurried to close her office door and directed her toward the love seat against the wall, right below a watercolor by Peter Goetz, one of her favorite Canadian painters. But Sarah didn't sit. She stood as still as a statue, arms loose at her side, as if she didn't know what to do with her body. "Oh, Claire." Tears burst from her. "I've been traded."

"You...what?" Claire's mind spun. She knew what *traded* meant for an athlete. Matt had been through the very same thing in his career, more than once. *Shit. Shit. Shit. Sarah's been traded. Oh, God.*

"I've been traded," she said again.

Claire squeezed her eyes shut. Maybe she was dreaming, conjuring this whole thing up. "Where?" she whispered.

"Boston. I have to leave tomorrow."

They reached for one another, held each other close. Claire, pressed tightly against Sarah's chest, felt the life that had awaited her the next couple of months, and beyond that, dissolve into grief. Grief over losing Sarah. Grief over losing something before it had barely had time to be hers. Their breathing and a distant ticking clock were the only sounds for a long time.

When they finally collapsed onto the love seat, holding hands, Claire pressed for more information. Sarah said she was in shock, that she'd been informed less than an hour ago, that she'd wanted only to see and talk to Claire before anyone else, even Brett. Her voice was flat when she spoke, like something vital had died inside her. Claire wanted to cry too but she pushed back against the press of tears. It hadn't ever occurred to her that Sarah might be traded. She was the team's captain, a star, an Olympian. It didn't make sense. When Matt was traded, he was not one of the most indispensable players on his team. "How can they do that?"

"They can." Emotions deepened the lines in Sarah's face.

"There's, what, still two months to go for the regular season?"

"Yes, then the playoffs."

"And after that?" Out of desperation, she was reaching for something she knew was hopeless.

"I'm signed for another year."

Another year. Another year of being in Boston? And then what? Another city? What would it mean for them, all that separation when they weren't even an official couple yet? Two dates and some fooling around gave Claire no jurisdiction over Sarah.

"But your career...Sarah, you're what, thirty-six? I mean, how much longer are you planning to do this?" They should have talked more about this. When she had asked Sarah before about what the end of her career might look like, Sarah had grown uncomfortable, hadn't been very forthcoming, and Claire had too eagerly dropped the subject. She should have pressed her.

Sarah's expression hardened—something unyielding had taken the place of her sadness and shock. "I've not finished my career yet, Claire. It's been the only thing I've wanted to do since I was eight years old. I'm one of the top players in the league. Don't you understand? I'm still at the peak of my career. Why would I give that up now?"

"Sarah, I promise you I understand. I was married to a professional athlete once, remember? Endings come, and sometimes sooner than you think."

Claire tried to keep the exasperation out of her voice. Her own words about endings repeated in her head, because, *fuck*, this felt an awful lot like an ending. "I had assumed that you had plans, after-hockey plans. I assumed that your hockey career was in...I don't know, overtime or something. Near the end."

"Claire, I know my body isn't what it was ten years ago or even five. But I am not in the overtime period of my career. Third period, yes, but definitely not overtime. I'm not going to reject the trade and retire. I can't. It's not time for me to leave the game."

Like a flower folding into itself against a threatening frost, Claire felt her heart closing up. She'd hurt Sarah, and Sarah had hurt her, too. The rising panic in her chest threatened to become a geyser and mostly because she'd been in this exact place before. The last time Matt came home and told her he was traded, she was working on her master's degree and Maddie was barely out of diapers. She refused to move to yet another city, to put off her career any longer. She could not fathom another round of instability. So Matt had gone off on his own. The sadness and desperation of that time was something she would do anything to avoid reliving.

Oh, she'd been stupid, stupid, stupid, letting her heart and body get ahead of herself with Sarah, when they should have worked all of this out right from the start. It was so unlike her not to hammer everything to death, examine every side before she dove in. Her desire for Sarah had blinded her, given her amnesia too. She dropped Sarah's hand. They both stood.

"Oh, Claire." Sarah's face twisted into a mask of sorrow; she'd been reading Claire's mind. "Please don't say what I think you're going to say."

They held on to each other as if they were drowning. She pressed her lips into Sarah's hair and kept them there.

Later, on her drive home from work, Claire had to pull over. It was impossible to see through the blur of her tears.

CHAPTER TWENTY-NINE

The nine-hour drive alone to Boston was misery, but it was exactly what Sarah needed—time alone with her own misery for company. The first hour, she steered with one hand and wiped tears with the other. She could cry for weeks, but that wasn't going to get her safely to Boston—her and all her hockey gear, two suitcases, and three boxes. She was leaving behind her best friend, her teammates, and worst of all, Claire and Maddie.

Saying goodbye to Maddie this morning—her heart still clenched at the memory. She had hugged the girl so hard, she worried she might crack one of her ribs. Tears had clogged her throat, but she wouldn't let Maddie see her cry. Heroes don't cry, at least, not in front of kids who admire them.

"You'll be back, right, Sarah?" Maddie sobbed. She was inconsolable.

"Of course I will." It took all of Sarah's willpower to force a smile. "You can't get rid of me that easily, I promise. The season will be over before you know it, and then I'll be back here for the summer."

But Maddie couldn't be consoled no matter what Sarah said. And Claire… Claire had hardly spoken more than a few words since Sarah dropped the bomb in her office yesterday. She didn't need to. Her withdrawal told Sarah all she needed to know. It was over. And Sarah was plunging, free-falling, standing but unable to feel her feet. The team in Boston wanted her in town as quickly as possible. There was no more time for discussions— discussions that had zero chance of changing anything anyway.

"Sarah." Claire had walked her to her car. "You know I will always care for you. That will never stop, okay? Please know that."

Sarah had felt herself starting to cry. Why the hell had this fucking trade happened now, exactly at the moment she'd finally found someone she wanted a future with? She and Claire had come so close, but it was as though the universe had decided there would be no falling in love for her, no partner in her future. Or at least not while she played the sport she loved. Apparently, she was not allowed to love both things at the same time.

"Claire, we can't just be friends, so please don't." She walked around the back of the car to the other side because she'd lose it if she stayed next to Claire any longer. She leaned over the roof. "If I can't be with the woman I'm in love with…" She couldn't finish. And then Claire's tears started, and that's when Sarah got in her car. She couldn't stay there any longer.

The weight of the low sky as she drove to Boston, the endless chill to the air, left her listless and drowning in self-pity. She hated feeling this way. It was time to give herself a kick in the ass. The truth was, she couldn't afford to keep crying over Claire. The hollowed-out feeling inside had to stop, because her career, especially with a new team, demanded everything she had right now. Everything. She needed to eat right and sleep, and she needed her mind focused on hockey. There weren't many seasons left in her tank, she wasn't in denial, but her career was *not*, as Claire suggested, in "overtime" yet. She would work harder now than at any other time; her aging body would demand it, and now she had something to prove. To prove that she was still in the game, still at the top, still a good team leader. She would expend all her mental and physical energy on the task at hand, and she would forget the sting of Claire's words. Eventually.

She stopped for a quick sandwich at a deli in upstate New York, but otherwise made good time. The weather, for February, was cooperating. She had numerous texts from Brett, other teammates too, waiting for her attention. Brett and Kelly were predictably devastated by Sarah's news. The three of them had spent an hour together last night, but she had so many things to do to get ready for the trip today, there hadn't been much time to talk.

It was dark when she arrived in Boston. Exhausted, she dragged herself and her luggage into the hotel that would be her home for the next two months. The rest of the stuff, she'd leave in her car for now. A hot shower helped her relax, but her brain wouldn't shut off. What was Claire doing this minute? Was she hurting as much as she was? Or was their parting as simple for Claire as closing a book and putting it back on the shelf? What was she feeling? Thinking?

Sarah looked over at the king-sized bed, to its massive sea of emptiness. She'd never shared a bed with Claire, but she wanted to. Like, right this minute. And not for sex, but to hold on to each other, to look into one another's eyes and figure out how the hell to navigate this shit. How to get through to the other side together. There had to be a way.

Her cell phone rang. Of course it wasn't Claire, she saw with disappointment. It was Brett for about the fourth time. Sarah hadn't felt like answering all day, but she did now, if for no other reason than to let Brett and Kelly know she'd arrived safely.

"I still can't believe it," Brett complained. "We're all in shock here, Sar. We had a team meeting this afternoon and everyone is pissed as hell. Even Coach Saunders. We're not just pissed, we don't even feel like playing right now."

"Newsflash: I don't much feel like playing right now either." Pep talks weren't Sarah's thing. Hockey was its own motivation, a streak of happy that ran through her like a giant, rushing river. But not now. Not today. Still…they were professionals. Paid professionals.

"Look, Quince, it's what we do. It's our job. I'm sure after rough days at the hospital, Kelly doesn't feel like going back, either." The talk was as much for her benefit as Brett's. "You know the team will be better because of the players and draft picks they got for me."

"But it'll be two or three years before any of that pans out. You were producing for our team *now*. It's like management is saying 'fuck it' for the next couple of seasons. And they think we're going to give them our best effort because of it? Fuck them."

The anger in Brett's voice was alarming. She was probably the biggest cheerleader on the team, the glue in the locker room. It sucked hearing her so deflated.

"I know." Sarah's hand rose to her forehead, where a headache was forming. Leaving her team, her friends, her city, her sort-of girlfriend, and her incredible kid… *Fuck*. But what could she do? She was a hockey player. A hockey player with a contract to fulfill. The Boston team wanted her because they understood she could be a difference maker in playoffs; they had given up a lot to get her. And yet Claire had the nerve to act like running off was her idea. Like she *wanted* to be nine hundred kilometers away from her and Maddie? That was fucked up. And wrong. She'd have stayed forever in Toronto had she not been traded.

"Look, Quince, it's been a long shitty day. The business part of hockey sucks big time, especially right now. But I can't talk about this any more tonight, okay?"

A sympathetic sigh from Brett. "I get it. I just miss you like crazy."

"I miss you, too."

Moments later, after an awkward goodbye, she flopped onto the bed and stared at the ceiling. Life was so easy when all she had to do was play hockey. Now, the sense of having lost something significant, something as great or maybe greater than hockey, fell on her like a great weight. Loneliness and its twin, neediness, were new to her. Hockey, for the first time in her life, wasn't enough.

She grabbed her phone because she knew she wouldn't sleep for a while and scrolled through her social media feeds. They were filled with outrage from Toronto hockey fans and even beyond. There were about six hundred notifications and about half as many messages. None of them would give her any comfort, because the person she wanted to hear from most had gone silent.

She tossed the phone back onto the nightstand and wondered, for the seven hundredth time, what Claire was doing, and whether she missed Sarah as much as Sarah missed her.

CHAPTER THIRTY

Claire closed her laptop. It was pointless to try to get some work done—because she couldn't think. She couldn't concentrate, wasn't sleeping well, found the days interminable to get through. It didn't help that Maddie was barely speaking to her, behaving as if Sarah's departure was somehow her mother's fault, as though Claire had scared her off or done something to make her leave.

The worst was when she'd yelled, "Mom, why do you always make everyone leave! First Dad and now Sarah." That one was a knife that went straight to Claire's core, and while Maddie apologized hours later, the sting hadn't gone away. At ten, Maddie was old enough to understand that being traded was part of pro sports, but what she wasn't capable of understanding was the complexity of adult relationships. She'd never, or at least not for a long time, be able to understand why her mother had needed to end things with Sarah.

There was a quiet knock on Claire's office door. Good, a distraction. She opened it to find Matt standing there, fiddling with his coat and toque. He'd only ever come to campus two or three times that Claire could remember.

"What are you doing here?"

"Take you to lunch?"

"Something's not wrong, is it?" She hated that she always expected Matt to drop some unpleasant news on her. Especially hated the idea of it because she'd had enough unpleasant news lately. She didn't need any more.

"No, nothing is wrong. But you need to eat and so do I. Plus, something tells me you could use a friend right now."

Claire was about to protest but decided against it. His appearance at her office was so unusual she couldn't say no. They stepped outside, where the day was gloomy, mirroring her mood. At the deli a block away from campus, she made him spell out the real reason he was taking her out for lunch.

"I don't have much time. Now, what's so important that you took time out of your schedule to come over here?"

"You're upset that Sarah got traded, and you need to talk about it."

"With you?" That was a laugh. How could Matt possibly understand her point of view? He was the one who'd never been fazed by the business of pro sports, and with his last trade, he went off without hesitation, as if Claire's desire to separate was merely a distraction he'd deal with later. Without a doubt he would take Sarah's side. Discussing it with him was pointless.

"I do know a thing or two about pro sports. And trades. And…" His gaze slid away. "Losing something—or someone—you love because of it."

It was weird, talking to her ex about her relationship, but it wasn't as though she had an army of friends with whom she could talk it out. Claire pushed her half-eaten tuna sandwich aside. She would not rehash their marriage or its end.

"You're saying I love Sarah? How could you possibly decide that?"

Matt had the audacity to roll his eyes. "Duh. The chemistry between you two is off the charts. I can see it, Laurie too. The way you two look at each other, well, you've never looked at me like that."

Claire felt a flush work its way up her neck. "I like Sarah. She's fun and nice and she's super with Maddie." Her chest released some of its tension. "She's a great person, okay? I'm not arguing that."

Matt took a massive bite of his corned beef sandwich. "She's crazy in love with you, you know."

"What?" Where was he getting *that* from? Sarah, when they said goodbye outside her house, said she couldn't just be friends with the woman she was in love with. But if that were true, how could she just run off to Boston without a second thought? How could she give up so easily on them? It was like Matt leaving all over again. Nope. Claire wasn't buying it. Sarah couldn't possibly be in love with her.

"She *is* in love with you, Claire. I can tell. Everyone can, even Maddie."

Claire crossed her arms over her chest. "It doesn't matter whether she is or isn't, Matt. It's a moot point. She's gone to Boston, in case you haven't noticed."

"For the rest of the season. She'll be back in the summer."

His cavalier attitude was infuriating. "And then back in Boston again next year. Jesus, Matt. I know how this works, okay? Her home is in Boston now for the next year or five, I don't know. My home is right here. With Maddie. Sarah's career is there, mine is here." She felt like she was talking to a kindergartner.

"No one is saying you have to move or make huge changes to your life."

"Good, because it will never happen. Matt, my God! I have tenure here, we co-parent Maddie. I have plenty on my plate without trying to do a long-distance relationship that has no end date in sight."

"I know. But…won't you always wonder what if?"

When had Matt ever been so insightful? So reasonable? In fact, where did the old Matt go? She hadn't noticed he'd changed, grown. *Huh.* "Look. Sarah and I barely…started dating. You're making a pretty big leap with the what-if comment."

"I don't think I am. And I don't think you can turn off your feelings for her that easily." He pushed his empty plate aside. "I've had therapy since our divorce, remember? And I know you. The way you've let Sarah in, trust me, your feelings for her aren't going away because she's been traded."

His arrow had hit the bullseye, but he didn't need to know that. Her heart hurt and she had no idea how to make it feel better. Her fatal flaw was that she sucked at relationships. They were hard, and she was an idiot about them, a loser who stepped up to the game booth at the county fair only to discover all the prizes had been won. She hadn't been trying to fall for Sarah, but when she started being so nice, coming around and spending time encouraging Maddie with hockey, the falling turned into plunging. The way Sarah looked at her, like she was the only person in the room. Check that, the world. If she knew a way out of her predicament, a way to keep loving Sarah despite the distance, the differences, she would do it in a heartbeat. But it was hopeless. "All right. You've made your point." She finished the last of her coffee, though Matt looked like he had all the time in the world. "Why aren't you working, by the way?"

He spread his ham-sized hands on the table. "Because this is more important."

"More important than work?" Where was *this* when they were together?

"It is. You're the mother of my child, Claire. Don't you think I don't care about you?"

She stopped herself from saying something sarcastic about his use of a double negative. Her default was to mistrust people when they said they cared about her, but here he was, taking time out from work and his life, *showing* that he cared about her, when he didn't need to be here. He didn't need to be doing any of this. The least she could do was return the favor with honesty.

"Matt, I'm not exactly confident about relationships. Especially relationships with athletes." There was an implication in her words that he was to blame, and she saw by the bunching of his eyebrows that he knew exactly what she meant.

"Oh, give me a break."

His anger surprised her. "What?"

"Stop blaming sports for all this. Or athletes. Or whatever narrative you've designed around this. Sarah is a human being first, an athlete second. It's not like she's going around saying she can't possibly be in a relationship with a professor, is she? You're not being fair."

Dammit, she *knew* he'd take Sarah's side.

"Don't tell me you can't understand how a pro athlete's life doesn't exactly lend itself to healthy relationships. How many birthdays and anniversaries did you miss? Jesus, you missed Maddie's birth by nine hours."

"Because I was on the other side of the country. Working. When she came two weeks earlier than expected." He looked away, retrieved a toothpick from his shirt pocket, and popped it into his mouth. "This isn't about me. Let's not make this about us."

"You're right." That ship had sailed a long time ago. "Okay, fine. It's me who can't seem to figure out how to adjust or compromise or share or…" Claire threw her hands up. "I can't seem to do it, Matt, okay? When things get complicated, I freak out, I get scared that it's all going to go bad anyway, so why bother. I knew this thing with Sarah was going to blow up. I just knew it."

"No, you didn't know it. Those were your expectations, and your expectations were met. You always set the damned bar too low, Claire. When are you going to learn to expect more than the lowest common denominator from people? When are you going to give someone a real chance to prove they love you? Even if they're not doing it in some, I don't know, some orthodox way that you happen to approve of. Like, working a nine-to-five job. Doesn't mean that person's feelings aren't genuine. Or worthy of your respect."

Is that what she was doing? Disrespecting Sarah by not trusting her to be enough? Expecting her to fail to meet Claire's expectations? Was she holding Sarah to an impossible standard?

"Matt, this is too weird for me. Talking to you about Sarah."
It was only making her feel worse, like it was all her fault, like
she alone had fucked everything up. She'd lost—again—at the
game of love, because she was no damned good at it.

"Then talk to someone." He stood and retrieved his coat
from the back of the booth. "Because you're going to lose
something that could be really good if you don't get your head
out of your ass."

Claire sat motionless and watched him leave, holding on to
the indignation she was entitled to have.

CHAPTER THIRTY-ONE

Four games with her new team, and so far Sarah had only notched one assist. One. Stinky. Point. In four games. She was no rookie. She had the confidence, the experience, to know that the points would come. They always did. But the waiting sucked, not least because of the pressure to perform well for her new city, her new teammates, her new fans. Everyone was waiting for the real Sarah Brennan to show up and wow them. Instead, she was playing like a bum.

"Give it a few more games," the coach told her between periods. "You're solid, Brennan. You'll be fine." Following the pep talk, he shuffled her linemates for the third period in an effort to get her going, but it hadn't worked.

In the locker room afterward, she chucked her stick in the giant garbage bucket near the door. Had to be the stick's fault, because this was getting ridiculous. Her entire career, she'd pretty much been able to score at will. Her new teammates were skilled, but every time she set one of them up with a timely pass, the puck went into their skates or skittered off their sticks. It was beyond frustrating.

"Hey." The assistant coach, a woman only a year or two older than Sarah, slung her arm around her shoulders. "You okay?"

"Fine. Just pissed at this stupid game at the moment." She sat down and pulled off her jersey, followed by her elbow pads and shoulder pads. Her T-shirt was soaked. Everyone was doing their best to reassure her, and the last thing Sarah wanted was to come across as an insecure diva. She couldn't stand selfish, self-absorbed teammates.

Janna Robertson smiled her encouragement. "Give yourself some time to adjust to being here, that's all. Listen, the media wants you out there for a scrum."

"You're kidding." Just what she needed. *Not.*

"Sorry. Wish I was."

No player in the history of sports wanted to go before the cameras and microphones when their game was flat. Or in Sarah's case, nonexistent. But she dutifully removed her skates, threw a ball cap on her head, and slipped into her shower shoes. When the media asked for certain players to interview postgame, there wasn't an option of saying no. It was business, pure and simple. Feelings of hurt or frustration got shunted aside.

The lights were bright to keep the television cameras happy. There were a half dozen reporters waiting, a few photographers and videographers, a sound person holding a microphone on a large pole. None of the attention was new or intimidating to her. She'd stood before media crowds six times this big at the Olympics. She knew what the reporters were going to ask her. And she didn't have an answer.

"Sarah," the first reporter said. "Your team scored seven goals tonight. How do you account for your not getting on the score sheet?"

Wow. No easing into things. "I don't know," she answered curtly. "I think I played almost twenty minutes tonight. Five shots on net. My plus/minus was good. I don't think I played badly."

"Do you think you're still adjusting to your new team?" another reporter asked.

Sarah shrugged. "Probably. But I'm loving the clam chowder here. Still tastes as good as I remember from my college years here."

That earned some chuckles. But then the first reporter spoke up again. He wasn't smiling. "You were brought here to do some damage, to help the team with what should be an excellent playoff run, yet you have one point in four games. Do you think the team made a mistake in trading for you? I mean, they traded away some of their future to get you here. Did they do the right thing?"

There was a collective gasp. Sarah froze. She was used to hard questions, but this one took the cake. She gazed unblinking at the reporter as though he might rescind the question. He wouldn't, of course. She took a calming breath, refusing to be baited into an emotional display.

"I'm sorry, I can't speak for team management. Do I personally feel like the team made a mistake in acquiring me?" Yes, she wanted to say, because she never wanted to leave her old team, and she never wanted to leave the life that was waiting for her there. *I didn't ask for this fucking trade!* "I think my career speaks for itself. I bring a lot of things to the table, and I think that's why the team wanted me, not just for the points I'll score. And I will score points. A lot of them." *There. Take that, asshole.*

"Do you miss Toronto?" another reporter shouted.

"Of course I miss my old city and my old teammates." We're not machines, she wanted to say. We're human beings with feelings and attachments and disappointments, all of us living in that stew called life.

"Anyone important you left behind?"

Sarah smiled to keep herself from tearing up. She thought of Claire in front of a classroom, looking studious in her glasses as she quizzed her students on James Joyce's style or Roddy Doyle's brilliant dialogue or why Claire Keegan wrote such lonely characters.

And then there was the vision of Maddie with her poster of Sarah. She choked down a sob, then cleared her throat to disguise it. She was Maddie's hero and she'd let her down. Not personally; it hadn't been her decision to leave Toronto, but in a ten-year-old's mind, it was all the same: the adults had let her down. God, how she missed the two of them. How fucking sorry she was that she was here instead of there, with them.

"I have many important people I've left behind. Many good friends I care deeply about. But I look forward to making new friends here, as well. Boston is a great city."

The questions turned more specific about the game, and Sarah answered as succinctly as she could. She wanted this press conference over. She wanted to go back to her hotel suite, sink into comfortable old sweatpants, find a movie, and zone out until she fell asleep.

"That was a bit rough," Janna said to her moments later. "Sorry."

"Not your fault. I know they're just doing their jobs."

"They're not exactly the welcome wagon, are they? Hey, speaking of which, would you like to go out for a drink? I know it's been a tough couple of weeks."

Major understatement. "Honestly, I feel like going back to my room and vegging out."

"Veg out after we have a drink. Come on. You look like you could use a friend."

She did need a friend or at least a distraction. She had been doing her best to be cheerful, to put on a good front with her teammates. She'd gone out for beers a couple of times with them, even though beer wasn't her thing. She'd gone running with teammates, and in the gym, which was nestled in the bowels of the arena, the players worked out together. She was slowly getting to know everyone, but mostly she was a stranger in a place she didn't want to be.

"All right. As long as we don't dissect my performance. Hold on. You're not a shrink, are you? Hoping to get to the bottom of why I suck since I got here?"

"Ha, nope, I'm no shrink. But I do have a pretty good set of ears."

"All right. As long as you don't expect me to do all the talking."

"Deal."

CHAPTER THIRTY-TWO

For more than a week, Matt's words burned a hole in Claire's mood: "You're going to lose something that could be really good if you don't get your head out of your ass." God, what an egotistical jerk he could be! Of course he blamed her for the breakup with Sarah, because good ol' Claire wouldn't compromise. Good ol' Claire demanded too much. Good ol' Claire didn't play well with others.

Well, good ol' Claire wasn't anyone's doormat, either, not anymore. Which is exactly why she'd waited so long to get involved with anyone, because inevitably, she never took priority in the relationship. Something else always did.

But a funny thing happened once her anger at Matt—and by extension Sarah—slowly spent itself. She began to wonder if maybe the line she'd drawn was too harsh, if she'd been too rash, because at the end of the day, she was alone—like always—though with her principles intact. Sometimes the cost of those damned principles wasn't apparent until all that was left was her and the scorched earth. The thing was, she didn't want to wait for the earth to be scorched anymore. She simply wanted to stop hurting.

Maddie's attempts to heap on the guilt hadn't helped. First, she took the poster of Sarah off her bedroom wall, rolled it up, and stuffed it in the back of her closet. She refused to watch any games on television. And when she tried to make her mother promise to get Sarah back, and Claire of course refused because it wasn't in her power to get just "get Sarah back" like a lost dog, Maddie stopped talking to her for three days. What Claire had worried most about—Maddie getting hurt—had happened anyway, in spite of it all.

She craved a return to normalcy. Plus she missed Sarah. Like crazy. Her absence was the one thing that had changed in her life, and yet it had changed everything. Her daughter was angry at her. Even her job felt hollow, pointless. It was a little like walking through a forest at night, trying to pick her way around the obstacles in the pitch black. She was sick of it.

There was only one salve that might help—seeing Sarah again. There was no naïve expectation that a reunion might end happily, where all their problems disappeared like so much melting ice. But whatever might happen had to be better than what she was enduring. She had to try *something*.

As the plane winged its way to Montreal, she thought how upset Maddie would be if she knew her mother was off to see Sarah play. Maddie was away with Matt and Laurie in Florida for her school's winter break, so Claire wasn't exactly hiding anything from her. She had pored over the Boston team's schedule, dismayed to see that the team had already played their games for the season against the Toronto team so she would have to see Sarah in another city. And since she only had a couple of days free from work, Montreal made the most sense.

After checking into her downtown hotel, Claire made the trek on foot to the arena, joining hundreds of other fans, most of them decked out in fan gear. She felt a little naked because she wore no fan jersey, but she was only here to see one player.

Claire arrived intentionally early enough to catch the teams warming up on the ice. She stood at the top of the stairs, watched as Sarah circled the rink below her, stick handling a puck as she skated around. God, she was the picture of grace, and it reminded her of the All-Star game, in which Sarah scored two goals and quarterbacked her team the entire game. Fans now lined the glass to get a closer look at the players, some with signs, some hoping to get something autographed if they could get the players' attention. Should she go down there and join the hopeful fans? Would Sarah even notice her standing there with all the others? She hadn't let her know she was coming, had hardly had any communication with her at all these last three weeks, save for a couple of how-are-you texts. Would Sarah ignore her? If she didn't ignore her, would she be happy to see her? Upset?

There was only one way to find out, butterflies be damned. Claire hadn't hopped on a plane and come this far only to chicken out at the last second. All right, she told herself, squaring her shoulders. *Let's do this.*

Down alongside the glass, she found a free spot to stand beside the other fans. She stood out like a sore thumb, she supposed, standing mute, feeling more than a little stupid. *Some fan you are*, and she wanted to laugh at the silliness of it all. At *her* silliness, in thinking that seeing Sarah again would…what? Make her fall out of love with her? Make her ready to move on and forget her? How could she possibly think coming here would change anything?

She watched Sarah wheel around the net, picking up speed. Nope. Nothing had changed. Nothing at all. Sarah was the most delightful thing that had happened to her in years. Perhaps ever. And seeing her now made her remember how the sunshine, when they were skating outdoors, had lit up the gold in Sarah's hazel eyes. And how those eyes had looked at her, sort of in wonder, seemingly dazzled by the mere act of looking at her. Which floored Claire, because…really? Was Sarah nuts?

And here she was, coming to such a quick stop in front of Claire that a shower of mist flew up and spattered the glass. Her eyes were wide with surprise, her mouth a bit agape.

"Claire? My God, you're here!" she shouted to be heard through the thick glass. When she smiled and shook her head in a pleased way, Claire relaxed. She could finally halt the overthinking.

"I am. I-I wanted to see you in a game and your team isn't back in Toronto this season, so I—"

"Where's Maddie?"

"It's the winter school break, she's with Matt and Laurie. They're doing Disney World."

"She'll love that." The buzzer droned out any further talk. Warmup was over. The players would head to the locker room to wait for the Zamboni to do a final cleaning of the ice before puck drop. "Can we talk? After?"

Claire hadn't thought that far ahead. Hadn't really thought anything through, beyond simply seeing Sarah one more time, in her element...and maybe...something more, she hadn't decided what that might look like. Having no plan was a lot like drifting, and all she wanted was the sheltering shores of Sarah, if even just for a few hours. "Yes, okay."

"I'll send someone to get you and bring you back to the media room after the game."

And then she was off. Claire bought some popcorn because, why not, and headed to her seat to wait for the game to start. The arena was packed, mostly with women and girls, but there were men in the stands, too. People of all ages, people happy to be here, including Claire. Maddie would kill her, though, if she knew she were at a game without her.

The puck was dropped at center ice, Sarah on the starting wing. It was strange to see her wearing gold and not blue, but she moved the same as always, driving straight into her opponent in the faceoff circle before racing past her to retrieve the puck. Claire had seen this move before, something Maddie once explained to her was a signature move of Sarah's. It worked more often than not, because, again as Maddie explained, it usually caught the defenders flat-footed.

Claire moved to the edge of her seat and watched Sarah speed down the ice, puck on the end of her stick, the two defenders clearly caught by surprise. Sarah hunched her shoulders, slid her hands further down her stick. She flipped the puck to her backhand and lifted it straight over the goalie's blocker and into the net. She threw her hands up and was swarmed by her teammates. Someone grabbed the puck to keep. *Right*, Claire remembered. She hadn't been able to help herself from Googling Sarah every few days to see how she was doing in her new city. Statistically, it hadn't been going well for her, so the goal was hopefully a watershed moment. Claire cheered loudly, which earned her a few dirty looks from her seatmates. It was Sarah's first goal in…well, sometime. A long time. She swore to herself that Sarah looked her way as she skated to the bench to receive more high-fives. She looked ecstatic, relieved, and Claire felt the press of tears. Happy tears.

The first period ended with both teams tied at one. Claire seemed to be the lone Boston supporter in the crowd. She wanted to stand up and shout: "Don't worry, I'm not a traitor! I would normally support the Canadian team except…" *Except my girlfriend plays for Boston. Past tense. Ex-girlfriend.*

Sarah was equally inspired in the second period. She was skating her ass off, playing as good or better than ever, Claire could see. She scored another goal that was nearly identical to her first one, and she looked equally surprised but thrilled by the goal. The dam had broken, finally, and Claire laughed, did a little fist pump. This time Sarah did look at her and gave her the biggest grin. "Yes!" Claire mouthed to her. She wanted Sarah to thrive and play well, how could she not, looking at those shining eyes and Sarah's smile, bright enough to rival the sun. She wanted Sarah to accomplish everything she wanted to accomplish in hockey, even though it meant rooting for the very thing that was a wedge between them. And if that meant Claire loved her, then yes, okay, she loved Sarah.

When Sarah scored again in the third period, a hat trick, Claire was out of her seat and banging on the glass. Channeling her inner Maddie perhaps, but she was over the moon for Sarah. The goal ended up as the game winner, and Sarah was mobbed at center ice by her teammates. Coming here had been the right thing to do. She wouldn't have wanted to miss this night for anything.

An usher in a gold jacket came to her seat and held out his arm. "This way," he said, and handed her a lanyard and badge that said VIP in large block letters. He escorted her to the basement level and deposited her inside the visiting team's media room, where a dozen or so reporters milled about. There were others too who looked like friends or family members of the players, standing around waiting.

Claire checked her phone for something to do. The whooping and celebrating from what she guessed was the locker room drowned out everything else. She assumed Sarah was at the center of the hoopla, her hat trick having propelled her out of her scoring slump in one hell of a flashy way. She overheard one of the reporters saying tonight's victory assured Sarah's team of a playoff spot. It would be a long playoff run, the guy predicted, and Boston might even win it all.

Which meant the season for Sarah would carry on for quite some time yet—weeks and weeks. A sense of deflation pulled at Claire. Sarah would be expected to be one of the leaders of a potential championship run. It would be all-consuming for her, would take over every aspect of her life. Claire knew what playoffs meant for a pro athlete. Their bodies, their minds took priority over everything—and everyone—else. When they slept, when and what they ate, who they saw. It was about keeping stress and distractions away so that the focus could remain on exactly one thing. The athlete disappeared into their own little cocoon that no one, save for the other members of the team, was truly allowed inside. It was isolating. She had never felt more alone than the times when Matt was either at training camp or in playoffs.

The second Sarah emerged from the sanctity of the locker room, the reporters descended on her. Some of her teammates filed out too to watch and support her, to bask in her success with her. "I'll just be a few minutes," Sarah mouthed at Claire, who stood at the back of the room.

Watching Sarah conduct the media interviews was a thing of joy. She was animated, laughing with the reporters as if they were old friends, recounting (at their insistence) with a great amount of gesticulation the fine details of each of her goals, praising the rest of her team.

Breathless from all the excitement, Sarah apologized to Claire as soon as the last of the camera lights was switched off.

"It's fine. It's a great night for you." *My love* had almost slipped out.

"Hey, Bren, you coming with us to celebrate?" one of Sarah's teammates called out.

"Yeah," said another. "We just made the playoffs thanks to your hattie. Come on, Sar."

"Nah, can't tonight," Sarah replied, sliding a look at Claire that revealed she had something much more important to do than hoist a celebratory glass.

"You can go ahead," Claire told her. "I don't mind." Her heart had begun to sink a couple of notches. Seeing Sarah like this filled her up, made her love her even more. But it was also clear that Claire wasn't part of this world. She never would be, and the thought broke her heart a little. She'd already learned that lesson a long time ago with Matt. Had she been stupid, or maybe it was weakness, in allowing herself to think that maybe things would be different with Sarah? To think that she, or *they*, could be on equal footing with pro sports this time around?

Another teammate gave Sarah an enthusiastic slap on the back as she walked past her. Sarah turned her attention back to Claire. "No, I can see those guys anytime I want. Let's go somewhere and talk. Is that okay?"

"Yes, let's."

She should be happy. She was with Sarah, who'd had an awesome game. And they were going to share a drink together. Alone.

Yet all she felt was a creeping sense of defeat. Of being lost again.

CHAPTER THIRTY-THREE

They went to Claire's hotel for a drink because it was closer to the arena than the hotel where the team was staying.

Claire ordered a glass of wine, Sarah a soda and water. Alcohol after a game was something Sarah could easily pull off a decade ago, but not so much anymore. She buzzed from the game. What a relief to finally score again—it was like the boulder that had flattened her had finally been plucked off, allowing her to get herself up and dusted off. She was stiff and sore, though, and exhaustion wasn't far off. She'd have to be at the airport with her teammates in about seven hours for the flight back to Boston, but sleep could wait. Claire had come all this way to see her. It was a shock, but the best kind, the exhilarating kind. She smiled.

"I think you need to share in my hat trick tonight, so thank you for that."

The faintest blush materialized on Claire's cheeks. "Full credit goes to the athlete on the ice. That would be you."

"Ah, but I was motivated to show off for you, don't you see?" She winked to make a joke of it, but she wasn't kidding. Not really. Having Claire at the game tonight meant…she wasn't quite sure what, but it sort of felt like it meant everything.

"Well, in that case, is there a trophy my name should be on?"

"Hopefully we'll win the whole shebang next month. So yeah, there will be a trophy. I'm sure of it."

"Are you always this confident?"

"After the way my scoring dried up the last few weeks, I think you know the answer to that." Claire knew her well enough to know that it was pure bravado talking, not confidence. Her scoring slump after the trade to Boston was reminder enough that the magic she had enjoyed for so long could not be summoned so easily. Suddenly, hockey was hard. Maybe she should be thinking about retiring if she couldn't cut it anymore. Claire obviously wanted her to. But did Claire understand how daunting it was to think of leaving behind the only life she really knew? Did Claire understand that she had no idea what her life might look like without hockey in it? How she would earn a living? What might make her happy? Clearly she did not.

"I have to confess, it's not as easy as it once was."

"Are you sure? I mean, you look the same out there, you look—"

"I know I do. And you're the only person I'm telling this to. But yeah, my body is starting to sit up and notice that it's thirty-six, almost thirty-seven." Her knees ached, her back was so stiff most mornings that it took twenty minutes of stretching to loosen it up. Things she could no longer attribute to a bad day or a rough game or a sleepless night. "The trade didn't help." Losing Claire and Maddie hadn't helped either, her body absorbing the stress.

"I'm sorry it's been rough."

She met Claire's eyes and examined the loveliness of her face. She looked more worn, like more worry frowns had caught up to her the last few weeks, but she was as beautiful as ever. "I'm guessing things have been rough for you too?"

She could see that Claire was trying hard to hold it together, but the tears wobbling in her eyes betrayed her. She ached for her. Ached to be with her, if only things could be different. She reached across the café-sized table to touch Claire's cheek. "I'm so sorry," she whispered. The tears slid down Claire's face and onto Sarah's hand. At the wetness, Sarah felt sick to her stomach. Claire's pain physically hurt her. "Claire, please talk to me."

Claire took a moment to collect herself. It gave Sarah a pang of hope that, together, they could figure this thing out. Maybe Claire had changed her mind about having a future again with a professional athlete. Was that the real reason she was here?

"It's been awful," Claire said. "Maddie is barely talking to me. I can't seem to concentrate very well on my work. I can't watch or even think about hockey. Or you. Well…the not-thinking-about-you part, I've not been very successful with. The truth is, I miss you, Sarah. I miss you so much. It's…so hard."

Sarah took a long drink of her soda to buy some time. There had to be a path forward for them. What they had started deserved to be finished. All she needed to do was look at Claire's tortured face to know she felt the same.

"Please don't give up on us," Sarah implored. "I know my hockey career has come between us. But there has to be a way. What can I do to change things? To make it work?" She'd happily fall on her sword, as long as that sword wasn't her career. *That* she could not do.

She could see from Claire's hesitation, from the sorrow on her face, that she had no answers.

"I don't think there's anything you can do. Seeing you play tonight, scoring those goals. You were so happy, so much in your element. You're a gift to this sport. I can't ask you—I wouldn't ask you—to quit what you do, what you clearly love so much."

"So why can't I love you and hockey at the same time?"

"The life of a professional athlete, it doesn't work with a love life, a family life. It just doesn't. It's all-consuming, it's nomadic. And I know it's not your fault, but I've been through all of this before, remember?"

"But I'm not Matt, and you're not the same person you were then. You wouldn't be sacrificing your career, your independence for me. I would never ask you or expect you to do any of that." This wasn't anything like Claire's life with Matt all those years ago, and it wasn't fair to tar her with the same brush. "We seem to be at an impasse. Tell me one thing. Right now. How do you feel about me?"

Claire's face rearranged itself into a smile that Sarah could only describe as beatific. "I first started falling for you when you gave us those tickets to come see you play. Well, probably before that. And definitely when you took me skating, how you held on to me like I was precious cargo. The way you were with Maddie, too, it was like you were a gift that appeared in our lives. You made me feel alive. Happy. You always..." Claire's voice wobbled. "Had the ability to make me feel special."

Tears pricked at the back of Sarah's eyes. *I don't know what the fuck I'm saying, but I know what I want.*

"Claire, be with me in whatever form it takes. It doesn't have to be complicated if we don't let it be." She would be in Toronto as much as possible, including all summer, she explained, which really wasn't that far away now. All it would take was for Claire to go with her heart, to *try*, to give Sarah something, even if it wasn't meeting halfway.

"I can't, Sarah."

What? "Why not? I love you, Claire." It felt like an opponent had just slammed her with a crosscheck to the back. "And I think you love me. Doesn't that count for something?" Exasperation hardened her voice. "It has to."

"Of course it does. But love isn't always equal or fair, and sometimes it can even hurt, when it's not on a level playing field."

"I don't follow." She slowed her heart rate, her breathing, to concentrate on every word. It was like standing before a judge and jury, preparing to hear a verdict.

"The thing is...I've had too many years of being someone's afterthought, of being too far down on their priority list. I won't allow that to happen anymore. I can't. It hurts me too much."

How could Claire think she wasn't important enough to be on Sarah's mind every minute? That she was somehow an afterthought, a footnote in her life? And yet, the pain of the declaration was clear on Claire's face. This was the hill she was prepared to die on. How was Sarah supposed to fight back against that?

"Jesus, Claire, you are not an afterthought to me. You are my first thought in the morning and my last thought before I fall asleep." And every hour in between, yet her words seemed so inadequate, useless. Defeat was staring her in the face, and she had no answer for it.

Claire downed the last of her wine, reached for her coat. "I'm sorry. It's not enough. I just...can't. And I wanted to tell you in person."

"But I thought..." She'd been stupid to hope Claire was here to reunite or that she'd at least throw her a bone. "You mean you already knew that before you came here?" *Like, why the hell didn't you just do it over the phone?*

Claire stood, shrugged as though she too were helpless against any other outcome. In the next instant she was gone, and Sarah was alone with the mashup of her thoughts. Claire hadn't said it in so many words, but it was clear that it was either her or hockey—move back to Toronto and leave hockey behind or forget about them. Always, running parallel to the reality of Sarah's career was a phantom version in which she led a full life of someone to come home to, of trips and events to attend together, of a house with a yard, maybe a dog. Always, she'd told herself, there would be time in the future for things other than hockey. Her life off the ice had mostly stood still while her hockey life took off like a rocket.

For the first time in her life, she realized, hockey wasn't enough. She wanted more.

CHAPTER THIRTY-FOUR

Claire took the empty seat beside Matt. It hadn't been hard to find him in the stands.

"Brought you a coffee," she announced. It was her olive branch. "Laurie's working, right?" She had a moment of panic that she hadn't brought an extra cup. Laurie managed a restaurant, and her hours were unpredictable, at least to Claire.

"Great, thanks!" His meaty hand accepted the hot paper cup from her. "Yes, she's at work. The game is just about to start. And I'm nervous as hell. You?"

"Butterflies at breakfast this morning, but I'm okay. I'm actually glad Maddie's back to playing." Hockey season for the kids was all but over, but at least Maddie would get in a couple of games first.

"You are? Did you hit your head or something?"

"Ha ha, very funny. I did not hit my head, but I was worried she wasn't going to go back to it. Which would have been okay with me, but she *loved* it so much, you know?"

"Do I ever. Man, she's been so mopey since Sarah got traded. Almost unbearable."

"Yup." He didn't have to tell Claire.

The two teams skated onto the ice. Matt and Claire waved furiously to Maddie, who grinned back at them. Her collarbone had healed nicely, and she waved her stick at them to show that it was okay. She'd hedged, though, about whether she wanted to play hockey again—and not because of her injury. It was Matt who finally convinced her, saying athletes don't give up because they don't feel like playing or because they're upset about something. "When you commit to something, you do it," he told Maddie in a tone that brooked no argument. "You committed to your team, to your coach. You go back and you play for them, if not for yourself." The tactic had worked. Maddie pretended to mope for another day, but then got to unpacking and packing up her hockey bag again, like always. Claire thanked Matt for being a good father. When she married him, she wouldn't have predicted it, but he'd changed a lot since leaving football. She always knew deep down that he was a good guy. She wouldn't have married him if she'd felt otherwise.

He turned to Claire. "How was Montreal?"

She'd told him in a text that she'd gone there while they were in Florida, but had provided no further details. She figured, or maybe hoped, that he'd forgotten about it. "It was fine."

"You saw Sarah?"

"I did." Personal conversations were often awkward with Matt. They usually needed a long runway to get to the heart of the matter. Well, except for the impromptu lunch when he told her to get her head out of her ass.

"Good for you. And?"

She pretended to fiercely concentrate on the game. Maddie was on the ice anyway, so the timing was perfect, and she seemed to be having a ball. Claire yelled out some encouragement before turning back to Matt. "It, um, was good to see Sarah again. She looked good. And she scored a hat thing that night."

Matt laughed. "I saw that she'd scored a hat trick when I caught the sports news. So you pulled her out of her dry spell, eh?" His teasing grin made Claire frown. She did not want to engage in cheap talk about Sarah.

"She had a great game." Claire remembered Sarah flying down the ice, as fast and as skilled as ever, looking like the Sarah of old, the one who could have her way with the puck anytime she wanted. She was the undeniable star that night, as though the years had not touched her body, as though the trade were a distant memory. She'd triumphed over it all.

"So why don't you seem happy to have seen her?"

"I am. I was. She played probably one of her best games ever. She was incredible, actually." So incredible that Claire knew she didn't need to worry about her anymore. Sarah was doing just fine without her and Maddie.

"I'm glad you went to see her. So what aren't you telling me?"

It was still awkward talking to him about Sarah, but a shade less each conversation they had about her. Not that she would admit it to him, but he'd been right that day at lunch, that she really had nobody else to talk to about Sarah.

"It's just…seeing how she was playing, the incredible goals she scored, the way her team mobbed her afterward. She looked so damned happy, Matt. She looked on top of the world."

"Okay, well, you do actually feel on top of the world when you have a great game."

"I understand that. But it seemed like, I don't know, like the game was everything to her again. Like she didn't need me or her life back here anymore."

"Oh, come on, one does not cancel out the other. You caught her in a triumphant moment, that's all."

The logical part of her understood that, but not her heart. Her heart said Sarah didn't need her anymore. Her heart said the game of hockey was all Sarah needed, that it was the only thing that truly filled her up. That night in Montreal, watching the cheers and the congratulations, she knew it was pointless to try and make Sarah choose between her and the game. Sarah and hockey were meant to be together.

"She was made for the game of hockey. It's her first love," Claire finally said, her voice sandpaper. "I can't come between that. I won't."

They both swung their gaze to their daughter, who was zipping up the ice on a breakaway. She didn't look nervous at all, her eyes lasered onto the puck so she wouldn't lose it. Matt was already out of his seat yelling, "Go, Maddie, go!" In another instant, the puck was in the net and Maddie was jumping up and down. Her teammates threw their arms around her, and it reminded Claire so much of the scene with Sarah last week.

Sarah. She would be so proud of Maddie scoring in her first game back from injury. She made a mental note to encourage Maddie to write an email to her about her goal, but it probably wouldn't happen. Maddie didn't seem to want to communicate with Sarah, so deep were her feelings of abandonment. No matter how Claire tried to make her understand that Sarah had no choice but to accept the trade to Boston, Maddie refused to forgive her.

"So what are you going to do?"

Claire shook her head. "I don't know." As much as it was clear she couldn't be with Sarah right now, neither was she ready to completely close the door. Doing so felt too final, too much like another heartbreaking failure.

She leaned her head against her ex-husband's massive shoulder. It could always hold anything. His strength, inside and out, his ability to keep cool under pressure, had attracted her to him all those years ago. She needed a friend.

"Here's the thing, Claire," he said softly. "And I'm telling you this because I care about you. I always will. Until you start feeling worthy of being loved, you're going to find excuses to reject it. To run away from it."

Heat rose up her neck and into her face. *Worthy of being loved?* Just because he'd gotten some therapy, he was an armchair psychologist now? Quietly, she ground out, "If you think you know me better than I know myself, you're mistaken."

"Now, hold on. I'm not trying to piss you off, okay? I'm saying let Sarah love you, and let yourself love her back. Yes, she's an athlete, and, yes, the game of hockey means a lot to her. It makes things a little complicated, I'll grant you that, but so what. Welcome to life. Like I tell Maddie, don't be a quitter."

"You think I'm too willing to take the easy way out? That I can't do hard? Come on. I can, and I did with you, remember? Maybe I don't want to do it again. Maybe I don't want to have to do something *hard* anymore. Maybe I would like a relationship that's easy for once. And please stop condemning me for that."

"I get that, and I'm not condemning you. But the hard part isn't actually Sarah."

"I don't know what you mean."

"Claire, I think you need to go back to Ireland."

"What?" What the hell did Ireland have to do with anything? "Why?" The last time she'd gone there was seven years ago. She'd taken Maddie, who was only three, to see her grandparents. Every Christmas and birthday, Claire's parents sent cards and gifts, but the contact was minimal, and it was how Claire, and obviously her parents, wanted things. There'd been no visits since.

"Because I think that's where the root of your problem lies."

What the hell was he talking about? "I've been there exactly twice in twenty-three years. There's nothing there for me anymore."

"Your parents are there."

Claire pulled a face. Her parents were so far outside her life, they barely counted. "You know I'm not close to them. Why on earth would you suggest I go see them? Did *you* hit your head?"

Matt smiled, his eyes following the game on the ice. "I did not, as a matter of fact. But I do think your parents hold the key."

"The key? Stop talking in riddles. It's not your forte."

"Fine." Matt sighed loudly, swung his brown eyes to her. "I think your parents, your childhood, is why you have trouble feeling worthy of being loved."

Claire would have laughed if it were funny. "Look, I know you're trying to help. I know you're fond of Sarah and I know you want me to be happy. I get that. But enough of the fortune cookie advice, okay? The less I see my parents, the happier I am. There is nothing for me back in Ireland. Everything I want in my life is right here." Everything except Sarah, of course.

"Fine. But if you love Sarah, don't you want to pull out all the stops?"

Okay, that was a low blow. She did love Sarah, but she'd gone as far as she could go with her. Revisiting her earliest years in Ireland would be nothing but a wild goose chase. A waste of time. And it certainly wouldn't bring Sarah back. Nope. She would not go back there. "Can we just watch the game, please?"

CHAPTER THIRTY-FIVE

The last game of the regular season was anything but a sleeper. Sarah's team had already qualified for the playoffs but was still jockeying for position, while their opponent, the Chicago team, needed the win to make the playoffs. The rivalry between the two teams was well-established, and she and her teammates needed no extra motivation tonight. They were on edge, Sarah uncharacteristically so. Normally she fed off an emotionally charged game, but tonight she was ill-tempered. It had started last night, when she and her teammates went out for a night of bowling. One of the coaches thought it would be the perfect opportunity for the team to let off some steam and have a little fun before the grind of playoffs. A group of girls around Maddie's age, celebrating a birthday party, came in and occupied the lanes beside them. The kids wore birthday hats, even brought a cake with them, and before long, Sarah and her teammates joined the kids, whooping it up with them, signing autographs, trading bowling tips. Which all would have been totally great except it made Sarah miss Maddie even more.

And Claire. Being away from them, and not just away, but out of their lives, was unbearable any time she wasn't on the ice. Playing hockey was the only time she forgot her loneliness, and yet it was the game that had taken her away from those she loved.

Just last week, she'd bought a Boston team sweatshirt and track pants for Maddie and mailed them to her. An extremely brief emailed thanks came back. Sarah was still being punished, and the impasse was all the more heartbreaking because there was no obvious solution, no way to fix what was broken. She kept trying to come up with an idea, a plan, something to make things better, but the more she racked her brains, the more it only distracted her from hockey. Each practice, each game, was becoming tougher and tougher to focus on, and it was absolutely the wrong time for her brain to take a hike from hockey. Playoffs were days away. The team needed her. And frankly, there weren't many more seasons left for her to go deep into the playoffs, perhaps win the league championship. She needed to drag her head back into the task at hand and the sooner the better.

Sarah didn't see or hear the opponent skating up behind her. The player clipped her in the hip, which spun her around, nearly made her fall. *Goddammit!* She committed the player's number to memory. Seconds later, the same player delivered a bone-shattering check to Sarah's teammate that was vicious and uncalled for. Sarah had had enough.

"Come on!" she yelled to the nearest referee. "That was a blindside hit! Did you seriously not see that?"

The ref flashed her a look of surprise before her gaze swung back to the play. It was rare for Sarah to yell at the refs. Almost unheard of. She possessed a well-earned reputation for being fair-minded, calm, someone the refs could reason with.

Sarah shouldered her way to the net, planted herself in the blue paint. She was mauled and pushed, hacked at by an opponent's stick, but she held her ground. When the point shot came, she muscled her stick into the right position to deflect the shot into the net. "Fuck yeah," she yelled. As she raised her arms to celebrate the goal, a Chicago player shoved her from behind. Hard. Blisteringly hard. Sarah's shoulder slammed into the steel frame of the net, which should have moved on impact, but didn't, meaning her shoulder absorbed the entire force of the hit. A lightning bolt of pain lanced through her arm, the intensity of it sucking the air out of her lungs. With effort she straightened herself. Shoved the pain to a far corner of her brain as she watched the player who'd hit her glide toward the bench. It was the same player who'd clipped her a few seconds ago, the one who'd then delivered the blindside hit on Sarah's teammate. She raced after the human wrecking ball, hell bent on revenge, adrenaline taking the wheel. She would make the player pay for her intentionally harmful play.

The target of Sarah's anger was almost at her team's bench when Sarah hit her in the back with a two-handed cross-check, sending her flying face-first to the ice. Pain sliced through her arm and into her neck in the aftermath, but it was worth it.

"Take that, you dirty bitch!"

The lineswomen quickly jumped in and pulled Sarah away, while Sarah's opponent remained on the ice, down on all-fours, and instead of feeling remorse, Sarah was glad she'd made her pay. Maybe it'd make her think twice next time. Two Chicago players skated over to Sarah, yelling threats at her, but the lineswomen kept them away.

"You just earned yourself a major penalty, Brennan," the referee snapped at her. "And a match!"

"What? You're kicking *me* out of the game?"

"That cross-check was intent to injure. Your night is done." She blew her whistle.

"But what about *her* intent to injure?"

"She's getting two minutes unsportsmanlike for her hit on you after your goal."

"Only two minutes? You gotta be fucking kidding me!"

The lineswomen, one on either side of Sarah, began escorting her off the ice. *Fuck this bullshit*, she told herself. The referees were obviously blind. Or perhaps they were homies for the Chicago team. In any case, it was bullshit.

By the time she reached the locker room, her shoulder was on fire. The pain radiated down past her elbow, and it was excruciating. *Shit.* She sat down and wondered how the hell she was going to get her equipment off by herself. Her shoulder was fucking killing her, worse by the second as her adrenaline receded. Something was badly wrong. One of the team's trainers popped her head into the doorway. "Everything okay, Bren?"

Sarah shook her head. "I think my shoulder's partially dislocated."

"All right, let's take a look."

"Oh, no," Sarah muttered, as the realization hit her that a match penalty came with an automatic suspension. Which might be moot anyway, given the unhappy state of her shoulder. Either way, she would be missing the start of playoffs. "Fuck."

CHAPTER THIRTY-SIX

Claire was loading the dishwasher when Maddie yelled at her to hurry into the living room.

"How come, honey?"

"Sarah! It's Sarah, Mom. She got suspended or something. And she got hurt, they're saying."

Claire dashed into the living room, where the evening's sports news was playing on television. They were showing a clip of Sarah forcefully cross-checking another player to the ice, the sports anchor saying that Sarah had been handed a three-game suspension. Not that the suspension mattered, he said, because she'd injured her shoulder during the game and had been placed on the injured reserve list.

When she could speak, Claire asked, "What does injured reserve mean?"

"It means the player is out for a while, like at least a week or two," Maddie answered. "Or longer. I'm not sure."

Claire sat down heavily. So Sarah was out and would probably miss playoffs or at least the first round or something like that. "Have they said how bad her injury is?"

Maddie shook her head. "They don't usually talk about that kind of stuff, cuz they don't want the other teams to know."

"Oh. Right."

"I can't believe she hit that player the way she did, Mom. Why would she do that?" Maddie's eyes shone with disbelief.

"I don't know, honey, but it's not like Sarah, is it?" She'd never seen her strike out at an opponent like that before, and she could not imagine what egregious thing the other player must have done to deserve it. Knowing Sarah, there had to be a good reason for her losing her temper.

God, it was going to kill her to have to miss the playoffs. She'd once told her and Maddie that playoff season was truly the only season that counted. The regular season was just the appetizer, she said. Claire's heart clenched for her. She should send her a text, tell her that she and Maddie hoped she was okay. She pulled her phone from her pocket just as it rang. It was her parents, calling from Ireland—something that only happened at Christmas and birthdays. Claire's breath quickened. "Hello?"

"Hello, Claire, dear." It was her mother. An awkward and predictable silence fell.

"Mum, is anything wrong? How are you and Dad?" Claire left Maddie in front of the TV and went to the kitchen, her phone to her ear.

"We're fine. Just, well, thought we'd say hello."

Every phone conversation was like this, a re-creation of all Claire's frustrations from the past—the withholding, the inability to discuss anything that possessed an emotional element. She decided to wait her mother out. It was she, after all, who'd called.

"Are you still into the snow there?"

Claire sighed to herself. *Really? We're going to talk about the weather?* "It's pretty much gone now. Spring is around the corner."

"And Maddie? How is she?"

"She's good. She, um, broke her collarbone playing hockey a couple of months ago, but she's okay now." She felt a pang of guilt for not telling her parents about the injury, but not for long. Her parents' disinterest in her life and her daughter's life was to blame. She should be used to the fact that they were two spheres separated by an insurmountable physical and emotional distance, but it still had the capacity to bother her, this chasm between them, especially during the couple of times a year they spoke on the phone.

"Oh, dear, isn't that a violent sport?"

No worse than hurling, Claire thought, an Irish sport her parents used to love and probably still did, she guessed. "It is a bit, but Maddie loves it and she's really good at it."

"Speaking of hurting oneself...Your father, he's a little banjaxed at the moment."

Claire closed her eyes. She knew it. Knew something was wrong, and knew that as an only child, any problems with her parents were destined, ultimately, to fall into her lap, whether she wanted them to or not. Of her many faults, irresponsibility was not one of them.

"What happened? Is he all right?"

"He had a little spill, right here in the kitchen. He swears the floor was wet, I don't know how. But anyway, he broke his arm in three places."

"Oh no. When did this happen?"

"Yesterday. I had to call the ambulance for him. He was onto screechin' like a banshee, so he was. They gave him surgery, some bolts or screws, a plate, I think, too. He's to come home tomorrow. Oh, he'll be right scorpy," her mother complained.

"Mum, do you want me to come?"

"Here?"

"Yes, of course, there." She didn't want to. God, did she ever not want to go to Ireland. But the second semester was just wrapping up, and her slate was clear until the start of the summer semester in six weeks. Intellectually she understood that her parents were aging, but how much and how fast? She hadn't laid eyes on them in years, and she couldn't trust them to tell her the truth.

"Well, you can visit anytime, we've always told you."

"No, I mean..." Claire held her breath, reminded herself it was too late to back out, she'd already made the offer. "Would you like me to come for a couple of weeks to help the two of you out?"

"Help? Oh, we manage, dear."

"But with Dad's broken arm, might it be a good idea to have an extra pair of hands around the house, do you think?" Why did it feel she needed to convince them that her offer was for their benefit? That she was doing them the favor, not the other way around.

Silence, then her mother said, "Well, if you would like to, dear, that would be grand."

It was as much gratitude as she would get. "All right. I'll start making the arrangements. I'll email you later tonight or tomorrow morning."

"All right. I must crack on, dear."

Maddie stood in the doorway as Claire pocketed her phone. "You're going to Ireland, Mom?"

"Yes. Granddad had a fall in the kitchen and broke his arm. I think it's kind of bad. I should go to help them out for a little bit, I think." Maddie knew very little about Claire's childhood, the roots of her emotional remoteness from her parents. She'd frequently asked to see her Irish grandparents more, and Claire had always shut her down with excuses. Perhaps she was old enough for a frank discussion, but not today. Not yet. Claire had enough on her plate.

"You're not going to let me come, are you?"

"I'm sorry, honey, but no. You have school. And I'm going to be busy running errands and doing chores for Grandma and Grandpa. It's not exactly going to be a vacation."

"But I haven't been there since I was a little kid. When can I go again?"

"Soon. I promise. Now look, I need to call the airline and I need to talk to your dad, okay? You'll have to stay with him and Laurie while I'm gone."

Maddie flashed her a look of what promised to be digging in for a battle, but she seemed to think better of it.

Claire turned away and got busy with her phone.

CHAPTER THIRTY-SEVEN

Sarah sat at Brett and Kelly's kitchen island with a cup of coffee cradled in her one hand, her sling leaving her with one usable wing for a while. She'd just finished giving her friends a summary of what the orthopedic surgeon in Boston had told her: x-rays and an MRI revealed that aside from the shoulder dislocation, she had a small fracture in her humerus. She could avoid surgery and rehab it through physio, but the joint wouldn't be stable enough to withstand the violence of professional hockey. There was a chance it might continue to dislocate, and every dislocation could cause more damage. If she opted for surgery this summer, it was a long recovery that would wipe out all of next season, and even then, surgery was no guarantee. Both choices sucked.

"And yesterday, I saw an ortho here at Sunnybrook for a second opinion."

"And?" Kelly prompted.

"Same opinion as the Boston doc."

"Good God," Brett said. "Talk about being between a rock and a hard place. Get surgery and miss next season, or skip surgery but not be able to play hockey again." She slung her arm around Sarah's good shoulder. "So what's it going to be, Door Number One or Door Number Two?"

"I'm going for Door Number Three."

Kelly peered at Sarah from over her glasses. "And what would that be?"

"Disappearing on a desert island. With some hottie to give me back rubs and wave palm fronds over me."

Brett laughed. "While you're sipping a mai tai?"

"Hell, yes! And maybe rub some suntan lotion on me, too."

"Nice life if you can swing it," Kelly said with a smile in her voice. "But I don't actually think it's in the cards for you."

Sarah sighed. "Unfortunately, no. But I need to decide. Soon."

"You're not thinking of calling it quits, are you?" Brett looked like she was only just now realizing the immensity of her best friend's decision. Her fear of Sarah quitting made sense. They were the same age and shared the same stubborn attitude about hockey. If she left the game, Brett was probably scared she was next. In the meantime, Brett was healthy and she was not.

"I don't know if I have it in me. Missing a whole year at our age is like a twenty-five-year-old having to miss two or three seasons. Jesus, Brett. I'm not coming back just so I can play on the third or fourth line. Or worse, be a healthy scratch. I'd be thirty-eight by the time I was ready to come back."

"Whoa. You're getting awfully far ahead of yourself. If you want to get healthy and get back to playing, you will absolutely be able to do that and you'll be great again. Right, Kel?"

"Yes," Kelly agreed. "But you have to want to do it to the exclusion of everything else, because it's going to take *everything* you have to get back in the game, to get that shoulder back to where it was. It will have to consume your life for the next year."

"Sheesh," Brett complained to her wife. "You don't have to try so hard to talk her out of surgery, you know."

"Sorry. You know me, I can't quite shake the stethoscope from my neck."

Sarah rested her chin on her hand. "No, you're right. And that's it: I just don't know if I've got it in me to do what I need to do."

What she really meant was that she was no longer so dismissive of the costs, the sacrifices. She was no longer inching her way toward forty; she was bearing down on it as if on a speeding train. At what point was continuing to play no longer worth it? Did she want to be one of those athletes who sticks around long enough to embarrass themselves? To be a laughing stock? No, she did not.

"You can do it if you really want to." Brett was trying to sound positive, but her eyes gave away her worry. "I mean, Sar, you're still one of the best players in the entire league. If you retire, what the hell hope is there for me?"

"You're doing just fine, Quince. Ugh! There's just so much to think about. My head hurts."

Sarah wouldn't voice it, but Brett didn't have the same legacy to consider. Sarah was a superstar in the game, there were expectations of her. She was an Olympic gold medalist, a world champion, captain of the national team and captain of their Toronto team until the trade. No. This was for her alone to decide.

"What would retirement look like to you?" Kelly asked, not looking at her wife, who was predictably shooting daggers at her with her eyes. "Someday, I mean. Does anything interest you?"

She'd often wondered what she might do with her math degree. At one time engineering interested her, same with teaching, but those options meant she'd have to go back to school full time. "The only thing I enjoyed as an adult besides hockey was the two summers I spent in Calgary building homes."

"I remember that," Brett said. "You said it helped keep you in shape. And that you looked like a total babe wearing a tool belt."

"Ha, you're putting words in my mouth about the babe part, but it was fun, you know? There was a real sense of accomplishment, seeing the progress of your work each day. It helped pay the bills and it definitely kept me in shape."

"Claire's ex builds homes, doesn't he?" Kelly asked.

"He does." She should talk to Matt about his contracting business—when she had the guts to do it. Maybe he could even use another pair of hands one day.

"Speaking of Claire," Kelly continued. "Have you seen her since you got back here?"

"No. Her phone just goes straight to voice mail. I stopped by her house this morning, but there was nobody home, and there was, like, mail piled up in the mailbox." Where the hell had Claire gone? Was she at a work conference for a few days? She couldn't begin to consider the possibility that she had met someone and gone away on some little romantic getaway.

"I've got an idea." Kelly reached for her cell phone and started tapping on it. "English Department please," she said into the phone. "Oh, hello, I'm looking for Professor Claire Joyce. Do you know if she would happen to be in?"

"Why didn't I think of that?" Sarah whispered to Brett.

"That's because she's Mensa Club material and you're not."

"Gee, thanks, buddy."

"Oh, I see," Kelly replied. "Do you know when she'll be back?"

Back? So she's not in town?

Kelly put her phone down. "She's in Ireland."

"Ireland?" Now, that was a mystery. Why would she go there, when she never wanted to talk about the place? And wouldn't she have gotten word to Sarah that she was leaving the country? What the hell? "When is she coming back, did they say?"

Kelly's eyebrows were doing that dancing around thing when she couldn't provide an answer to a question, which was extremely rare. "They're not sure."

"What about Maddie? I wonder if she went with her?" Sarah's mind raced. She pulled out her phone and Googled Matt's contracting business. "I'll call Matt. He'll know what's going on."

CHAPTER THIRTY-EIGHT

The strangeness of returning to Dublin soon disappeared, thanks to the familiar accents, the narrow roads, and the taxi driver's endless complaints about the Garda. Very little had changed in the city since Claire's visit seven years ago. Still no skyscrapers (they weren't allowed), and the same throngs of tourists trudging in packs to Trinity College, St. Patrick's Cathedral, and Christ Church, to the Temple Bar, to the shops that catered to them—bookstores, whisky shops, and shops selling the woolens Ireland was known for. It was nothing like the sleepy town Claire had grown up in—Nenagh, County Tipperary. Claire's parents had lived in Dublin ever since her father's post with the Irish Consulate General's office in Toronto ended twenty-four years ago. They wanted to be close to culture, as they called it: museums, the national library, the theatre. They'd become proud *jackeens*, the derogatory term by which rural Irish referred to Dubliners.

Claire waved the taxi off and paused at the bottom of the concrete steps leading to her parents' rowhouse in Rathmines.

She looked up at the thick, wood door with its brass lion's head knocker, admiring it but feeling no affiliation. The bright red of the door, darker now in the dusk, was so at odds with her parents' modest personalities and the quiet life they had lived since retirement—a life that, as far as Claire could tell, included a stiff gin cocktail at five o'clock each evening before dinner, followed by watching the telly or reading. The ritual rarely wavered, except for their annual summer week at a resort in the south of Spain. They barely went out anymore. This more than anything floored Claire. They'd never been homebodies, not as long as there was a cocktail party somewhere, a symphony, or a horse race.

"Claire, dear." Her mother's smile was stiff and her brief hug was more like a facsimile of a hug. They were not a demonstrative family. "Come in. Set your bags down here and you can take them upstairs later. Your father's already gone to bed for the night. The pain pills leave him knackered."

The house was its usual tidy self, everything in its place, the antique furniture polished to a gleam. It barely looked lived in, except for what had once been the dining room. Her parents converted it to a library years ago, adding floor-to-ceiling oak bookshelves crammed with books about everything from history to astronomy. There was a healthy collection of fiction, and it was this collection, in its earlier iteration, that had sent Claire down the rabbit hole of literature. As a kid, she would lose herself for hours with the books, propelling herself into their worlds, welcoming the sense of purpose they gave her.

Claire and her mother settled on comfortably worn chairs next to the stuffed bookshelves with cups of tea, Claire having already eaten dinner on the plane.

"How is Maddie?"

"She's good. Back to her old self after her hockey injury."

"Ah. Grand. And your flight? How was all that?"

Conversation was as stilted as ever, but it was safer this way, considering the last time they'd had an honest discussion it had devolved into an epic blowup upon the news that she was divorcing Matt. Their objection wasn't only because of her parents' Catholic religion, but also because they loved Matt. Loved him probably more than they did her, Claire was pretty sure, and so they hadn't taken well to the news. Blamed it all mostly on her, but she wasn't about to revisit old wounds. There was no point. Support for her was absent then, as it would be now.

"Flight was fine, Mum. How are things here? With Dad? How's he doing?"

"He complains about the pain and about not being able to go about his gardening. I have to help him with dressing, and he can't drive, so he hates that. He gets knackered easily."

Claire studied her mother, mentally cataloging the changes that had occurred since her last visit. She was thinning, shrinking into frailty, the way old people do as they begin to lose the battle with their bodies, sometimes their minds too. It was hard to imagine her mother now as someone who had worked a chaotic job as a clerk at University College Dublin upon her return to Ireland. Or as the woman who would spend two days in the kitchen each June making cottage pie and soda bread for the annual Castlefest, back in Nenagh. Now, she noticed, it took Mona Joyce half a minute to sit herself in a chair or to get up from it.

"How's your arthritis?"

"Oh, you know. It's not going anywhere, I guess. I manage."

"Do you have help coming in?" Claire looked around again at the supreme neatness of the place. Her mother had always been fastidious, the old "cleanliness is next to godliness" nonsense. "Cleaners? Someone to help with the cooking or the groceries?"

"Your father helps me." Her face twisted for a second. "Well, not now, of course, with his broken arm and all. But we manage."

Claire could see that she was going to have to spend some time finding and arranging more help for her parents because they couldn't keep on like this, doing everything themselves. They might be *managing* now, but they wouldn't for much longer. It would keep getting harder for them, things around the house would begin to slide. The real challenge would be in convincing her parents of the need.

"I'll help as much as I can while I'm here. I thought I would stay for a couple of weeks, if that suits you and Dad."

"Whatever you think, dear." She gave Claire the same not-quite-warm-but-not-quite-cold smile she gave to the postman or the shopkeeper. The makes-no-difference-to-us attitude was simply par for course.

Claire drained her cup of tea and stood, feigning exhaustion, and reminded herself that she was here to help, that she would get through it, that she was not here to expect or initiate some sort of miraculous reckoning of all that was wrong between them. She would keep busy. The time would fly. She would be back home, back to Maddie and her own life in a couple of weeks.

The next morning, thanks to jet lag, Claire rose shortly after dawn. She enjoyed a cup of coffee and made her way through the pages of the *Irish Independent* in the gray silence, the chime of the grandmother clock her only company. She'd left her cell phone in Toronto, declining to spend the extra money for overseas service. It was a great relief, not being leashed to a phone. Matt and Maddie knew how to reach her at her parents' home. That was all that mattered.

The clock struck seven, prompting her to start thinking about breakfast. And to remember how her father used to make breakfast for them every Sunday. He'd start before she and her mother were up, and they'd find him at the hob in his pajamas and plaid bathrobe, making a mess, whistling some old song as he worked. The eggs and sausage and fresh jam were always delicious, and she always ate slowly, prolonging the event, because it was her job to clean up. Then off to St. Mary's Church they'd go, a short walk from their home. It was the one day a week they pretended to be a family.

She heard her father coming down the stairs before she saw him. One heavy, halting step at a time, an occasional grunt. He was no longer that man who got up early and made breakfast. He was becoming stooped, his steps more of a shuffle and less certain. The tide was going out for both her parents, and she was struck by the difference between these people and the people who'd once been in charge of her life.

"Claire, my girl. Howya!"

"Hello, Dad." She went to him and one-armed hugged him so as not to interfere with the massive cast on his right arm. "How's the arm?"

He shook his head. "What a holy show, this." He made a tiny gesture to raise his broken arm, but the effort made him grimace. "Let's get me some coffee. Your mum will be up in a bit. She likes to sleep in."

That was different. Her mother was usually an early riser. Claire put a coffee pod in the coffee machine for her father. She wondered when they'd switched to this more modern amenity. They used to use a bulky glass percolator made in the fifties, the only proper way to make coffee, her father used to say.

The two of them sat at the small table for four in the kitchen with their cups of coffee. Another thing that felt familiar and yet not.

"What can I help you with today? Groceries? Gardening? Appointments to be driven to? I want to make a list of what needs doing for the next couple of weeks." The list, Claire hoped, would be her salvation, eliminating the need to have to sit and invent conversation with her parents day in and day out.

"No need for lists." Ronan Joyce's blue eyes had paled over the years, much of their luminescence gone, though they were not rheumy like those of the very old. "How about we just enjoy each other's company. Be good to spend some time with us oul ones before we go, eh? Let's make a good go of it and catch up right, so." He reached across the table and patted the top of Claire's hand.

Claire blinked at her father, at the new softness in him. She had been completely unprepared for this, his happiness in her being here. It was liked being dropped into another house. Another family.

"All right, Dad." She hoped her smile looked conciliatory, even if it didn't mirror what she felt. She had no idea how or where to start. Or if she even wanted to make the effort.

CHAPTER THIRTY-NINE

"How's the shoulder?" Matt asked her.

The shoulder could wait. She wanted to talk about Claire, as in why she was in Ireland and when was she coming back, but she tamped down her impatience and told Matt all the details of her injury, including the prognosis.

He leaned back on his side of the booth and listened, the glass of beer made small by his hands. They were in a quiet bar on Queen Street West called The Bar Poet. Sarah had called his business and asked him to meet her so she could find out more about Claire. As a bonus, she was eager to pick his brain. Matt was once a pro athlete who'd been forced to retire from injuries. Even if retiring wasn't uppermost in her thoughts, it couldn't hurt to talk to hash things out with him. He'd been in her shoes. In more ways than one, she supposed. And he had a successful business building homes, which intrigued her.

"What are you going to do?" he asked bluntly, after she told him her medical options.

"I don't know yet. There's no guarantee the repair will work, that I will be back on the ice in a year and able to pick up at the level I'm at now."

"I once missed a season too—for an ACL repair in my knee. I won't lie. It was a bitch rehabbing and getting myself back to playing. It's a lot of work, but it can be done, Sarah. If that's what you want, you're certainly capable of it."

The problem? She didn't know if it was what she wanted. A year ago, most definitely. But now? The decision didn't seem so cut-and-dried. "How old were you then?"

"Thirty."

Sarah sipped her gin cosmo. It was sweet, though the gin smoothed it out. "I wish I were thirty. The decision would be easy."

"You think you're too old to come back?"

Sarah wished she knew. "Maybe. I don't know, and that's the part that's killing me. I don't mind putting in all the work, but if it isn't going to get me back to where I was before the injury…"

"You don't want to play if you can't be at the top of your game."

It was said without judgment, without any veneer of meanness. But man, did this guy know how to get to the point. The least she could do was to answer honestly.

"I don't want to play if I'm just going to be a shadow of my former self. I don't want to end my career that way, fighting for playing time." What she didn't say was that continuing her career meant enduring the loss of Claire and Maddie for as long as she kept playing. And perhaps forever. What seemed so clear, so important in her priorities when the trade came along, wasn't as clear, wasn't so important anymore. Everything, it seemed, had changed.

"I get it. You want to finish on top. Nothing wrong with that."

"You make it sound narcissistic. Or maybe just selfish." She smiled to soften her words.

Matt grinned back at her. "Show me an elite athlete who isn't at least somewhat of a narcissist. And you have to be a little selfish to be good. You know that as well as I."

Sarah sank into her own thoughts. She had a lot to show for her decades of sacrifice—Olympic and world championship medals, scoring titles, records she'd set, even the odd endorsement on television. But now what? What if it really was over? What did she have in her life that filled her up the way hockey did? Would she be able to find something again so fulfilling? She was lost without a map.

"I'm afraid it's a decision only you can make, Sarah, but I do have one piece of advice for you."

"Please."

"Don't make your decision from a place of fear. Fear that you won't be able to come back if you try. Fear that you can't be happy if you decide to give it up. Trust me, there *is* life after sports. And it can be great, if you're brave enough to take that leap. You can do anything you want, kid. Including being a partner to someone. If"—his face reddened a little—"if that's what you want."

Ah, good. They were finally getting around to talking about Claire. Who best to do that with than someone who knew Claire much better than she did. "No," she said quietly. "I don't want an empty life away from sports."

"Then don't do what I did." Matt's voice roughened. "I let Claire and Maddie get away. I was stupid. I mean, I tried, but not nearly hard enough. I ignored all the warning signs in my marriage because I just didn't want to deal with it, not when there was practice or a game to get to. Don't give up the way I did."

"It might be too late."

"I don't think so. I know she's crazy about you. You're the first person I've seen her fall for, since, well, you know."

Sarah couldn't quite believe him, though she ached to. If he was right that Claire was nuts about her, how could she have cut her out of her life so fast, so clean, so sharp? Claire didn't even want to *try*.

"She doesn't want to be with an athlete, Matt. She's made that clear from the start, and it's not something she feels she can compromise on, I guess. Getting traded was the last straw." How familiar this must sound to Matt. "She can't seem to see me as anyone other than an athlete." That hurt more than she cared to admit. She'd taken a risk in opening herself up to Claire, in revealing the other parts of her that made her who she was, including that she was pretty much an ace at literature. And for what? So that Claire could lump her in with all the self-centered, not particularly bright athletes? She was so much more than that, she knew was. Her family knew it too, or at least, they'd come to know it. They just liked pushing her buttons now and again about her career choice.

Matt nodded solemnly. "Yeah, yeah. I've been there. It's her personal hangup, and she's being stubborn and unfair. Mostly, though, she's scared." He looked off in the distance, thought for a while. "She's so damned scared to give all of herself to someone." His gaze returned to Sarah. "Convince her you're worth it. That the two of you are worth it. Claire and I...By the time she asked for a divorce, we didn't even know how to talk anymore, how to work things out. There was no way for me to make her see that my sports career wasn't forever, that I wasn't going to split my priorities forever, that things would get better someday. I kind of gave up trying to convince her." He rolled his eyes. "I gave up even *wanting* to convince her. It just seemed easier to...stop."

"But you guys managed to stay friends." At the end of it all, Claire didn't hate Matt. Maybe that was good news for Sarah.

"We did stay friends." Matt lifted one shoulder in a half shrug. "Laurie's wonderful, and I wouldn't have met her if I'd still been with Claire. So it was for the best. I mean, you can't force someone to feel something for you. I think Claire fell out of love with me long before everything came to a head. But she's still in love with you, Sarah. Don't let her do it again."

Sarah raised a questioning eyebrow.

"Don't let her push you away without a fight," he insisted. "Because that's what she's doing. She's pushing you away instead of trying to work on the problem. Make her talk to you about it."

How the hell was she supposed to do that? "Why is she in Ireland, and when is she coming back?"

"Her father hurt himself in a nasty fall and she flew to Dublin to help her parents," he said. "I don't know for sure when she's coming back. Probably two weeks, but it could be longer, depending on what's happening with her parents. I do, however, know where to find her." He looked at Sarah for a long moment, gauging her commitment to getting Claire back, she supposed. "I can give you the address right now."

"You think I should jump on a plane and go to Ireland?" She'd never been to Ireland before, hadn't the faintest idea about anything to do with the country, including how to get around in it.

"I think you should. I mean, what else have you got to do?"

He had a point. Still…"I can't imagine that her parents, or Claire herself, would exactly be thrilled to have me show up on their doorstep." It would be one hell of a surprise. And what would she do if they slammed the door in her face? What if Claire didn't want to talk to her?

"If Claire never wants to see you again, then let her tell that to your face. And if worse comes to worse, well, then, you have an entire country to roam around in while you figure out what you're going to do about your shoulder. And your career."

Sarah thought about that as she finished the last of her drink. A trip to find Claire could go one of two ways, and maybe Matt was right. If nothing else, it was an opportunity for a bit of soul-searching.

"Go get her."

"Thanks, Matt. And thanks for being a friend."

"Anytime. Something tells me you're worth it."

"One more thing. Tell me a little about your business building homes."

"Think you might be interested?"

"I don't know yet. But I might."

CHAPTER FORTY

The open air, the expansiveness of the beach at Malahide, especially with the tide out and all that velvety sand, tiny rivulets of water trenching their way back to the Irish Sea, was perfection for Claire while her parents napped at home. The sun was high, the spring temperature warmer than back home, and she pulled in a deep breath, feeling, for the first time since she'd arrived, a lifting of the curtain of fatigue she'd felt for some time now. Her parents were trying not to be too demanding of her, which she appreciated. It was a balancing act for them all, living under the same roof. So far she was enjoying the thaw in their relations, though some tension remained. It was as if both sides were afraid of saying the wrong thing and reigniting the hot fury that had been so damaging in the past.

Gulls dove toward the water, their screeches splitting the silence. A couple walked ahead on the beach, holding hands, their dog trailing obediently behind, stopping occasionally to sniff something before running to catch up. A solitary figure some distance off walked toward her, too far away yet to tell if it was a man or a woman.

Claire's gaze drifted toward the sea and across it to the spit of land where Wales sat. Liverpool, the place made famous by the Beatles, was just north of that. Sometimes she could hardly believe she'd come from Éire, and other times it felt like it was the only place she could have come from. There was something about growing up on an island that was, yes, confining at times, almost claustrophobic. But it was comforting, too, all the ties that bound them, the common experience of subjugation and repression at the hands of a foreign country, the great diaspora too, that produced an almost militant sense of solidarity with other Irish folks. She missed that.

Being around her parents was altering her sense of gravity, her sense of control. Back in Toronto she went about her own daily life without giving any thought at all to them unless she had to, like at special holidays. If she were to let herself actually consider and care what their everyday lives were like while she went about her own, it would only unleash an avalanche of feelings—disappointment, anxiety, even resentment—that threatened to bury her every time she had to deal with them. She should long ago have moved on from such confusion, but her parents unsettled her. It wasn't an easy position to be in, to only love your parents out of a sense of misaligned duty—the very opposite of when she had been *their* duty. The similarities in their positions surprised her, because she hadn't thought of it before.

The solitary figure moved closer. Claire could see now that it was a man, a tall man in a clerical collar. A priest, his dark pant legs rolled up, his feet bare, his black shoes in his hands. They greeted one another politely, but just after he stepped past her, he stopped and snapped back toward her.

"Claire Joyce? Is that really you?"

Claire almost said no, he was mistaken. She was content being in her own head on a solitary walk, a quiet reprieve from her parents' house, in a country where no one else knew her anymore.

"It *is* you, isn't it?" His smile ate up his face, his blue eyes crinkled at their edges. He had red hair that was short, graying at the temples, but it was his ears Claire recognized. They stuck out like paddles, and oh, how the kids at school were mean to him, calling him Cabbage Ears. And worse.

"Tommy O'Brien!"

"It is, so. I would recognize you anywhere, you haven't changed a bit. What are you doing here? Finally disenchanted with America?"

"Canada, actually."

"Right, so." A lot of Irish called the entire continent America. "I remember when you moved there. You broke this young boyo's heart!"

Claire laughed. She'd always been able to laugh with Tommy. As kids, neighbors in Nenagh, they shared the same dry humor. And the same love for books. Claire was Tommy's closest friend, his ally who would stick up for him when kids called him names.

"So my moving away sent you straight into the arms of the priesthood, did it?"

Tommy clutched his heart. "The only solace for me."

Claire turned serious. "I didn't know you were, you know, so devout."

"I was an altar boy, remember?"

"Yes, but so are most boys in this country."

Tommy shrugged. "Come along. Let's go catch up for a bit. I have some time. My parish isn't far, but let's go have a swift one at the local. I'm trying to clear my head anyway, which is why I'm walking the beach. Tricky funeral mass tomorrow morning, so I'm dossing a bit today."

"Ah," Claire said, as if she understood what the tricky funeral mass was all about. "Yes, it would be lovely to catch up." It might be nice to have a friend during her stay, even if he was a man of the cloth.

The pub, a short walk from the beach, was dark and quiet at this time of the day. A few pairs of eyes darted to them for a quick glance as they entered and took a table. A large fire burned in a grate in the middle of the room, the smell of peat thick in the air. She'd never forgotten its smell. Coal, too, though it was acrid and smelly.

"I made a bargain, is the truth." Tommy sipped his Guinness, a foam mustache forming above his lip. "With the Church. A long time ago."

"Tell me more."

"My little brother, Declan. Remember him?"

Claire did, but barely. Declan was three years younger, an annoying little kid who insisted on following Claire and Tommy around, wanting to do everything they were doing. "I do. Go on."

"He was eight, so it was maybe a year after you'd left. One day, our family went to Limerick for the day, to have a picnic by the river. Declan, he wanted to look for frogs. He was always on the hunt for bugs, butterflies, you name it. Our Da said no, but he took off, promised he was only going to look for stones and that he wouldn't go near the river, that he wasn't interested in the frogs anymore." Claire watched Tommy's face tighten, a sadness materializing in his eyes that hadn't been there a minute ago. "I was supposed to go with him, to keep an eye on him, but I didn't want to. I refused. I was already mad at him because he'd won my favorite marble off me earlier that morning. Anyway, he was gone a while, and out of guilt I finally went to look for him."

Claire's stomach sank. "Was he all right?"

A stark shake of the head, a slight tremble in Tommy's chin, and then he shook it off as if he were recounting a story that had happened to someone else, to another family. "He drowned, Claire. He didn't know how to swim, you see. He must have slipped in the mud along the edge."

"Oh, Tommy. That's awful. I had no idea! I'm so sorry."

"Thank you. It was awful. I became an only child, like you, and I felt so guilty about that because so many times before, when I'd wanted to go off on my bike or something, Declan tried to come with me. He'd follow me, always acting the maggot. So many times, I'd just wanted him to bleedin' go away."

"You were a kid, Tommy. You can't blame yourself for how you felt as a boy."

"I know that now, but I don't think my parents forgave me for not watching him when he went near the river. They withdrew, went through the motions of life after that. And I told

God I would join the priesthood if he would spare my parents from anything bad happening to them again. And, well, it made them happy to see me go into the vocation. So there's that."

What a burden to carry, Claire thought, putting his whole family and their troubles on his shoulders. "Poor you. Are you sure, you know, that the cost is worth it? I mean, are you happy?" She felt awkward, inadequate, talking about the Church with Tommy, but she wanted to know if he felt like he'd finally paid the debt. Was his guilty conscience going to be a perpetual burden? Did he plan to commit his *entire* life trying to cleanse the guilt of a long-ago tragedy?

Tommy grinned at her. "I'm sure about it, I really am. I enjoy it, actually. I didn't go in it for the right reasons at first, but now that I'm here, I can't imagine doing anything else."

Claire sipped her stout. She wasn't a beer drinker, but Ireland indeed was the best place in which to drink Guinness. "I'm glad, then. But you should know that I haven't been a very good Catholic."

"Oh?"

Claire held up her left hand, bare of jewelry. "Divorced."

"I see. It happens, Claire. It's okay, I won't judge you on it."

"I don't go to church any more either."

"You should come to mine, you might even like it. How long are you here? What's the story, my oldest friend?"

Claire explained that she'd come back to help her parents, but that it wasn't easy, that they were so *old* now. "It sort of happened before I realized it was happening. I need to arrange some regular in-home help for them." She rolled her eyes. "If they'll let me." Simply mentioning the idea to them had sent them spiraling into immediate resistance. Denial, too. She'd need to keep working on them.

"Perhaps I can help with some contacts through my church."

"All right, that would be nice."

"And how are you…getting along with them?"

It was clear by the hesitation in his voice that he understood the friction between Claire and her parents that had always been there. He'd seen it for himself back in Nenagh.

Claire told him they were all on their best behavior, tiptoeing around anything uncomfortable, almost as if they were strangers. She recounted the blowup, in all its painful detail, that had followed when she'd announced she was divorcing Matt. How they'd taken his side. How they'd assumed with the confidence of trial judges that it must be all her fault.

"That's rough. Claire, I hope you're all right with me saying, but your parents, back when you were a kid, sort of treated you like—"

"I was an inconvenience? A nuisance?"

Tommy squeezed his glass harder. "Yes."

Claire made a show of glancing at the big clock on the wall over the bar. She no longer wanted to talk about her parents, or Nenagh, or any of it. The memories would only leave her in a dark mood, a combative mood, before returning to her parents. "I should probably be getting back. They'll be wondering—"

"Claire." Tommy's big hand covered hers on the table. "I know I'm overstepping, but please listen for a moment. Time is running out for them, as it does for all of us. There may not be much time left to make things right between the three of you. If it's what you want," he amended.

"I appreciate that you care, Tommy, but—"

"But you don't want a priest saying these things to you. Would it matter if I wasn't wearing a collar? If we were just two old friends drinking the black stuff on a sunny afternoon?"

Claire shrugged. "I suppose it wouldn't matter."

"Look, if there's one thing I know about, it's forgiveness. I have finally, with God's help, forgiven myself about Declan, and I think my parents have too."

"I'm glad, Tommy, I really am."

"You know." He leaned a little closer. "Have you tried forgiving your parents?"

"Me? Forgive *them*? I think it's the other way around."

"No. It is for you too, my friend. They may never get to that point, but you can. And you should."

"Why?" Claire dug in her heels, basking in her righteousness. She'd reached her expiry date on compromises.

"Because if you don't forgive them for being imperfect, how can you ever forgive yourself for being imperfect? Or anyone else? You must start there. With them."

Could that be why she'd refused to forgive Sarah for choosing to go to Boston? Because she hadn't forgiven her parents or herself for being imperfect? Had she somehow hardened herself against love? Taken to heart the lessons from a childhood starved of love and affection? Starved of forgiveness too? She told Tommy she would think about what he'd said, but she was in no mood to promise.

"Here," he said, scribbling on a napkin. "My private number at the church. Call me before you go back to America, all right?"

"Canada." Claire smiled.

CHAPTER FORTY-ONE

"You're a professional athlete, so? Like Matthew?"

"Um, yes, as a matter of fact. A professional athlete, that is, but not, you know, football. Hockey is my sport." At the blank expressions on Claire's parents' faces, Sarah added, "Ice hockey."

After an awkward silence, Claire's dad said, "Ah, lovely. Like the Toronto Maple Leafs."

Almost as an afterthought, Mona Joyce added, "Our granddaughter plays hockey."

"She's a very good player. Smart, mature. Loves to score." Sarah smiled, picturing the goal celebration Maddie had perfected, getting the slide on one knee just right. "You would be very proud of her."

Mona Joyce said, "I don't know what's keeping Claire. She went up to Malahide for a visit. She should have been back by now."

"And she doesn't know you're here, like? In Dublin?" Ronan Joyce asked again. He winced every so often from the pain of his broken arm, or at least, Sarah hoped it was from pain and not because of her unexpected presence.

She had arrived on their doorstep like a lost dog, feeling unmoored, feeling like a bottle containing a message that had drifted for kilometers and days before washing up on a random shore. She needed to see Claire. Claire was the only person who made her forget she was a hockey player. The promise of another life, a different life, lurked in the background, waiting for her, a little out of reach still. Until she saw Claire again, nothing about her future made sense. She couldn't even imagine it, not yet.

She swallowed nervously. "No, she doesn't know I'm here. She didn't bring her cell phone apparently, so I decided to take a chance. Matt kindly gave me your address, though I'm staying at a hotel downtown."

Sarah's father considered her with appraising blue eyes exactly like his daughter's—eyes that were intelligent if a bit on the cynical side. "It must be important for you to see her."

"It is."

"Well, then." Sarah's mother raised herself arthritically from her chair. "I'll get the tea on."

Ronan Joyce stared wordlessly at Sarah. She stared back, the mutual appraisal continuing as the tap ran from the kitchen; there was the sound of a kettle being filled.

"You and Claire must be very good friends, is that so?"

Ah, okay, here it comes. "Very, yes." It wasn't her place to enlighten Claire's father any further about the nature of their relationship, but at the firm way she had answered his question, he sat up straighter, softened his gaze a fraction. Perhaps he understood.

"Come over here," Ronan said, getting up awkwardly from his chair and ambling over to a bursting bookshelf, where he pulled out a heavy, unadorned hardcover. It was Edna O'Brien's *The Country Girls*. "First edition. Signed."

Sarah gently took the book from him, turned it over in her hands. "Read this cover to cover in an afternoon when I was in high school. Read it again a few years later, to see if my older self felt the same about it."

"And did you?"

"I did, but with a better appreciation of how revolutionary the book was. Or must have been."

"Oh, indeed, it was. Caused an awful sensation." With a stern look that reminded Sarah of his professor daughter's classroom presence, Ronan said, "Now give me your best two-minute summary of why the book is such a noteworthy representation of Irish literature."

"Well…" Sarah sensed Ronan was a man who was used to his commands being obeyed. "It shone a light, or you might say it pulled back the veil, on women as much more than wives, mothers, servants to the Church. O'Brien laid bare how poorly women were treated by the cultural institutions here, by the Church, by men in particular, but not only men. Her writing gave voice to the voiceless, washing Ireland's dirty laundry in public in an era where it just wasn't done. But what I love about the book actually is that it's much more than a battle cry for female emancipation, much more than its political messaging. I found it beautiful, funny, haunting. I loved it."

Ronan grew visibly animated. Clearly the apple hadn't fallen far from the tree when it came to books. "It's fascinating that *The Country Girls* has outlived its political and religious critics who called it filth. It's only grown in stature, if anything. A watershed in freeing an entire generation of Irish women. It's really a novel of heartbreaking empathy, unvarnished honesty, and—"

There was a clatter at the front door, the sound of Mona exclaiming, "Oh, you're finally home."

Claire entered the room, pausing in perfect stillness as she took in Sarah's presence. Only her eyes showed surprise. Time slowed, stopped altogether, and Sarah felt herself go numb. Now that the moment was here, she panicked, if only in her mind. What if Claire threw a fit? Turned around and walked out? What if this, her last chance to really talk to her, to find out if anything was left between them, turned into a disaster? Had she made a terrible mistake coming here?

"Claire…"

Claire rushed to her. Collapsed into her, almost, and held on to Sarah like a lifeline. Sarah blinked back her surprise and relief, gathering Claire tighter to her chest with her good arm. She wasn't wearing a sling anymore but she was careful with her movements. She felt Claire's tears seep into her sweater, and as she sent a glance the Joyces' way, she could see that they were moved by the display before them. Their silence—respectful, patient—was evidence enough that they were not surprised that their daughter's love interest was a woman.

Claire finally pulled back, her eyes shining with emotion. Her voice, too. "Um. You're here. And…your shoulder? Are you okay?"

Sarah wanted to laugh. "My shoulder will be okay. Eventually."

"And you've met my parents I see." She looked around as if realizing for the first time that her parents were in the room as well.

Ronan Joyce cleared his throat, stepped forward. "It's grand, Claire. Sarah here knows her Irish literature."

Claire kept her arm loose around Sarah's waist. "She had a good, er, professor, Dad."

"The best," Sarah added.

CHAPTER FORTY-TWO

"How do you manage to drive on these narrow roads?"

Claire watched with amusement as Sarah lunged again for the safety of the dash. She was driving her back to her hotel in her parents' Toyota, and while her left-hand driving skills might be rusty, Claire knew she was doing fine. Sarah was just being a wuss.

"It takes some getting used to. Would you like to try?"

A look of terror swept over Sarah's face. "I'm not sure I'm that brave."

"You? Not brave?" Claire smiled at her. "I think coming all the way over here to see me was kind of brave. Don't you?"

"Brave or stupid." Hope flared in Sarah's face, but she turned away quickly, as though she didn't want Claire to know that she teetered on the thin line that separated success from disaster, hope from despair. Claire knew that line well.

She reached over and gathered Sarah's hand in hers, rested them on the console between them. "Don't be afraid, love."

Sarah turned her face to her. A tear raced down her cheek, chased by another. Claire disengaged her hand from Sarah's and reached up to wipe the tears. In that moment, with the wetness of Sarah's tears on her fingers, Claire knew she loved this woman and wanted to be with her. How that would look, she had no idea. Not yet, but she would never again question whether she loved Sarah, whether they weren't meant, somehow, to be together. She was certain now.

"I have a few things to be afraid of, at the moment." Sarah's smile revealed more pain than joy. "Come in and have a drink so we can talk?" They'd arrived in front of the Grafton Hotel, the bright yellow cladding of the Hairy Lemon pub across the street standing cheerful in the evening's fading light. Sarah had booked a stay at the hotel without an end date.

"Absolutely. At the hotel or at the Hairy?" Claire asked.

"Quieter in the hotel, I think."

Minutes later, they each sipped a gin and tonic. It was safe here, Claire knew, because if they went up to Sarah's room, she didn't know what would happen. And she wanted things to happen, she wanted everything with Sarah, all of it. But not yet. They needed to talk, figure out a path forward. She didn't want to screw this up again. Her heart would not be able to stand it.

"I think my dad likes you," Claire started off. "I'm not surprised. He liked Matt too. A little too much, however."

"What do you mean?"

"They took his side in the divorce. It was ugly."

"I'm sorry. Because they didn't want their daughter getting a divorce or because they really loved Matt?"

"Both."

"That really sucks, Claire. I'm so sorry." Sarah fiddled with the stir stick in her drink. "Back when you came to see me play in Montreal, when you told me it was over between us, you said something I don't understand. You said you were tired of being someone's afterthought. What did you mean by that? Were you talking about your parents taking Matt's side?"

Claire's mood tumbled. She didn't want to talk about her parents, didn't want to dredge up a lifetime of hurt, but if she couldn't talk about it with the woman she was in love with… She made a swift decision to tell Sarah everything.

Over a second drink, and then a glass of water, she told Sarah how, all her life, she'd felt unwanted by her parents, how they'd had a mental checklist of the right parties to attend, the right vacations to arrange, the proper people to impress for the sake of her father's career and for their social standing. Claire, when she'd come along, was the intruder, the fly in the ointment of their perfect lives. She wasn't on their checklist, not really.

"Even as a small child, I never felt the warm reassurance of my mother's hand when we were in crowds. One day, I was four or five, when the three of us were in Dublin, we got separated in a large department store. My parents left. They'd forgotten about me." Sometimes she would grip her mother's skirt or coat, something to hold on to to ease her fears, but that day she hadn't. Clearly it was *her* responsibility to stay safe—a child keeping a child safe. "I had to get a guard to help find my parents. It was an hour before they realized I wasn't with them and came back for me."

"I can't imagine how scared you must have been." Sarah looked alarmed. "Does that mean you pretty much raised yourself?"

"Pretty much. As soon as I was seventeen and heading off to university for my undergrad, they came back here and settled in Dublin."

"Did they come back to Canada often to see you?"

"They've been back to Canada exactly twice since then. Once when I got married and then again when Maddie was born." Claire loved her parents in a dutiful way, but their presence pulled at her emotions in a much more dramatic way than phone calls and emails did. Deliberately she drew a long breath, told herself to relax, that she was okay, she'd made it through the other side of a lonely childhood. Others weren't so fortunate.

Sarah shook her head. She looked disturbed, bewildered, pained. Sometimes Claire forgot how the details of her childhood surprised and upset others.

To clarify, she added, "I wasn't abused or neglected."

"Being unwanted is a form of abuse and neglect, Claire."

"I suppose. But I got through it. I don't hate them. I just feel like they're strangers that I've known for a very long time."

Softly, Sarah said, "I understand now what you meant by feeling like you were an afterthought to others. You certainly were to them. And I hate that."

Claire could cry at how much Sarah cared, except she didn't cry anymore when it came to her parents. "I was an afterthought in my marriage, too, or at least, that's how it felt to me for a long time. It seemed like a repetitive pattern in my life, one that I couldn't live with anymore. And then when you came along…"

"It reminded you of all that stuff. *I* reminded you of it."

Claire wanted to scream inside at the tears brewing in Sarah's eyes. Scream because she was so tired of being imprisoned by her past. Tired of being a victim. Tired of seeing pity on others' faces. Tired of letting the actions of others hurt her.

"Yes," she answered simply. "And it's exhausting feeling that way." She thought back to her talk with her childhood friend Tommy and his advice about forgiveness. "I think I'm beginning to realize that when I feel like I'm someone's afterthought, it's just the old crap coming back at me, paralyzing me, screwing with my relationships. It's *me* who needs to change, Sarah. It's me who needs to feel worthy, because I sure as hell can't change my past."

Was forgiveness, like Tommy implied, the key to it all? Not that it would change anything about the past, but would it help her find happiness *now*? Could forgiving her parents free her from this trap she'd been in all her adult life? She had a right to be happy. She had a right to move forward with her life.

Sarah grew quiet, rolled the empty glass around in her palms. "And where does all of this, your problems with your past, leave me? Us?"

Claire wished she could gather Sarah in her arms, reassure her that she wanted her in her life. Permanently. But there were things she had to work out for herself before she could do that. "I hope it leaves you giving me a little more time and patience." It was her turn to choke up. "Please. I don't deserve it, but…"

"Of course I will. I'm not going anywhere." Sarah's confidence was back. "In fact, I think I just might stay here in Ireland while I wait."

"Oh, good. You can look after my parents."

"Ha ha, not funny. Though I do get the feeling that, I don't know, maybe they're ready to be closer to you? Maybe they want to try to repair things? Maybe growing older has changed their perspective?"

Claire bit back a sarcastic retort, because maybe Sarah was right. Maybe the ground was more fertile now for her and her parents to sort things out. Aging had caught up to them. Was there an infinite amount of time to rectify the mistakes of the past? An unlimited number of do-overs? Not likely.

"Tell you what. I'm close to arranging for a neighbor's college-aged daughter to look in on my parents in the mornings and evenings for a few days. Why don't you and I head over to the Atlantic coast together? It's beautiful there. Magical, really."

"I would love that. Thank you. But on one condition."

"Oh?"

"*You* drive."

Claire laughed and leaned over the table to kiss Sarah. "You've got a deal."

CHAPTER FORTY-THREE

"Where exactly are we going?" Sarah asked. She loved watching Claire drive the narrow winding roads, her hands expertly on the wheel. She looked as though she'd been driving here all her life, which she hadn't, of course. Then again, Claire had had to become an expert at navigating things on her own, and her competency was one of the things that attracted Sarah to her.

"We are going, my love, to some of the most gorgeous scenery you'll ever see in your life."

"Oh, I'm quite sure of that." Sarah let her eyes roam over Claire, not caring how obvious she was about it. She'd behaved herself until now, giving Claire space, not rushing her. Claire hadn't shared the accommodation plans yet and she didn't want to jinx anything by asking or by appearing too eager. As much as she wanted to know where Claire was taking them on the island and what was going to happen tonight, mostly she just wanted to know where Claire was steering them as a couple. To distract herself, she gazed at the scenery whizzing by.

"Look, there's a castle!" She pointed in the distance.

Claire chuckled. "One of thousands, my dear."

"I can't believe you can drive across this entire island in less than a day. It's wild."

"And yet every county is so different. Even the accents, especially once you leave The Pale. The regions are like mini countries themselves."

"Speaking of accents, yours is stronger now that you're here."

"Really? That's funny, because Maddie would say the exact same thing."

"Do you think Maddie will ever forgive me for being traded?"

There had been some brief email exchanges, but Maddie had been noticeably distant with Sarah since the move to Boston. One-sentence answers, for instance, when Sarah wrote to ask her how her hockey was going. It bothered her. A lot. There would be enough disappointments ahead in Maddie's life. Sarah was sorry she'd taught her an early lesson in it.

"I think," Claire said, her eyes on the road, "no, I *know* she forgives you. You're one of her favorite people in the world, so how could she not? She's just at that age when everything seems personal. Every hurt is intentional. She's also at the age of learning that anger can be a weapon. She's certainly used it on me since you got traded."

"Oh, Claire, I'm sorry."

"Not your fault. It was the circumstances." Sarah could see that Claire's eyes were misted. "It's not easy for a kid her age to understand why adult relationships don't always run smoothly. So, yes, she will eventually understand, but I think you and Maddie need a little heart-to-heart when we get back."

It sounded like such a sure thing, "When *we* get back." A foregone conclusion that the three of them would work things out, be together, once they were back on Canadian soil. It wasn't a lot to go on, but it was enough for Sarah to feel hopeful, *really* hopeful, for the first time in a long time. The sun broke free from the clouds, glinting off Claire's glasses, and Sarah felt that maybe it was beginning to poke through her own clouds as well.

And God, Claire looked so goddamned beautiful. She could hardly pull her eyes away from her.

Claire began fiddling with the car's sound system. "Let's see what CD my parents have in here. Shall we guess?"

"Sinatra? Bing? Wait, Maria Callas?"

"Good try, but they were always sticklers for listening to Irish musicians. Hey, maybe it's Thin Lizzy in there!"

"Or Van Morrison!"

They both laughed, and Claire's pleasure immediately softened her face. Her finger poised over the play button. When she hit play, The Cranberries exploded from the speakers, singing "Dreams," and the two of them exchanged a look of disbelief, followed by another round of laughter.

"Hey, don't tell me your parents are actually cool?"

"Hell, even I didn't know they liked The Cranberries. Which also happens to be Maddie's favorite group. And mine. Huh. Weird." Claire started singing along.

"Wait, no fair, I don't know the words." Sarah pulled out her phone and Googled the lyrics so she could join in. Claire laughed when she did a little gyration dance in her seat.

They drove around what was probably their fourteenth roundabout of the day when a sign announcing County Galway appeared.

"Ah-ha! I finally solved the secret of our destination."

"I knew you were a smart one."

Sarah smacked Claire's arm in jest. "Is that anyway to talk to your star student?"

"Hmm, well, I don't know about *star*, but...let's see. You're definitely my cutest student ever."

"Ah, I wouldn't have pegged you for the looks-over-brains type of gal."

Claire bit her bottom lip, and it was adorable. "You caught me out. I am a sucker for both, actually. Luckily, you happen to fit the bill."

Sarah clutched her heart. "Oh, thank God. You'll keep me around for another day?"

Claire raised a single eyebrow but kept her eyes on the road. "Well, professor?"

She turned her head and gave Sarah a wink that was full of promises. "You'll have to wait and see."

Sarah clutched her heart playfully as Claire pulled the Toyota into a lot behind a three-story, white stucco inn called Morning's Glory. She turned the engine off and looked at Sarah, her face set with worry. "I booked us a room for three nights. And…yes, one room. Is that all right? Because if it's not, we—"

Sarah tenderly cupped her chin in her palm. "It will be perfect."

Out of the car, the breeze brought a whiff of salt, and Sarah filled her lungs, looked around. The Atlantic Ocean was just beyond. "So. Galway, eh?"

Already she knew this town was going to mean everything.

"Oh, good, the rooms are exactly as they looked on the Internet." Claire dropped her bag at the foot of the queen-sized bed. "I wasn't sure. I was hoping—"

"Stop worrying. I love it. It's romantic."

The Juliet balcony looked out over the ocean, and Claire immediately opened the French doors to let the sea breeze in. The floors were made of wood, the furniture vintage Art Deco style. A bright red-and-gold area rug brightened up the room. It was cozy, simple; it was everything they needed.

"Hungry?" Claire asked.

Sarah sat down on the edge of the bed. "Oh, Claire, I'm hungry for many things. *You*, mostly."

Claire pushed at her glasses. "Sarah, you should know that I haven't been with a woman in a long, long time."

"I'm not any *woman*, Claire. I'm me. We're us. How we feel about each other is all that matters. Not our past histories, nothing else."

Slowly, she stood up. Something welled up in her and burst, like a great bubble, and she knelt before Claire, her good arm encircling her waist, her head against her warm belly. She hoped the inarticulateness of her actions expressed the depth of her feelings. She wanted Claire to realize that they would go slow, that they would simply love one another, in whatever ways they chose to express it here, in this room. No timetable, no rules.

CHAPTER FORTY-FOUR

"Sarah, wait." Claire gently touched the back of her head until her soft eyes looked up at her—full of love, full of quiet anticipation. "How did I manage to get so lucky in finding you?"

Sarah grinned, pulled herself up. "You said something a minute ago about being hungry?"

"Food, my love. Hungry for food." Sarah had that look in her eyes that said she was ready for anything. Sex right here, right now, no problem. But Claire needed a little time.

"I'm famished, actually. All that clutching onto the dash for dear life has made me hungry." Sarah fabricated a pout for Claire's benefit, but it was only seconds before she strode to the door.

Laughter rose in Claire's throat. She enjoyed the fact that she was braver than Sarah about driving around Ireland. Probably the only thing she was braver than Sarah about. She took a steadying breath and followed her out the door. They'd made huge strides in their relationship, but there remained hills ahead. Hills that would challenge them. And that was okay. She wanted this.

The pub was within walking distance, a place painted bright red and called O'Sullivan's. Most of the public houses were simply named after an owner, either previous or current. Not exactly inventive, but predictable nonetheless.

"What's good in-house?" Claire asked the server, a young woman with flaming red hair.

"The fish and chips are to die for." She lowered her voice to a whisper. "But I'd skip the coleslaw."

"All right then, fish and chips for me."

"And me," Sarah replied.

"And what'll ye have to drink?"

Claire looked at Sarah, who shrugged and mouthed, "When in Rome."

"Two glasses of Guinness," Claire told the server, who left whistling a tune.

"Okay. I'm a bit tense," Sarah announced, sitting up stiff and straight like she was waiting for the teacher. "Can we hurry up and get this part over?"

"What part? Dinner?"

"No. The talking part. Because right now my stomach feels sick and my knees are shaking because I need to know if this is all some little lovefest before a giant goodbye or something, this little Galway getaway." Sarah stopped long enough to take a breath. "Are we just going to have a *thing* here, Claire, or is this the start of something real, something permanent? I just really need to know, okay? Because I don't think I can handle it if it's just a little a holiday fling. It…would hurt me too much."

Okay, then. It was all on the table now, no more waiting to address the elephant in the room. Here was Sarah, practically prostrating herself before her, probably dying inside, because she was the one who held all the cards and was making her wait. She hadn't meant for all the suspense.

"Sarah…I love you." Claire's emotions formed an untimely knot in her throat. The pause was good timing, though it protracted Sarah's agitation. Two glasses of Guinness were plunked on the table.

"I love you too," Sarah said quietly, too quietly. She had trouble holding Claire's gaze.

"No." Claire pushed out the words, for Sarah's sake, as fast as she could. "Wait. Sarah, this is *not* goodbye. This is not a fling. The time for that was over a long time ago. We could have had a fling the minute you stopped being my student. Except… you're not fling material, you know."

"I'm not?"

"Nope. At least not for me."

"O…kay. So what am I, exactly? To you? I know I said I would give you as much time as you need. And I'm really, really trying to be patient, honest. But this is sort of killing me."

Calmness wrapped itself like a blanket around Claire, and everything slowed. Sarah was the one she wanted. There was zero doubt anymore in her head and in her heart. It was all the details that needed sorting, the obstacles that were out there, waiting to trip them up—Sarah's career for one, Maddie and her anger for another. But she loved this woman. She wanted to be with this woman, however that would look. Somehow, they would make it happen.

"To me," Claire said, clearing her throat so she could speak clearly and with composure, because Sarah, if she began tearing up, would be the undoing of Claire. "You are perfect. To me, you're my love, the one I want to be with. You're the one I want next to me as we try to navigate ourselves through this crazy world, this thing we call a life. I don't want to do it alone. It's…"

Sarah was shaking her head back and forth, and Claire's breath left her. *Oh no.* "What?"

"I haven't figured out yet what I'm doing about my shoulder, about my hockey career, and you deserve to know that. That I haven't made a decision, that it's still up in the air."

"Sarah, it's okay."

"It is?" Sarah's mouth hung open. "But it was this, this major obstacle between us, this—"

"I know. Look. I'm not being very clear here, am I? It's, sorry, it's been a hell of a week in more ways than one."

"You're right. And it didn't help, me showing up here unannounced like some crazy stalker."

"Are you kidding? You're the only good thing that's happened to me this week."

Their food arrived, and Claire could see that Sarah was fighting her impatience to understand what Claire was doing such a crappy job of trying to explain.

"Oh!" Claire exclaimed. "This fish really is to die for." She was toying with Sarah a bit now, making her wait, but it was because she was so happy to be here, far from home, with Sarah, eating fish and chips of all things, at a pub in Ireland just steps away from the ocean. If this moment lasted forever, it wouldn't be long enough.

"You're enjoying this, aren't you?" Sarah's eyes narrowed playfully.

"The fish and chips? Absolutely. Best I've had in years."

A chip ended up in Claire's lap, then another. In seconds, they both erupted in laughter.

"All right, all right, you win," Claire said. It felt good to laugh, felt good that Sarah was the one making her laugh.

"I win, eh? The chip-throwing contest? Or do you mean I can do whatever I want with my hockey career and you will love me all the same?"

"Now *you're* the one toying with me."

"Guilty."

Claire looked at the woman she loved, let her eyes wander over her, and then back to her face. She'd never get tired of looking at her. "Yes. That's exactly what I'm saying." It was time to trust that what they were building together was strong enough to weather whatever the future might throw at them.

"Are you serious?"

"I am. I've been stupidly unfair to you. To me, too. And Maddie, while we're at it."

"Want to throw a few other names in there too?"

"Nah, I think that's enough guilt for one person."

Sarah reached across the table for her hand. "I love you for trusting me. I love you for overcoming your fears enough to love me back, to give us a chance." She beamed, and instantly Claire felt warm all over. "Most of all, I love you for not needing to know the end of our story before we really get started."

The phrase brought her back to the first time Sarah leveled the accusation at her. It had hurt then, because it was true.

"I guess I have changed a little, haven't I?"

"You have. I'm proud of you, honey. So proud."

"I want us to write the ending ourselves," she said softly. "Me and you. And Maddie, if you're okay with all of that?"

"Okay? Are you kidding? Claire, you have no idea."

They looked into each other's eyes for a long time in their shared appreciation that it wasn't a dream, that it wasn't a long-wished-for fantasy, that it was actually happening.

"Come on," Sarah said. "Let's get out of here."

CHAPTER FORTY-FIVE

Performance anxiety was something Sarah hadn't felt in a long time. Not on the ice and not in the bedroom. But she did now. Panic was in her throat and in her hands and Claire was going to see right through her. Claire with her big eyes that were looking at her not with apprehension but with hunger, their blue as hot as a gas flame. How the hell had she managed to banish her nerves and send them Sarah's way? Was Claire going to expect fantastic sex? Like, the best ever? Would she disappoint her?

"Claire, we can wait if you want. I—"

"Come here," Claire said in a voice husky with want. She moved to the bed and patted the spot beside her.

Sarah did as she was told. She knew what to do, how to pleasure a woman, but the impulse to protect herself, just a little, remained, and it had to do with getting hurt. With making love and then Claire pulling away, dumping her for good this time. Claire had said all the right things to soothe her fears, she knew that, and yet she couldn't quite contain the tiny kernel of doom sitting in the middle of her chest.

"Sarah my love, talk to me. What's wrong?"

"Nothing. Nothing at all. I want you so much it almost scares me, that's all."

"But…?"

Sarah hated having doubts. "There's no buts, not really." She was sliding down a slope and desperately needed to grab onto something to halt her descent.

"Not really?" Claire's eyes softened, her smile so gentle that it made Sarah want to cry. "I know I hurt you. And I'm sorry. I understand if you don't trust the things I've been saying. About wanting us to be together. I'll prove it to you if you're patient with me, I promise. If you'll just…let me try?"

They could talk more about it, but there was no need. A wave of longing—acute, heated—crushed her doubts. She tilted Claire's chin toward her and began to kiss her. Everything she'd felt for Claire for months found its way into the kiss—desire, fear, joy, confusion, and finally, love. All of it had been worth it, every painful and joyous moment up until now, because she was sitting on a bed in Ireland, madly kissing Claire, and she'd do it all again if it brought them to this exact place.

"Wait one sec," Claire murmured against her lips. "There's something I need to do first."

Sarah groaned, but she wasn't annoyed, not really. She'd stay in the moment, let things happen and be okay with whatever that was, she reminded herself. *Be where you are.* Brett's wife, Kelly, had once told her that, a clever piece of advice that she tried to remember both on and off the ice.

Claire rooted around in her suitcase and pulled out a small scented candle in a travel tin. It said lavender-tangerine on it, and something like "Love is in the Air," and Sarah had to smother a smile. Claire's attention to detail was sweet. "Oh crap, I forgot a lighter."

"It's okay, we can skip the candle."

"No. I want this to be romantic."

"Claire, honey, it *is* romantic. Even if you put a towel around your hair and a bathrobe and big floppy slippers on, it would still be romantic." Her heart tripped over itself at the thought that Claire wanted things to be perfect for their first night together. If it was that important to her, she'd find a way to light the candle.

"Ta-da!" She held up a book of matches from the night table drawer. There were only three matches in it and the whole thing was coated in dust. Claire snatched it from her. "Careful now. There's only three."

A silky, sly smile from Claire. "Trust me, nothing is going to get in the way of…us tonight." She lit the candle successfully and blew out the match with a sexy puff. She set her glasses down on the nightstand and gave Sarah a look that was pure smoke and sex, raw desire that took her breath away. *How did she get so confident in the making-out department?*

"Um, so…" Sarah swallowed against her dry throat. Claire was so fucking hot and here she was, a lifelong, card-carrying lesbian, feeling like it was her first time. Claire unbuttoned her blouse, standing next to the scented candle, in a strikingly simple act that brought Sarah back to herself, back to them. She watched the thin wisp of smoke rise from the burning candle, which actually did smell of lavender and tangerine. "Guess you, like, planned all along you were going to get lucky tonight, eh?" She gave Claire an indulgent smile that left no doubt that Claire would, indeed get lucky tonight.

Claire threw her a sheepish smile. "Hoped, anyway."

"You get bonus marks for being romantic, professor. I love it."

Claire's blouse dropped to the floor. "Is my plan working?" Next she slid her Capri pants down her legs, slowly, and into a puddle on the floor with her blouse.

"Wow." Sarah couldn't breathe. Seeing Claire in only her bra and underwear—sexy, vulnerable, exceedingly beautiful— rooted her in place. She felt dumb, unworthy, but cocky enough to mumble, "I think the odds are pretty good."

Claire moved to the bed again, but this time she lay down and made room for Sarah beside her.

Take the leap, Sarah commanded herself. And so she did.

CHAPTER FORTY-SIX

Claire had no playbook, no detailed plan other than the scented candle, but if nothing else, it broke the ice and signaled her intentions. If it backfired, so be it. If she was willing to have Sarah back in her life no matter what she decided about her hockey career, then she had to let go of wanting to control things, of needing to know the end of a story before it began. Sarah had been right about that. She had been right about a lot of things.

"Let me look at you." Claire's breath came out in a long, ragged exhale as she watched Sarah slide off her button-down shirt and her jeans. She looked nervous as she sat on the edge of the bed, and it made Claire love her even more. Because, surely, Sarah was an ace at sex like she was at hockey. She would know plenty about making love to a woman, and more than anything else, Claire wanted her to make her come. She whistled low and long at the sight before her.

"God, you are gorgeous, Sarah Brennan." Long, thick muscles. Strength and grace. It was a heady combination, reminding Claire that it'd been a very long time since she had been with a woman—college and that was almost two decades ago. A man's body was no comparison. How could she have forgotten? "May I touch you?"

"Please."

Claire sat up, brushed Sarah's hair back from her forehead, trailed her fingers down her cheek, and relished how Sarah leaned into her touch even as she closed her eyes. Her hand skimmed lower, down Sarah's neck and to her shoulder.

"Is this the shoulder you hurt?" When Sarah nodded, Claire leaned in and kissed it tenderly, thoroughly. She lowered the strap of Sarah's bra so that her lips could graze there too.

"Claire…" Sarah laid down beside her, facing her but not touching. "I'm afraid to touch you."

"What? Why?" Arousal—a raging, water-swollen river—coursed through her body. And now Sarah was afraid to touch her? What the hell? She was going to *die* if Sarah didn't touch her. Like, now. "I'm not going to hurt you, Sarah, I promise. Please don't think—"

"It's not that." Sarah's flimsy smile dissolved. "I'm afraid of disappointing you."

"Disappointing me? Oh, Sarah my love, believe me, there's zero chance of that happening."

Sarah's bottom lip trembled the tiniest bit. Enough. It was time to show her how much she wanted her, how much she loved her. She moved on top of Sarah, kissing her mouth until lust replaced the startlement in her eyes. It was rewarding to watch those hazel eyes darken, to feel Sarah's body begin to relax under her and then tighten again, this time with arousal. Claire peeled the bra's other shoulder strap down, removed it altogether. She didn't want to stare at Sarah's chest, but God, she couldn't help it. "I think I might be the one to disappoint *you*."

"That's never going to happen." With her teeth, Sarah pulled gently on Claire's bottom lip, then began to kiss her madly, greedily, her hands moving up and down her back, finally landing on the clasp of her bra. Sarah unclasped it, pulled it away from her body, tossed it to the floor. Skin on skin. Claire would be content to lay with Sarah like this for hours, if only her desire wasn't pounding as hard as a bass drum, demanding attention.

Sarah, as if reading Claire's mind, pressed her body deeper against her own, began to move and writhe sensuously beneath Claire. It felt amazing.

"You feel so good," Claire hissed.

"Then touch me."

Claire paused long enough to vanquish all thought from her head—doubts about her body, doubts about her skills in the bedroom, and the crazy disbelief that Sarah could and did want her this way. She directed her focus to how her body felt, how it throbbed hotly, and then to the feel of Sarah's body down the length of her, hard and strong, yet impossibly soft, too. Sarah's mouth was on hers—hot, demanding, yielding at all the right moments.

Claire snaked her hand between their bodies, felt Sarah rise enough to make room for her explorations. First stop was Sarah's ass, mounds of muscle disguising silent power. She had always thrilled watching Sarah skate, seeing on display such raw power but also incredible finesse, and she felt both those things at her fingertips as she stroked. Sarah drew in a sharp breath when her fingers found the edge of her underwear. She slipped beneath the cotton material and was met with hot, wet flesh. Sarah gasped against her mouth.

"Claire, you're killing me. I want you so much."

Claire clenched her thighs together against the desire ripping through her, threatening to derail her mission to pleasure Sarah first. She stroked her, inching her fingers along until she found exactly the right spot. And she knew she'd found it by the jolt Sarah's body gave, the pleasurable full-body shiver that followed.

Sarah's mouth, hot and wet, fell away from Claire's and landed on the hollow between her neck and collarbone. Her teeth nipped Claire's flesh. "I'm so fucking turned on. I'm going to come. You're going to make me come."

Claire smiled against Sarah's cheek. She wanted to make her come in the most glorious way. She stroked harder, faster. Loved the powerful rolling swells, the gentle troughs that followed, when Sarah moved beneath her. She loved how hard and slippery she was in her hand. Loved every single way her body responded to hers. She groaned with pleasure. She could come herself if she let it happen, but she narrowed her focus again on Sarah. She slipped a finger inside, Sarah drawing it in, riding it, her hips rocking. She palmed her at the same time, felt her breath rush from her body as she tensed beneath her, cried out. Raggedly, she shouted, "I'm coming for you, Claire. Oh! Yes! Yes yes yes yes."

Claire kept with her through the spasms of orgasm, planted kisses on her throat and face, and finally claimed her mouth as if she could swallow the orgasm right back. "I love you," she said against her mouth, Sarah limp and spent as the tension left her body.

"I love you too. That was…fast. Sorry. I couldn't keep it going. I was too turned on."

Claire pressed her fingers against Sarah's lips. "Never apologize in bed. Just…"

"What?" Sarah was smiling against her fingers.

"Just, you know, make improvements."

"Ah, I see. I think you've just thrown down the gauntlet."

"I did no such thing."

"Oh, yes you did. You think you won't come as fast?"

Claire blushed. She had no idea how fast she would come. Probably not fast at all, given the cobwebs down there and her lack of experience. "It sounds like you're challenging me to a… duel of sorts?"

"A sex duel. An orgasm mano a mano."

"An orgasm face-off?" Claire quipped.

"Oh, now we're using hockey analogies, are we? I might remind you that I'm an expert in the field."

Claire raised a single, teasing eyebrow. "So I've heard. But it's not the field I'm interested in. It's the bed."

Sarah flipped her over in one swift move, then crawled on top. "How about *your* field, my sexy literature professor. Want me to show versus tell?"

Claire laughed, but she couldn't sustain it, not when Sarah's tongue landed on her nipple. It was almost game over for her right there. She wanted to be ravaged by this hot lover. *Her* lover. She honestly didn't care who came fastest, she just wanted— needed—to come. As Sarah's tongue circled and stroked her nipple, Claire pushed up into her, urging her to keep touching her.

"Jesus, this feels so good, Sarah. So fucking good."

"I don't want you to wait anymore," Sarah whispered. She moved down Claire's body, pulled her underwear aside, and took Claire into her mouth.

Yup. Game over.

Claire's world exploded into a million starbursts.

CHAPTER FORTY-SEVEN

Any awkwardness from their first lovemaking didn't last—a second and then a third round before the sun came up saw to that. Sarah loved how in bed together they alternated between tender and restrained, wild and insistent. It was as though their craving for each other couldn't truly be satisfied, not yet, not until a thousand more lovemakings. With the morning's first light, muted by the muslin curtains, she watched her sleeping lover. She'd wanted a night like this with Claire for months. Had privately dreamed about it, fantasized about it. Her hopes at times dashed and sometimes not. In her mind, making love to Claire only solidified how she felt about her—the period to an exclamation mark. She wanted to live inside this moment forever, breathing in the sweet fragrance of sublime happiness, nothing else existing inside the little world they'd spun but the two of them.

It was a nice thought. No. A beautiful thought.

Claire's eyes blinked open.

"Good morning, beautiful."

"Oh, Sarah." A faint blush appeared on Claire's cheeks, which Sarah began kissing away. She didn't want to give Claire any time to feel weird about them waking up together this way.

"I love you," she whispered in Claire's ear, felt the tiny shiver from her as a puff of her breath grazed her neck.

"I love you, too. And…" The blush was back.

"Yes?"

"Was I…okay last night?"

Sarah swallowed down the giggle caught in her throat. "Are you kidding me?" Claire's adventurousness, not to mention her combination of vulnerability and assertiveness, had been incredibly sexy. Clearly, she trusted Sarah enough to be completely open and accessible in bed; she had not been shy to ask for what she wanted and when she wanted it. It made Sarah love her even more.

"Not kidding, actually." Fathomless blue eyes beseeched her.

"You were perfect, my darling."

A low chuckle started in Claire's throat. "I doubt that very much, though I promise to, er, practice. *You*, on the other hand. My God." Claire's voice trailed off, her eyes clouded with a sex haze, as Sarah liked to call it. Claire was already off on a private memory of their lovemaking.

"There's more where that came from. Like, a ton more."

"Does that mean we're never leaving this room?"

"Don't tempt me. But, number one, I'm starving. And number two, you promised to take me to the famous Cliffs of Moher today. And number three…"

"Yes?" Claire batted her eyelashes.

"I want us back in this room as soon as possible."

Claire grinned, threw the sheets off her naked body, and took her time prancing around the room naked. "You're sure you're still hungry? For breakfast, that is?"

Sarah shook her head. "You're incorrigible, do you know that?"

"What I am, my dear, is turned on. Come here and let me show you."

* * *

The coastal drive took them along winding roads, past herds of sheep being moved from one pasture to another, past the ruins of old churches and castles as commonplace as billboard signs back in North America. Every little town they drove through had a colorful pub at the center of it, a handful of shops, not much more.

At the Cliffs, the wind cut hard and swift off the Atlantic Ocean, and Sarah breathed in deeply air that was moist and faintly redolent of salt. They were hundreds of meters high up from the sea.

"Wow," she said at the vista before her. The cliffs were so steep, it was almost a straight shot down. The fierce waves of the ocean smashing into the rocks produced an occasional loud crack that sounded like a cannon being fired. The power of the wind and the sea was a visual delight but an auditory one as well. "This place is magical, Claire. What's that island over there? To the north?" She pointed to a lump of dark land in the hazy distance.

"That's part of the Aran Islands."

"What's it known for?"

"The best wool sweaters in the world. Oh, and Dun Aonghasa."

"What's that?"

"An old, prehistoric, stone fort. It's over three thousand years old."

"Cool! Can we go there?"

"Of course we can."

She was like a kid on her first trip away from home. There was so much to discover and not only about Ireland. Reconnecting with Claire had motivated her to come here, but there were decisions to be made about her future. She couldn't put them off any longer. It wasn't fair to Claire and it wasn't fair to herself.

"Do you mind if I set off on a little walk? Alone?"

A look of worry, a hint of confusion crossed Claire's face, but she smiled and said, "Of course."

Sarah wasn't worried. Her heart told her that Claire would support whatever she decided about her career. She kissed her gently on the cheek. "I'll be back in a few. Thanks for giving me the space."

It only took a couple of minutes to find a haven in which to lay about and think. "I love it here," she shouted into the wind. It was like being on top of the world, the open sky above, the sea below her, the cliffs seemingly endless as they stretched out along the coast for kilometers.

She got as close to the edge as she dared and sat down. It was almost disorienting, the height and the expanse before her, but the grass beneath her grounded her, allowed her to lie back and look up at the sky. How small and insignificant she felt, lying on top of these cliffs just as others had done hundreds, even thousands of years, before—contemplating, dreaming, deciding, forgetting. The cliffs didn't care. They, the ocean, and the sky went on as silent witnesses.

A sequence of moments made up a life; other people made those moments worth showing up for, worth sharing. To be alive, Sarah thought, was to keep moving toward more of those moments, to turn from the past, to look forward.

It was in this frame of mind that she began to understand that hockey was for her no longer the defining characteristic of her life, her identity. Claire had been right weeks ago when she indicated that her hockey career was in "overtime." Oh, how she had railed against that notion at the time, but it was because Claire was right. The forward momentum that had carried her through all the highs and lows and in-betweens of her hockey career had stalled. Or petered out, more accurately. She'd set a high bar for herself and had achieved all of it, every one of her goals and then some she didn't even know she had had. She'd crossed the finish line, not entirely intact but mostly. The shoulder was the last straw. She knew she didn't have it in her to push through surgery and rehab to continue her career in the way she wanted and expected and hoped. But being with Claire…being *here* with Claire…changed everything.

There was another life out there waiting for her, for them. She felt ready for this, realized that her thoughts had begun shifting this way for a while now. It was her heart that needed to catch up, because hockey had filled it in a way nothing else ever could. She would grieve its loss, but maybe it could fill her up in ways other than playing at the highest level—coaching kids, or becoming a referee, or working as a scout for her old team. There were so many ways she still could contribute to the sport. Helping Maddie and her teammates had reminded her how fun it was to teach a few skills to young hockey players. Perhaps she could do it on the regular.

Sarah stood up, brushed the dirt and grass off her backside, and walked back to Claire. Without a word, she wrapped her in her arms, breathed her in, felt her with her whole body, because she wanted to remember this defining moment. This moment when her life changed forever.

Softly, Claire asked, "You okay?"

"I am. I think we've both come here to change our lives. To figure out a future that's different. And I'm ready to do that."

Claire pulled back, took both Sarah's hands in hers, looked at her with patience and love as limitless as the sky. "Before you say anything, I want you to know that I will stand with you like this, holding your hands and loving you, in whatever you decide to do."

"I know. And I love you for that. For trusting me to do what I need to do for *me*." Claire was her hero. Because Claire already knew what she now understood: That love was a silent trust, an immeasurable belief in the other person. "Come on, let's walk."

After a few moments, she casually said, "I'm going to retire."

Claire stopped, a mix of surprise and joy and wonder on her face. "You are? I mean, you're sure?"

"I am. It's time to start the next part of my life."

"And what does that look like to you?"

What was she if she was not a hockey player? "I don't know, but it's time to find out. Are you—would you think it's silly if I worked for Matt building homes? I mean, once my shoulder is better."

They started walking again. "Of course I wouldn't think it's silly. Matt is very good at what he does. If it's something you want to do, then you should do it."

"You won't—I'm not trying to be Matt 2.0. I don't want you to think—"

"Sarah, honey." Claire squeezed her hand. "You're not Matt. You're you. And I love you. I think you're an amazing woman who can do anything she wants to do. And if it turns out building houses isn't your jam, there will be something else."

The stress of the past few months slid away with the relief of a decision having been made. "Thank you, Claire. Your support, your love, means everything to me. My life is with you and Maddie. That's all that matters."

"You've got that, my love. You've got that. But you're not doing this for me, right?"

"No. I'm doing it for me. Because I want to see what else life has in store for me. For us."

Claire stepped in for a kiss that Sarah felt all the way to her toes.

CHAPTER FORTY-EIGHT

Downtown Galway was a throng of shops, most of them catering to tourists, the streets so busy on any given day from spring to fall that vehicular traffic had mostly been edged out by pedestrians. But not entirely. As she walked side by side with Sarah, Claire noticed her suddenly step off the curb to make way for a family of three coming toward them. Accustomed as she was to cars traveling on the right side of the road, though, she had glanced the wrong way for traffic. Claire jerked her back onto the safety of the sidewalk just as a car whizzed past, missing her by inches.

"Jesus!" Sarah yelped.

Claire's heart pounded, but she gentled her voice, clutched Sarah's hand. "That was close, my love. Hang on to me. I've got you."

"Thanks, babe." Sarah kissed her on the cheek. "Lesson learned. Stay on the sidewalk and all will be well." She laughed with the consolation of having survived a close call. Claire laughed with her, but only to stem the fear that she might have lost her to such an unlucky stroke.

They stepped into a little storefront restaurant called Alma's for lunch. Over steaming bowls of cheddar and ale soup with a side of fresh soda bread, Claire admitted to Sarah that she wanted to find a way to stitch together her relationship with her parents. That her wounds had felt more raw and open since she'd come to Ireland, as though they were screaming at her to do something about it. Finally. She wouldn't leave the island until she'd at least tried, because it might be her last chance.

"I want things in my life to be different, to start over," she told Sarah. Being unable to forgive was relentlessly wearing down her psyche, leaving her feeling like a tree constantly bending with the wind, threatening to snap. But now, being in love, she didn't feel so much like that tree buffeting itself against the wind. She wasn't alone.

"I know my parents won't be around forever, that I have to do this now. I just don't know if I can, Sarah."

"You can. I learned a long time ago that there are times in the game where you need to take charge, where you need to put the game on your back and just go full out. And there are other times, because the game is so fluid from one second to the next, that you have to roll with it, let it come to you, and react to what you're presented with. What you've taught me is that sometimes you have to pull back, look at the bigger picture, examine things away from the chaos of the game. That's where the real balance is, I think, living fully in those moments, but also taking the time to think about where you're going, and whether or not you're happy. It sounds like you know what exactly you need to do."

"When I pull back to look at the messiness, or sometimes it's the tidiness, of my life, I know that my feelings about my parents, the insistent one that I've always had of being unwanted, is hurting me too much. It almost made me lose you. I can't risk that again." It also wasn't fair to Maddie to have grandparents so out of touch.

"But we didn't lose each other. That's the important thing."

She told Sarah about running into her childhood friend Tommy O'Brien when she was in Malahide and the advice he'd given her.

"He's right, but I'm not sure how to do it. How do I erase all the crap I feel about them and have a normal relationship? If that's even possible…" It might not be. If they couldn't mend things, she knew, she'd have to walk away. For her own self-preservation.

"I don't think you do erase it all." Sarah spooned soup into her mouth. "Maybe it's more about looking at your parents through a different lens."

"How, like?"

"Maybe you're still viewing them through the eyes of a hurt child instead of through the eyes of the intelligent, loving, gifted woman you are." Sarah leaned closer to make her point. "They can't hurt you anymore. They don't have that power over you. Once you realize that, you can have whatever kind of a relationship you want with them."

Claire sat back and tried to corral her thoughts. No one had ever framed it the way Sarah had. The only thing keeping her bitter, hurt, was herself. It was time for her to step up.

"You're too smart to be a hockey player."

"Nah. I'm smart *and* I'm a hockey player. Or was."

"Oh, sweetheart. Nothing stays the same forever, does it?"

"There is one thing that will."

"What's that?"

"My love for you."

The declaration looked good on Sarah, because she meant it. Claire smiled so that she wouldn't cry. "Come on. There's something we need to buy for each other."

* * *

The little jewelry store was about the size of a walk-in closet. Towing Sarah behind her, Claire went straight to the display case of rings. There were rows and rows of Claddagh rings, some in silver, some in gold, some even in titanium. A variety of them included gemstones like rubies and emeralds and sapphires. Claire asked the clerk to pull a tray out.

"What are these?" Sarah asked. "They're gorgeous rings."

"Claddagh rings. They've been part of Irish culture for centuries. Look, see how the hands hold the heart and on top of the heart is a crown?"

Sarah put her face up to the nearest tray.

"The heart represents love, the crown is a symbol of loyalty, and the hands mean friendship. They're meant to give as a gift of either friendship or love, and how you wear it denotes the intention."

"That's so cool." Sarah touched a gold ring that had a deep blue sapphire embedded in the heart. "Oh, Claire, these are the same color as your eyes. May I buy this for you?"

Claire placed her hand on her forearm. "I would love that. But only if I can buy one for you."

Sarah grinned. "We definitely need Claddagh rings." She asked the clerk if she could try on a thick band style made of sterling silver. "This one I love."

Outside with their purchases, Claire explained the tradition of wearing the ring on either your left hand or your right.

"The left was meant for being married or engaged. If it's on the right hand, it signifies friendship or that the wearer is in a love relationship. Now, on the right hand, if you point the tip of the heart toward your fingertips, it signifies that you're single. If you point the tip towards your heart, it means you're taken. On the left hand, pointing the heart toward your fingertip signifies an engagement and pointing it toward your heart signifies that you're married. Lots of people actually use them as wedding rings."

"So, um, how do we decide how we want to wear them?"

Claire grabbed Sarah's hand as they walked down the street. "Why don't we put them away for now and decide later, some other time, what we want to do with them?" She could tell that Sarah, too, understood the significance of the decision, but now wasn't the time.

"All right." Sarah picked up their joined hands and kissed Claire's. "That gives me time to plan something romantic."

"And what if I'm the one who wants to plan something romantic?"

"Why not have two romantic plans? Gotta be better than one."

"Then that's what we'll do." Claire sighed deeply. "But I think I'd like to get back to Dublin for now."

Sarah nodded. "Good idea."

CHAPTER FORTY-NINE

They didn't talk much on the drive back to Dublin. Sarah asked Claire if she wanted to stop in her hometown, Nenagh, but Claire said no, there was nothing there for her anymore. An hour from Dublin, she asked Claire if she wanted to drop her off at her hotel so that she could have a private talk with her parents, but Claire only looked at her like she had three heads.

"I need you with me," she said plainly. "You give me strength. You remind me that this is all worth it. I don't think I can do it without you."

"Claire Joyce, you're already the bravest woman I know. You have all the strength you need, trust me."

Claire's lopsided smile told Sarah that she didn't believe her. "All right. Anything for you, sweetheart."

At the Joyces' house, they ordered Lebanese takeout and ate on their laps to the evening news. As Sarah cleared away the plates in the kitchen, she heard Claire say to her parents it was time to turn the telly off, that they needed to talk, and that Sarah would be joining them. *I'm intruding*, Sarah thought, and yet, Claire wanted her there, *needed* her there, all of which meant she had to tamp down her outsider feelings and do what she could to support Claire.

She returned to the living room as Claire was trying, without much success, to start the conversation. Sarah sat down next to her and held her hand. She would keep silent; it was not her place. Claire squeezed her hand and started again, less haltingly.

"Mum, Dad. We need to talk about a few things. Things that…might be uncomfortable. I can't—won't—leave Ireland until we do."

"Go on," Ronan said.

"I don't want us to be like strangers anymore. I want us to actually *like* one another from here on. To, to…change things between us. To be more of a family."

"How do you mean, so?" Claire's mother asked, a frown stamped on her face or maybe the look was one of confusion. In any case, she didn't look happy.

"I guess it…No, it does go back to my early childhood. I felt unwanted by you both. I felt like I didn't matter to you, like I had intruded on your lives together. I'm sorry but that's what I've felt all these years."

Ronan Joyce's mouth slackened in surprise. "We never meant. Sorry, that. We gave you a good life, did we not? Your mum and I loved each other very much, we had a good life together. You came along, and we were delighted, especially your mum, you being a girl and all."

"But I didn't *feel* that, you see?"

"If we'd been able to have more children," Mona said flatly, "perhaps you wouldn't have felt that way."

"You mean you couldn't have more? I thought you didn't want more, that somehow having me soured you on having any more children?"

Claire's parents shared a private look that Sarah couldn't decipher. The silence was finally broken by Mona, whose shoulders seemed more rounded by the minute, her small frame swallowed up by the wingback chair. She looked defeated, misunderstood, trapped in the way of someone under attack.

"Of course we wanted more children. And when we couldn't…"

"Your mother took it especially hard," Ronan said, as if that were explanation enough.

"But the one child you did have—me—was never made the priority. Never cherished. Why? Why weren't you thankful for the one child you did have?"

Mona's mouth trembled, but she remained defiant. "There was never any doubt of our love for you."

"I disagree."

Sarah stiffened. This wasn't going well. She could feel Claire's anger coming off her like tiny shockwaves. She held her hand tighter.

"When I came here with Maddie, barely out of diapers, to tell you that I was divorcing Matt. Do you remember?"

Her parents nodded.

"All I wanted was to be taken into my mother's arms and held and told that everything would be all right. Instead, all you did was give me grief. How could you not have chosen my side? How could you have taken Matt's over mine?" Claire's voice broke. "Can't you understand how hurtful that was? How unloved that made me feel?"

More charged silence, followed by a paltry explanation. They'd been upset over the news of the divorce, they hadn't wanted it to happen, that was all.

Claire was not appeased. "You're my parents. I need you to take my side every single time, especially in something so important as my marriage. That is your job. And if you can't or won't support me, then I'm afraid I can no longer be in your lives."

Shock weighed heavy in the silence. Then chastened, awash in guilt, the tears came from both Ronan and Mona. Claire too. Followed by the apologies, the asking of forgiveness, the promise to do better at including one another in their lives. Atonement, for now, was complete. Or at least on its way to being complete.

Claire went to her parents and hugged them each. Reaching for Sarah's hand, she pulled her to her feet.

"We'll be running along to Sarah's hotel. She is my life partner, my love, and I'm going with her. We'll be back tomorrow morning."

Ronan put up his hand. "Wait. It'd be grand if you both stayed here. With us. Wouldn't it, Mona?"

Mona's smile seemed genuine for the first time since Sarah had met her. The tightness in her face was gone. "Right, so. Please stay as long as you like. I'll get the cards out. We can play Twenty-Five!"

"It'll be the craic." Merriment was high in Ronan's voice. "I'll get the whisky. We'll have hot whisky, how's that?"

Sarah had never heard of the game. Or the drink. "What's Twenty-Five?"

Claire took her arm. "Come on, love, I'll explain it on the way back to your hotel to pick up your things."

CHAPTER FIFTY

All Claire wanted to do on the plane ride home was sleep, but it was impossible. She was too pumped, almost bursting with the juicy plumpness of happy memories, for sleep. She must be living inside a dream. In just two weeks, her life had been redefined in so many ways it was hard to fathom.

Sarah coming to her, their reuniting and committing to one another, was the crowning moment. But the other surprise was discovering that her parents really did love her. It was in their eyes, in their tears, when it came time to say goodbye. They couldn't reasonably make up for the last forty years, Claire understood that, but it was a fresh start now. They wouldn't have to lose any more years to feelings of disconnect, to the not-so-buried resentments.

"Bring Maddie back to see us soon," Mona begged her.

"And Sarah," said Ronan. "Bring Sarah back too, as soon as you can. What about Christmas?"

"Oh, that's months away," Mona complained. "Come sooner."

"Christmas it is," Claire decided, with a nod from Sarah. The three of them would spend Christmas in Ireland. It would be the first Christmas in a long time that Sarah didn't have hockey games to play, cities to travel to. It would be Claire's first Christmas in Ireland since she was Maddie's age.

"Ah, the oul dear," Ronan said as he put his good arm around his wife. "We can wait until Christmas, but it won't be easy, love. You'll keep in touch?"

"Every week, Dad." That would be new, but Claire looked forward to it, and she knew Maddie would, too.

One of the visit's miracles was Mona and Ronan agreeing to daily help coming in. Just a couple of hours a day, they'd cautioned, for some meal prep and some cleaning. They weren't ready for a stranger to practically move in. But it was a start. It was a start in so many ways now.

Claire looked down at her and Sarah's joined hands and thought of the Claddagh rings they'd purchased, packed safely away in their luggage. She'd think up something romantic, something to The Cranberries' song "Dreams," and she would ask Sarah to marry her. But first she would ask Maddie if it was okay. They both would ask Maddie, together. Maddie would be ecstatic.

She leaned over and kissed Sarah's cheek until she began to stir. "We're almost home, my love."

Sarah smiled, rubbed the sleep from her eyes with her free hand. "I can't wait. But you're my home, Claire, wherever that is."

Bella Books, Inc.
Happy Endings Live Here
P.O. Box 10543
Tallahassee, FL 32302
Phone: (850) 576-2370
www.BellaBooks.com

More Titles from Bella Books

Hunter's Revenge – Gerri Hill
978-1-64247-447-3 | 276 pgs | paperback: $18.95 | eBook: $9.99
Tori Hunter is back! Don't miss this final chapter in the acclaimed Tori Hunter series.

Integrity – E. J. Noyes
978-1-64247-465-7 | 228 pgs | paperback: $19.95 | eBook: $9.99
It was supposed to be an ordinary workday...

The Order – TJ O'Shea
978-1-64247-378-0 | 396 pgs | paperback: $19.95 | eBook: $9.99
For two women the battle between new love and old loyalty may prove more dangerous than the war they're trying to survive.

Under the Stars with You – Jaime Clevenger
978-1-64247-439-8 | 302 pgs | paperback: $19.95 | eBook: $9.99
Sometimes believing in love is the first step. And sometimes it's all about trusting the stars.

The Missing Piece – Kat Jackson
978-1-64247-445-9 | 250 pgs | paperback: $18.95 | eBook: $9.99
Renee's world collides with possibility and the past, setting off a tidal wave of changes she could have never predicted.

An Acquired Taste – Cheri Ritz
978-1-64247-462-6 | 206 pgs | paperback: $17.95 | eBook: $9.99
Can Elle and Ashley stand the heat in the *Celebrity Cook Off* kitchen?